# Pearl White Peril

# Pearl White Peril

EMILY OBERTON

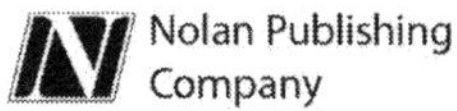

Publisher's Note: This is a work of fiction. Names, characters, places, and events are a product of the author's imagination. Locales and public names are sometimes used for atmospheric purposes. Any resemblance to actual people, living or dead, or to businesses, companies, events, institutions, or locales is completely coincidental.

Cover art by DLR Cover Designs

Internal images © Julien Eichinger/Adobe Stock; Tartila/Adobe Stock

Pearl White Peril/ Emily Oberton. — 1st ed.

ISBN 978-1-7347003-2-9

*For Noelle and Landon*

# CHAPTER ONE

Two champagne-gold pendant lights, suspended directly above the kitchen island, cast a warm glow on the glossy marble countertops and subway tile backsplash. The all-white kitchen in the Walnut Ridge home gleamed with cheerful opulence despite the untimely arrival of a mid-morning storm. Persistent waves of rain thrashed against the window above the sink, almost drowning out the angry chants of protestors in the backyard.

I approached the counter space between the stove and refrigerator and adjusted the items on a woven rattan tray, moving the stack of salad plates in front of the wooden cake stand and vase of lavender hydrangeas. The plates were part of the company's new Stantonville dinnerware set, and it was best to put them in the spotlight.

I turned around and surveyed the room. "Hey, Terence," I called out over my shoulder. "Can you please move the middle barstool a smidgeon to the right? I need it centered between the other two."

Terence Holt wiped his palms against his jeans as he walked from the adjoining breakfast room toward the island. "You got it."

He slid the low-back stool toward its neighbor then raised an eyebrow at me. "Good?"

"Yes, thank you. You know I couldn't do this without you. Everything looks perfect." Terence and his crew were the company muscles, doing everything from moving furniture and painting walls to hanging drapes, shelves, lights and artwork. They transformed rooms within the Walnut Ridge home two, sometimes three, times a day, making them look completely different. And fortunately, Terence was a pro at interpreting words like 'smidgeon.'

He tapped his knuckles against the white marble. "You'd better hope the rain lets up. What's on the other side of that window is just plain ugly. We might as well be taking photos at night, it's so dark out there." One of his braids fell in his face, but it didn't seem to bother him. The sides of his head were shaved, but the top held a thick stack of long black braids, which he usually tied back with a band.

I grinned and joined Terence by the stools. "Nah, don't worry about the storm. The graphics team can spiff up that window faster than you can say Photoshop. They'll make it look like the clear-sky spring day we should be having right now." The day's forecast promised a full day of rain, and we couldn't afford to delay the photo shoot.

It was early April, and Walnut Ridge's first-ever printed catalog was scheduled to arrive in mailboxes throughout the country on July 1. The tight deadline meant long workdays, including most Saturdays. We had started staging rooms and shooting pictures several weeks ago and we had at least five more weeks to go for the first issue.

But I didn't complain about the long hours. I loved nearly every aspect of my new, never-dreamed-it-could-happen-to me job.

"There you are," said a voice behind me.

Terence and I turned as Vincent Weatherford, owner of

Walnut Ridge Furniture and Decor, pushed his way past a tower of plastic storage bins and stepped into the kitchen. In a pressed blue dress shirt buttoned nearly to the top and well-worn dark blue jeans, his style wavered somewhere between smart and casual without directly hitting the trendy smart-casual look.

When Vincent started Walnut Ridge six years ago, customers could only order from his company's website. But when every southern woman became obsessed with his furniture and decor, Vincent decided to escape the digital confines of his website and mail monthly catalogs to customers. He moved from Baltimore to Darlington Hills, Virginia last year and bought a seventy-year old classic southern home with a wraparound porch, columns, and black shutters that contrasted nicely with the smooth white siding. His was one of the larger homes in the ritzy, heavily wooded North Hills neighborhood.

Vincent's gaze settled on Terence. "Don't you keep your phone on? I've been looking for you the past five minutes. I should have known Hadley had ensnared you in conversation. I need you to go do something about *them*." Vincent jerked his head toward the kitchen window. Half a dozen drenched protestors held soggy posters condemning the new catalog for killing trees. It was the same group that had been protesting outside, more days than not, for the past several weeks. Two men blew into long plastic noisemaker horns, while Sonya Bean, the leader of the six, shouted into a white bullhorn.

Terence, who was a month away from graduating from Old Dominion University with a psychology degree, was certainly the most qualified person on Vincent's payroll to try to reason with the protestors, but I guessed Vincent picked him because he was also the most physically intimidating, with his six-three frame and bodybuilder biceps.

"Go tell them I'm calling the cops if they don't get off my lawn," Vincent said. "They're going to destroy the grass."

Terence nodded and started walking toward the kitchen door, which led to the backyard.

"Remind them they're on private property," Vincent called after him. "Make sure they move to the street out front, or better yet, help them find their way out of this neighborhood."

"Help them find their inner child," I teased. "Go make Freud proud."

Laughing, Terence stepped out into the downpour.

Vincent's eyes swept across the kitchen. "How much more time do you need to finish staging the kitchen? Rachael is wrapping up photos in the entry hall, and her crew is shooting this room next. You did see today's itinerary, right? It said kitchen photos at 10:30 a.m. It's 10:15 now, and you clearly have a lot more work to do."

I straightened my back. "Actually, I'm done with the kitchen. I just finished arranging the Stantonville plates—"

"Done?" Vincent's eyes were wide. "I'm putting the kitchen on the cover of my new catalog. For some people, this room will be their first impression of Walnut Ridge. I cannot have them thinking I sell soulless junk. This kitchen should scream contemporary southern, but right now it's more of a sad whimper. Give me some warm dashes of color, Hadley. I need a kitchen that begs for lively Sunday brunches with maple pancakes and griddled country ham. This room should be so southern that it conjures Scarlett O'Hara herself and makes her cry tears of sweetened peach iced tea. Can you do that for me?"

I forced myself to hold his gaze while I took a slow, steady breath. "Of course." I strode toward the storage bin marked Serving Dishes and removed a small glass bowl. Tucking it under my left arm like a football, I moved across the kitchen to Vincent's refrigerator, scanned the well-stocked shelves, and removed five lemons from the fruit drawer. I set the bowl on the counter by the sink, stacked the lemons in a pyramid, then swung around toward Vincent, my wavy ponytail whipping across my face.

"There," I said.

He brought his hand to his face and massaged the gray and black bristles of his goatee. In the weeks since I had moved to Darlington Hills to work as Walnut Ridge's interior designer, I had learned Vincent was never pleased with anyone's work initially, no matter how good it was. He first ridiculed it and then educated us on how we should have done it. But I tried to not let his criticism bring me down; he was probably just nervous about his first catalog.

The deep creases between Vincent's eyes softened. "This is more like it. It's sophisticated yet sensible. Go tell Rachael we're ready to shoot the kitchen."

The back door opened and a soaked Terence walked through, followed by an older man, perhaps in his sixties, wearing a red raincoat that looked about three sizes too large for his slender frame. Next to me, Vincent swore.

The man's eyes fell on Vincent. "You are in a heap of trouble, Mr. Weatherford. Don't think just because you aren't responding to my violation notices that I'm going to back down."

"You can't just walk into my house whenever you'd like," Vincent said. "We're in the middle of a photo shoot. If you have an issue with my business, get in line. Go make yourself a sign and join the tree-loving group outside."

The man flipped back his jacket hood, revealing frizzy silver hair. He marched toward Vincent and me. "I don't care about trees. I care about rules. And as a new resident of North Hills neighborhood, you are required to abide by the rules set forth by the homeowner's association. Pursuant to Article Twelve, Section Four in the HOA's governing covenants, residents are not allowed to run a business from their home without prior approval."

My mouth fell open. Vincent hadn't gotten approval to run his business from his home?

The man glanced at me and gave a curt nod. "Willy Ellsworth, president of North Hills HOA. I assume you work with Mr. Weatherford?"

Before I could respond or offer my hand to introduce myself, Willy returned his fiery eyes to Vincent. "Given the nature of your business and the fact that you did not seek prior approval, I can assure you my board will not allow you to conduct your business in our upstanding neighborhood. We will take action against you, Mr. Weatherford."

Not good. If the HOA forced Vincent to cease business operations, we wouldn't finish photos for the catalog in time. Or worse, Vincent would be forced to move and I might not have a steady job anymore. Although my plan for moving to Virginia involved starting my own interior design consulting business, at the moment I needed the steady income from Walnut Ridge. So far I'd completed only one client job in Darlington Hills. It was a one-week project I'd snagged while I was here for my job interview with Vincent.

It hadn't ended well, to say the least. I most definitely would not be doing any more work for that client.

Vincent took a step closer to the man. "I am well aware of your HOA rules. You don't think my attorney reviewed them before I bought this house? Unfortunately for your HOA, its covenants do not give your board any real enforcement power. It's all in the fine print, Willy, and my attorney will be happy to spell it out for you. My company is one of the south's top home furnishing companies, and my neighbors are thrilled to live next to Walnut Ridge's new design home. Besides, it's not like I'm throwing wild parties every night."

"You've had a twenty-foot moving truck parked in front of your house for the past month," Willy said, his voice rising. "Not to mention all the parked cars in front of your home these days, and those hideous storage sheds in your side yard, which are visible from the street. Your neighbor, Mrs. Feldman, says her five kids can't ride their bikes in this cul-de-sac or play in their front yard because they're scared of that rowdy gang of protestors causing such a hoo-ha in your yard. Your business is a nuisance to this neighborhood."

There was a flicker of light outside, followed immediately by a fierce clap of thunder. The house went dark.

Vincent grumbled, casting an angry look out the window. But as fast as the electricity had cut off, it came back on—except in the kitchen and breakfast room.

Vincent stormed into the breakfast room, looking toward the dining room in the front of the house. Willy and I followed him. "Where did Terence go? He was just in here. Someone needs to go flip the circuit breaker for the kitchen lights. We have a photo shoot in here in less than fifteen minutes."

"He probably went to dry off," I reasoned, turning toward the garage. I could flip the breaker as easily as anyone else. But before I reached the door, one of Terence's guys, Josh Finney, walked into the kitchen carrying a can of paint.

"Go take care of the lights," Vincent barked. I was surprised he hadn't used the opportunity to flip the breaker himself as an excuse to dodge Willy.

Instead, Vincent widened his stance and faced the older man. "You will leave my home immediately or *I* will take action against *you*," he said, punching his words out like a series of rapid, powerful uppercuts. "Do I make myself clear?"

I flinched. Vincent could be moody and condescending, but I'd never seen him act like a rabid Rottweiler before.

Willy removed his raincoat and reached into the front pocket of his shirt, then pulled out an envelope folded in half. "This is a cease and desist letter, curtesy of your neighborhood HOA, which by the way most certainly does have the power to enforce its rules."

Josh popped his head through the doorway and checked the overhead lights. "No good. I flipped the breaker but it didn't do anything. Must be some sort of electrical issue." With his smooth platinum-blonde hair, tanned skin and paint-streaked sleeveless T-shirt, he resembled a twenty-something-year-old version of Hulk Hogan, only about a quarter of the wrestling star's size. His circa 1980s clear plastic-rimmed eyeglasses had a small smudge of paint on the right lens, and I had to use all my willpower to not march over and clean them myself.

Vincent checked his watch, then dismissed Josh with an impatient flick of his wrist. "Of course it's an electrical issue. You're the handyman; go fix it. Find Terence and get him to help if you can't do it." He stared out the breakfast room's three-panel bay window and shook his head. "This home has been one nightmare after another. It was a junkhouse before I got my hands on it, and despite all the money I dumped into it, this place continues to show its ugly bones."

"I can't believe old Ms. Henkle sold it to you," Willy said. "Considering the price you paid and my dealings with you thus far, I presume you intimidated her into selling."

Vincent yanked the envelope from Willy's hand and tossed it on the breakfast table. "Intimidated? No. I charmed that deed out of her hands." He laughed. "It didn't take much. She probably hadn't been charmed in years."

Terence moseyed back into the breakfast room, his face dry but his solid white T-shirt and blue jeans still soaked. He glanced up at the lights, then looked to Vincent for an explanation.

"Lights out, Josh can't fix it," Vincent said.

"I tried the breaker and nothing happened," Josh explained, his shaky voice obliterating his Hulk Hogan facade. He came and stood next to Terence. "But I can go take care of it."

Terence smiled appreciatively. "Thanks, man, but I want you to finish painting the dining room and then move on to the game room. I'll go check it out."

Dropping his eyes to the floor, Josh spun on his heels toward the kitchen.

"Dude. Other way," Terence said, one corner of his mouth lifting into a smile.

Josh shook his head and turned around, revealing already-reddened cheeks. "Right. I get turned around in this place."

"Hadley, tell me the upstairs bedroom is ready for photos," Vincent said. "I don't have time to wait on the lights. We need to keep things rolling. We're finishing everything on today's itinerary even if it means working until midnight."

"It's ready," I responded, thankful I had stayed late last night to stage the room. Whether or not Vincent would think it was ready was another consideration.

"Terence, go fix the lights," Vincent instructed. "Hadley, follow me upstairs and grab Rachael's crew on the way. Willy, you have ten seconds to leave my house. You will hear from my attorney."

"I'm not going anywhere until you read and acknowledge this cease and desist letter, Mr. Weatherford."

Vincent grabbed the envelope from the table, ripped it in half in one dramatic motion, then threw it back on the table. Grunting, he turned and walked toward the entry hall. I followed, stopping only to ask Rachael to move her team and equipment upstairs.

I caught up to Vincent at the top of the stairs just as he turned toward the bedroom. "I put some fresh peonies on the nightstand, and I had wanted to add a stack of books with blue spines to complement the cool tones in the Calypso rug, but I couldn't find any in your storage sheds. Do you have any in your bedroom?" Vincent was an avid reader, so there was a good chance he had a few books in his off-limits personal living area, which consumed about half of the home's upstairs space.

The graphics team, which worked remotely from its Detroit office, could easily superimpose a stack of books, but Vincent required all photos to be authentic—wallpaper, paint, and all. He wanted everything to be perfect. Because not only would these photos be printed in the catalog, they would also live in the products section of the company's website. He had never hired an interior designer to stage his furniture for professional photo shoots before, and now he hoped to take Walnut Ridge to the next level.

Vincent stopped walking. "Probably, but I'm not wasting time on that right now. Next time, try the attic. There's a bunch of junk in there from the woman who used to live here. I haven't gone through it but you might find something useful."

Vincent held up a finger, then dug his hand into the back pocket of his jeans and pulled out his vibrating phone. After glancing at the screen, he closed his eyes for a long beat, then brought the phone to his ear. He listened to a deep voice on the other end, clenching the phone so hard his knuckles turned white.

"I don't want any more delays," Vincent snapped. "You need to take care of it this morning." The deep voice continued talking, but Vincent pulled the phone from his ear and hung up.

"Contractor?" I asked.

He resumed walking, his eyes set on the open door in front of us. "No."

I didn't press him to elaborate. It wasn't my business who was on the phone.

Rachael and her crew joined us a minute later, set up their tripods and spotlights, then began shooting the room. After they photographed the bedding collection I had arranged last night, I replaced it with the Augusta Rose duvet cover and matching shams, which featured roses embroidered with stitching several shades darker than the rest of the pink cotton fabric. The extra-thick synthetic feather insert gave the duvet a nice full shape, and the two additional inserts I hid under the Augusta Rose duvet made the bedding look downright plush. To balance the angular lines of the tufted headboard, I'd placed a round mirror above the nightstands on both sides of the bed.

Rachael flitted around the room, snapping photos from every vantage point possible. She reminded me of Tinker Bell with her asymmetrical pixie cut and spry movements. Leaping from the floor to the chair to the rug to the linen-covered bench at the foot of the bed had never looked so easy. Rachael's two assistants, Silent Kyle and Harry the Hummer, worked alongside her.

Vincent remained quiet as we worked. Not once did he criticize my design choices or tell Rachael how to do her job. He spent more time checking his phone than watching the activity in the room. His eyes followed the photographers without seeming to focus on them. I wondered if Willy had gotten to him, or if the person he had spoken with on the phone had upset him. Or maybe he was just tired. The hypnotic drumming of the rain against the roof and window, interrupted only by the soft clicks of cameras and Harry's soft humming, was enough to put anyone to sleep. It made me want to slide under the stack of warm duvet covers and take a nap.

The harsh screeching of Sonya's bullhorn interrupted my mid-morning nap fantasy. In the front yard, just below the bedroom window, Sonya and her cohorts from the Forest Action League resumed chanting the same words they had chanted for nearly two weeks: "Stop the madness and insanity; kill the catalog, not the trees!"

Their yelling was irritating, but I sympathized with their concerns. I couldn't count the number of catalogs I had thrown away because they weren't relevant. I hoped Walnut Ridge's marketing agency would mail its new catalogs to only the most promising customers.

"If they want to stand in the rain all day and die of pneumonia, that's their business," Vincent said. "But we don't have to listen to them." He propped his phone on a metal stepstool near the door and tapped the big orange play button on his screen, dragging the volume slider all the way to the right. Classical music replaced the chanting instantly, and we enjoyed two entire minutes of a lively piano concerto before a rapid sequence of thwacks interrupted the music.

We all rushed to the window, just as a grapefruit-sized mud ball slammed against the glass.

"They're digging holes out there," Vincent shrieked. "That mud is from my flowerbeds." He made it to the bedroom door in several large steps. "This madness is going to stop right now. Keep shooting, I am not letting this delay us."

The spirited pounding of Vincent's feet on the stairs was a well-timed accompaniment to the rising crescendo of the classical ballad playing on his phone, punctuated by the swift slamming of the front door.

Rachael and I exchanged eye rolls. Someone yelled below us, but the loud music made it impossible to hear what they were saying. The mud ball assault stopped, and I continued fluffing pillows while Rachael's team snapped away. We finished with the Augusta Rose bedding collection and I went into the room's walk-in closet to retrieve the third and final bedding set that Vincent wanted to include in the catalog. The third set was my favorite and I intended to buy it for my bed once I earned a few paychecks from Walnut Ridge. The soft gray comforter featured evenly spaced pinch pleats, which gave it more depth and texture than any other comforter I'd seen.

"What are you doing?" Rachael asked. She was folding up a tripod. "We need to head downstairs for the next photo shoot." I could barely hear her over the music, but I didn't want to touch Vincent's phone and risk adding to his anger. "We're done in here."

"Vincent wants photos of all three bedding collections," I said, trying to raise my voice loud enough for her to hear me without sounding like I was frustrated. I avoided conflict like I avoided paisley prints and linoleum flooring. Pulling the folded itinerary from the side pocket of my navy tailored skirt, I pointed to the line on the paper that confirmed my belief.

Rachael nodded with a smile. "Yeah, but he told me yesterday he only wants us to shoot the first two bedding sets. Why don't we wait for him to come back up? Should be any minute now."

I frowned. It seemed like Vincent would have told me about the change yesterday before I steamed the comforter and matching pillow shams. "Hold tight, I'll go ask him."

I hurried down the stairs, opened the front door, and stood on the covered front porch while I scanned the yard. Other than an abandoned "kill the catalog" poster by the base of the sprawling oak tree, there were no signs of Vincent, Sonya, or the other protesters. A gust of wind swept a torrent of rain toward the patio, peppering me with cold water. I retreated into the Walnut Ridge home and moved through the family room toward the back door in the kitchen.

A new musical number from Vincent's phone echoed throughout the house, which felt hollow without its typical swarm of frantic workers. I checked my watch. The Walnut Ridge crew stopped work at noon every day, honoring their lunch hour as if it were a religion. But it was only 11:30 a.m., too early for lunch.

Curious about where everyone was, I continued exploring downstairs. I stepped into the sunroom, then swung an immediate right through the arched doorway into the dark kitchen. Without the warm glow from the pendant lights, the marble countertops reflected only the dim light from the window above the sink, giving the kitchen a greenish hue.

The back door was open, sprays of rain blowing into the kitchen. Several steps away from the door, the tip of my right shoe kicked something soft. It took me a moment to realize the bright yellow object rolling across the wood floor was a lemon. It settled next to another lemon amid a mess of broken glass and water.

My eyes snapped to the counter space where the glass bowl should have been but wasn't. Questions spun through my mind faster than I could process them. Had someone dropped the bowl of lemons? Why had they been moving it? Why would they leave them on the floor? I couldn't imagine making such a mess and leaving it for someone else to clean up. Who would do that?

I closed the back door, then picked up the two lemons near my feet, careful not to touch any glass, then reached for a third lemon that lay by the cabinet under the sink. I spotted another pop of yellow to my right, turned and reached for it, then whipped my hand back so fast I whacked it against the cabinet.

The lemon was half-hiding behind a shoe that stuck out from one corner of the island at an angle that told me it was still on somebody's foot. My heart launched into overdrive as I rounded the island.

I froze, unable to unlock my eyes from the wide unblinking ones of Willy Ellsworth, who was lying on his stomach with his head turned toward me. I dropped to my knees to check for a pulse, then bolted backwards when my eyes fell on the wooden knife handle protruding from his back.

I screamed loud enough to put Sonya Bean's bullhorn out of business.

# CHAPTER TWO

I crawled toward Willy again, then pressed two fingers against his neck. No pulse. I backed away from him, bumping into Rachael and Josh, who were running into the kitchen.

I couldn't find the words to form a sentence. Instead, I pointed to the body lying on the floor. Rachael's stuttered shrieking was soon joined by a chorus of yelling, swearing, and crying as others joined us in the breakfast room. Sonya rushed into the house, followed several moments later by Vincent, who bellowed obscenities louder than anyone.

My legs felt incapable of supporting the rest of my body. The only thing keeping me upright was the tight huddle of people around me. Sonya and Josh both whipped phones from their pockets and called the police while Vincent demanded that somebody tell him what happened.

"I came downstairs to find you," I told him. My voice, shaking violently with sobs, didn't sound like my own. "I saw the lemons and picked them up and then I saw Willy lying on the floor with a—" I gasped for air, unable to finish my sentence. As someone who gets squeamish slicing raw chicken, I couldn't think about the knife in Willy's back, much less talk about it.

"Lemons?" Vincent said. "What are you talking about? Was anyone down here when you found him?"

"No."

The back door opened and Terence came through, pulling wireless headphones from his ears. His eyes widened when he saw everyone in the breakfast room. "What's going on?" He strolled toward us, casually swinging his gaze down toward Willy. He jumped, his black toolbox falling from his hand, spilling its contents onto the wood floor. A black and yellow screwdriver rolled toward Willy's body.

As if by instinct, Terence bent over to pick it up, then jerked back his hands and hurried toward the chaotic cluster of people by the breakfast room table. He gripped the back of a chair near me. "What happened?"

"Do you want to sit down?" I asked. His dark brown face had paled to a scary shade of panic.

"I'm okay," he said, though his tone did little to reassure me.

Josh came up behind Terence and laid a paint-covered hand on his shoulder. "You alright, man? This is messed up," Josh said, keeping his voice low. "Who is this guy? He's the one who was in here earlier, right?" He was probably thinking the same thing I was: he was the one in here earlier arguing with Vincent. I looked at the table. The cease and desist letter Vincent had torn in half lay on top of a Stantonville dinner plate next to the napkin I had folded so precisely earlier this morning.

"Where are the rest of your guys?" I asked Terence, whose cheeks had regained some of their color.

"They're in Richmond," Terence said. "Vincent sent them there about an hour ago." Walnut Ridge's one-acre warehouse in Richmond was an hour drive from Darlington Hills, a small town which sat squarely in the middle of the Virginia Peninsula. The guys made frequent runs to the warehouse to exchange furniture sets and decorations for the photo shoots.

Terence nodded in the direction of Willy's body. "Did you guys hear anything in here when this happened?"

Josh shook his head. "I was painting up in the game room and didn't hear anything except for piano music."

"Same," I said. "Vincent had his music turned up on his phone. Didn't hear a thing."

Sirens sounded in the distance, silencing the frantic chatter in the room. Several minutes later two paramedics and four police officers paraded into the room, followed by a bald man with a thick gray beard in a blue linen sports jacket. The older man introduced himself as Detective Roy Sanders, then instructed us to move to the family room so they could get to work in the kitchen.

The family room seemed to spin as I walked through it, ceiling over floor over ceiling. I claimed the armchair in the far corner because its high back and cushiony arms seemed like a necessity should I pass out and slump to one side. I gripped the armrests and rubbed my shaking hands against the chair's whimsical array of happy daisies. The chair was the room's statement piece. It was like the life of the party—fun and vibrant amid a neutral landscape of beige, white, and taupe furniture. Now, in this room of despair and confusion, the chair was an unwelcome guest taunting us with its merriment.

The police had told us to wait for the detective to call us into a separate room for individual questioning. Even Sonya waited with us. She had tried to convince a young officer to let her leave since she had been outside the entire time, but he had refused her request. Her Forest Action League buddies had, according to Sonya, left for an early lunch break thirty minutes ago in the town square, which was Darlington Hills' miniature version of a downtown. I guessed the police would follow up with them later.

Sonya, who looked to be in her sixties, sat on the area rug with her ivory slender legs crisscrossed and hands resting palms up on her knees in a meditative pose. Long silver dreadlocks swept across her back and shoulders while thin wisps of hair hung next to the deep-set creases around her closed eyes.

A tall man in a charcoal long-sleeve sweater and black slacks entered the room and strode toward Vincent, who was sitting on the arm of a wingback chair. Vincent stood to face the man, then began talking in a low tone and gesturing to the kitchen and around the family room. Where Vincent's back arched in a tired slouch, the other man held his wide, thick shoulders at an angle that would have impressed a chiropractor. The profiles of the two men were remarkably similar. They shared the same commanding, angular nose and sculpted jawline set in a manner suggesting confidence and determination.

Vincent caught me looking at him and motioned me over. "Hadley, I need you to do something for me. My younger brother is moving out of Darlington Hills and hasn't been able to sell his home. I want you to help him stage it so it doesn't look like a thirty-five-year-old man-child lives there."

The man smiled and offered his hand. "Reid Weatherford. Nice to meet you, Hadley."

Great. Two Weatherfords. Vincent's brother, with his stunning honey-brown eyes and dark brows, likely had an ego as big as or bigger than that of his older brother.

I raised my shaking hand. Reid grasped it, enclosing it in an unexpected blanket of warmth. "Nice to meet you too," I said.

"I'm sorry to hear what happened this morning," he said, still grasping my hand. "You doing okay?" His sharp eyes were sincere, so I gave him points for that, even if he did turn out to be as arrogant as Vincent.

"I'm okay, thanks. I just can't believe this happened." Even though we had surpassed the normal duration of a handshake, I didn't pull away. Not only did my hands feel less shaky, but the room had righted itself and stopped spinning. "So I take it you're not in the home furnishings business?"

Vincent snorted. "Reid's in the business of puttering down the river all day. He doesn't know an armchair from an armoire."

Reid rolled his eyes and released my hand. "Puttering down the river? Really, Vinn?"

Sensing tension between the two brothers, I steered the conversation back to Vincent's original request. "How long has your home been on the market?" I was eager to find out if Vincent expected me to stage Reid's home for free. I wanted to grow my Hadley Home Design side business with paying clients.

"Two weeks," Reid said, running his hand through his dark brown hair. Unlike Vincent's mostly gray hair, Reid's was void of any silver patches. "I know that doesn't seem like a long time, but I'm in a bit of a rush, so I could really use your help."

I decided to not bring up the topic of compensation. As one of Vincent's employees, it was in the best interest of my job to help his brother. Also, I wouldn't mind feeling the electric warmth of Reid's hand again. Staging his home would likely mean many more handshakes. "Sure, I'd be happy to help."

Reid smiled. "Thank you. I'll get your number from Vinn."

Someone tapped my shoulder. I spun around to find Detective Sanders.

"Miss, I'd like you to follow me to the office please," he said. "I've got a few questions for you."

"Of course." I looked back at Vincent, who opened his mouth as though he were going to say something, but then closed it just as quickly.

I walked with Detective Sanders to the office in the front of the house, thinking about Vincent's argument with Willy this morning. Vincent was a volatile firecracker, with or without snippety HOA presidents threatening to shut down his business. Still, I couldn't imagine him stabbing a man in his own kitchen. Maybe I didn't know him as well as I thought I did.

My stomach churned as I envisioned talking with the detective. I had never been questioned by the police.

"Let's start with your name, miss," Detective Sanders said. "And by the way, have we met? You look familiar."

"Hadley Sutton, and I don't believe so. Everyone says I look like someone." I had gotten that question so many times that I'd often wondered if giant photos of my face were planted on billboards along major interstate highways. Either that, or there were a lot of other women with dark brown eyes, wavy light-brown hair, and a small scar above their right eyebrow. I'd had the scar since I was nine when a lamp fell on my head while I was rearranging furniture in my bedroom.

"Sutton...I know that name." He brought the tip of his pen to his chin, which was hidden somewhere beneath his beard. "You aren't by chance related to Debra Sutton?"

I brightened. "That's my Aunt Deb. She's the one who convinced me to move to Darlington Hills. You know her?"

"I know of her. We go to the same church, although I'm guessing she goes more than I do." He spoke slowly, stretching out his words in the true form of a southern drawl.

My stomach squeezed tighter when Detective Sanders clicked his pen and lifted his notepad. He asked me to describe the events of the morning from my point of view. He watched me through narrowed eyes as I spoke, jotting a few notes occasionally.

"So you didn't hear anything unusual when you were upstairs with the photographers?" he asked when I finished talking.

"I did hear some shouting, but I assumed it was Vincent yelling at the protestors to stop throwing mud at the windows." I shrugged. "I'm sorry I can't be more helpful, but it was hard to hear anything over the music in the room."

"The music Vincent turned on shortly before he went downstairs?"

I cringed, realizing I had left that detail out of my story. Apparently Detective Sanders had already interviewed Rachael's crew. "Yes, the music Vincent turned on to cover up the annoying chanting coming from downstairs," I clarified.

"Tell me more about Vincent's argument with the victim," he said. His eyes narrowed again, and I wondered if it was an intimidation tactic or perhaps he needed glasses.

I took a deep breath, the bitter fumes of the fresh paint stinging my nose. I told myself it wasn't my job to protect Vincent, it was my duty to tell the truth. The cops could figure out who was guilty; all I was doing was retelling the same story the others who had been in the kitchen would tell. I described the argument as best I could.

"Did Vincent threaten the victim, either physically or verbally?"

I paused to think before answering. Although Vincent had surprised me with his aggression, he hadn't explicitly threatened to harm Willy. "He did say he would take action against Willy if he didn't leave this house, but I'm certain he meant legal action because he mentioned his lawyer. No physical threats though." I gave a nervous laugh. "The only thing Vincent harmed was a letter he ripped in half."

Detective Sanders straightened his back. "Letter?"

I nodded. "It was a cease and desist letter Willy gave to Vincent."

Detective Sanders prompted me to continue with a nod. I had already told him about the HOA board's complaints against Walnut Ridge, so I didn't need to explain the backstory on the letter. "Vincent got mad and tore it in half without opening it."

"You by chance know where Mr. Vincent put this letter?"

"He threw it on the table in the breakfast room."

Detective Sanders stood and dropped his notepad and pen onto his chair. "Stay here, Miss Sutton. I'll be right back." He opened the glass-paned French doors but didn't close them when he walked out. My mind replayed everything I had told the detective. Although I didn't think Vincent would kill someone, the more questions I answered, the more I questioned my own assumptions. What if Vincent wasn't only quick-tempered, but also violent? I had, after all, known him for about a month.

Detective Sanders returned with a uniformed officer in tow. It was Officer Dennis Appley, whom I had talked with several times in March when I flew to Darlington Hills for my interview with Vincent. The circumstances of our prior interactions were as grim as they were now.

"Hadley, this is Officer Appley. He'll be assisting me with this investigation."

Officer Appley offered me a wide smile as he shook my hand. His sandy blonde hair was even shaggier than when I'd first met him. Apparently he didn't spend much time at the barbershop. "Good to see you again, Hadley." His tone was surprisingly upbeat considering the situation.

Detective Sanders set his intense gray eyes on me. "You're sure the letter is on the breakfast room table? None of my deputies have come across it, and unless I'm blind, it wasn't there just now."

"Yes. I'm positive I saw it on the table when we were waiting for you guys to arrive," I said. It had been on top of the Stantonville dinner plate. "Maybe someone moved it?" Or hid it. My mind immediately landed on Vincent for that scenario.

Detective Sanders nodded. "Thank you, Miss Sutton. That'll be all for now, but do let me know if you think of anything else that may help us."

"Do you still have the card I gave you when we met?" Officer Appley asked. Grinning, he swept back his bangs from his forehead, revealing blue, hopeful-looking eyes.

"Sorry, no. It must have gotten lost in the move." And I didn't think I would need to contact the police again. This was Darlington Hills, after all.

Both men gave me their cards, then Detective Sanders led me back to the quiet family room and pulled Sonya into the office for her interview.

Two hours later, the police and Detective Sanders had interviewed everyone who had been at the house this morning, including Sonya's friends when they came back from their lunch break, as well as Vincent's guys, who returned from Richmond with a truckload full of new furniture and decor to stage and shoot. Even Reid gave a statement, although he was in and out of the office in five minutes. He left Vincent's house as soon as he was done.

Vincent sent all of us home because the police had told him their investigation would take several days. So much for sticking to his tight timeline. Before I headed out, I ran to the upstairs bedroom to retrieve my tote bag, which held the composition notebook in which I keep my ideas, drawings and plans for upcoming photo shoots. On my way down, I found Vincent sitting on the bottom step, his head cupped in his hands.

I paused at the bottom of the stairwell. "I'm sorry, Vincent. Please let me know if there's anything I can do before we're able to resume the photo shoots."

"Thanks, Hadley," he said, keeping his head down.

I turned and started toward the front door.

"The cops think I did it." Vincent kept his voice to a whisper, even though the police were in the kitchen and the entry hall was empty.

"What makes you think that?" I asked, although I already knew the answer.

He tilted his head and gave me the classic Vincent eye roll. "Come on, I think you can figure that one out." He exhaled slowly. "I'm sorry, rough morning."

My eyes widened. What? Vincent apologized? That was a first. "I wouldn't worry too much. The detective asked everyone tough questions. I felt like I'd been sent to the principal's office when Detective Sanders called me in there."

Vincent laughed sarcastically. "Right, like you were ever sent to the principal. And you were in there with Sanders for all of five, maybe ten minutes? He kept me in there for forty-five minutes, Hadley. Don't tell me not to worry."

My mind scrambled to come up with something to make him feel better. "They would have arrested you if they were that convinced." I winced, thinking I could have come up with something better than that.

"The day's not over yet. The detective probably doesn't think I have a good alibi. I told him the whole story three times. I explained that when I went out front, Sonya's tree friends were there and I made them leave, but Sonya wasn't with them. I walked around the house and searched out back for her, but didn't see her until I came into the kitchen when I heard you screaming. I hope that detective grilled Sonya as hard as he did me. He wanted to know my exact path from the time I went outside to when I came back in, down to the square millimeter. He was drawing a map in that notebook of his. Did he do that when he questioned you?"

I considered lying to make him feel better, but shook my head instead. "He only made a few notes while I was talking."

Vincent pressed his lips together and worked his jaw. "Well he kept writing and underlining things—repeatedly underlining them—the entire time I spoke. Oh, and he kept asking me about that letter Willy gave me when he intruded into my house. I told him I tossed it on the table in the breakfast room, but apparently Sanders can't find it and he sure seems to think I know where it is."

I raised my brows, as if the letter's whereabouts was news to me. Vincent didn't need to know I was the one who had brought it to Detective Sanders' attention. It would be nice to still have a job after all this was behind us. And if Vincent turned out to be the killer, I didn't want to end up on the sharp end of another one of his knives.

Vincent looked toward the indistinct chatter coming from the kitchen. "What's your take on all of this?" he asked me. "Can you fathom why anyone would kill that man? He was annoying as anything, but why would someone come into my house and stab him?" He turned heavy steel-blue eyes toward me. If Vincent was guilty, his face showed no remorse.

"Was anything stolen?" I asked. "Maybe someone came in the house planning to steal something, saw Willy, attacked him, and—"

"Nothing's missing," Vincent interrupted, waving off my suggestion that it had been a random robbery. "Other than that letter, everything's still here as far as I can tell."

Unwelcome images of rolling lemons, broken glass, and the upright handle of a knife in Willy's back flashed into my mind, making my insides roil. It was well past lunchtime, but I doubted my body was capable of digesting both food and horrific memories at the same time.

I blinked as a fresh memory snuck back into my thoughts. "Willy was wet when I found him on the floor. Not drenched, but his hair was slicked back. His shoes were also wet. And where there wasn't blood on his back, there were large wet dark spots. That is odd, isn't it? Because before we went upstairs this morning, Willy said he was going to stay put until you read his letter."

I twirled my ponytail as I considered why Willy would be wet if he had stayed in the house. "I bet he gave up on waiting for you and left, but then came back inside for some reason." As upsetting as it was to think about Willy's body on the floor, I forced myself to remember other details. I snapped my head up. "His coat. Willy was wet because he wasn't wearing his raincoat. He came into your house this morning wearing a coat, then took it off. I bet he left your house, then quickly came back inside when he realized he'd forgotten it."

Vincent studied me. "You do have an eye for detail, don't you?" He spun around, giving the entry hall a 360-degree scan, then motioned me closer to him. "You know, if these cops get lazy they might try to pin this murder on me. And you'll be out of a job if I'm behind bars."

I didn't know where he was going with this, but the unemployed-Hadley scenario was becoming more likely as the day progressed. "I'm sure the police will make this investigation a priority. I doubt they're working on any other homicide cases right now." Darlington Hills' crime rate was among the lowest in Virginia. For ten years straight, the *Smith and Woodbury Travel Journal* had bestowed the town with its coveted title of 'America's Friendliest Town.' This designation was a frequent topic of conversation among townspeople.

"Actually, I'd like *you* to make this investigation a priority. You notice things most people overlook. Why do you think I hired you? And you like to talk—a lot. So start talking with people around town, talk their head off. Go irritate a confession out of someone."

I pulled my brows together. "Okay, so I'm a bit chatty. But that doesn't mean people are going to talk to me about the homicide. I'm not a police officer."

Vincent lowered his chin. "Can you just try? I'd like to think there's someone out there asking questions who isn't already convinced all the evidence belongs in the file marked 'Vincent Should Go To Jail.' Please, Hadley?"

Whoa. Vincent was desperate. He'd said "I'm sorry" and "please" within a record-breaking span of five minutes. If he were charged with Willy's murder, the company he worked so hard to grow would likely implode. He had a lot to lose and I could relate. I'd started my Hadley Home Design business in New Orleans after graduating with a degree in interior design, and I soon realized it was easier to attract a two-headed bee than a new client.

What would it hurt to ask around? If I learned anything interesting, whether it pointed the finger of blame toward Vincent or someone else, I would share it with the police. And I wasn't ready to start looking for a new job. I had recently moved to Darlington Hills and my chances of finding another interior design gig in this town were slim. I still had eleven months left on my apartment lease and I really wanted the five-percent employee discount on the Walnut Ridge pinch pleat bedding set.

"I'll try." It was all I could promise. I turned toward the dining room. "Before I leave, I need to speak with Detective Sanders. I completely forgot to mention Willy's raincoat when he questioned me. They might want to tag it as evidence."

"No, I'll tell the cops," Vincent said. "You go home and get some lunch. I'll be in touch."

# CHAPTER THREE

"Tell me you didn't agree to play detective." Carmella Jones, my good friend and neighbor, gave me a stern look even her feathery eyelash extensions couldn't soften. As the principal of a local middle school, she likely used that same expression dozens of times each day to discourage wayward tween behavior.

Carmella had come straight to my apartment this afternoon after leaving school. She was still wearing her standard principal attire: tailored dress, minimal jewelry and black heels. Today's dress was her signature color, emerald green, which emphasized the rich tone of her flawless black skin.

I poured a glass of freshly made raspberry-infused mojito into a stemless wine glass and set it on my kitchen table in front of Carmella, nudging aside a bin of craft supplies. We had planned to work on wreaths to sell at the upcoming Spring Flower Festival, but I was too upset to surround myself with happy-colored ribbons and artificial tulips. Thanks to Carmella, the waves of adrenaline thrashing through my body had subsided, leaving me less shaky but more exhausted than I'd felt in ages.

"How could I say no to those cold, venomous blue eyes of his?" I joked, then raised my hand defensively when she pretended to slap me. "Just because there's a chance he interprets the backstabbing metaphor more literally than most doesn't mean he doesn't deserve my help." I lowered my gaze and poured myself a mojito. "And I don't want to lose my job. I love this town and don't want to go back to New Orleans."

As the daughter of an Air Force airman, I had moved nine times in my life, beginning with my move from Mississippi to Florida when I was three months old. Packing and unpacking, leaving friends and making new ones was as much a part of my childhood as climbing trees and catching fireflies. After my parents dropped me off at college in Louisiana, they moved overseas for an extended tour at a U.S. base in Japan, and had been there ever since. They loved moving around, but I was tired of brown boxes and sad farewells. I had lived in a majority of the southern states. I'd loved them all, but felt at home in none. Three years in a city just wasn't long enough for me to grow my roots.

After college, I thought New Orleans would be my forever-home. I had a steady interior design job with a homebuilder and I'd fallen in love with a man I was sure I would marry. But when my Cajun heartthrob, Ricky, broke my heart and fed its pieces to the Louisiana gators, I quit my job and started packing.

I moved to Virginia because I'd always loved traveling there with my parents during Christmas. My dad was from Darlington Hills, and although he moved away when he turned eighteen, his older brother Bill never left. Uncle Bill married Aunt Deb, raised my cousin Michael and enjoyed the small-town life until the day he died on a fishing trip five years ago.

I considered Darlington Hills a fairytale town, with its gas-lit street lamps, stone-paved town square, and friendly neighbors who said good morning even though they didn't know me.

My boss told me before I left New Orleans that she'd always have a job for me if Virginia didn't work out. But I didn't want to live in the same city as Ricky. As a morning TV news anchor, his face lived on roadside signs, the sides of city buses, and digital billboards. I couldn't walk half a mile in New Orleans without seeing his smug, I-don't-have-time-for-a-relationship-because-I-need-to-focus-on-my-career face.

I would happily play detective if it increased my chances of keeping my job in Virginia.

"I'm going to start by talking to Vincent's brother," I said. "He probably knows more about Vincent than anyone in this town."

"Brother?" Carmella lifted her brows. "You never told me Vincent has a brother. And why did you say it like that? *Brother*. Like he's some sort of a mythical creature."

I brought my mojito to my lips, hoping it would hide my smile. "I didn't say it like that. Brother. See? It sounds perfectly normal, like any other word out of my mouth. And I've never mentioned Reid before because I just met him today."

"Reid? Why do you say it like that? *Reid*."

The door to my apartment opened and Aunt Deb let herself in, the charms on her bracelets jingling like a door chime. I gave Carmella a look to stop talking about Reid, but she'd already closed her mouth. She knew the drill: don't mention the words 'man' and 'Hadley' in the same sentence or else Aunt Deb would start talking about weddings and babies.

"Hadley, hon. After everything you've been through today and you still aren't locking your door?" Aunt Deb turned the lock, then swished over to the slow cooker on my counter, her long polyester skirt swinging at her ankles. It was the second time she'd come over this afternoon to check on me. She probably would have stayed if she didn't have a storage facility to run and a yappy, energetic dog to look after.

"I never lock my door during the day when I'm home." I understood why she was worried, but the town hadn't been overrun by evil lunatics. And I doubted my modest one-bedroom apartment would be high on a burglar's wish list. "But I'll do my best to remember," I added after seeing worry cross her pale blue eyes.

Aunt Deb flipped her auburn hair behind her shoulders and lifted the slow cooker's lid. "This smells delightful— Oh! Hadley, dear..." She closed the lid, then lifted it several inches and peered inside again. "What in the name of all things savory is this?"

"It's peachy pork tenderloin. I've been scouring Pinterest for new recipes now that I have a slow cooker. This one looked irresistible." I joined Aunt Deb by the counter and inhaled the sweet smell of dinner. I tapped the side of the slow cooker I'd bought last week. "This thing is going to solve all of my cooking difficulties." Growing up, we never owned a slow cooker because my mom was a microwave loyalist who believed in the ever-almighty power of the 800-watt box.

I opened my overhead cabinet and removed three plates. "Aunt Deb, Carmella, please help yourself. I have plenty." I removed the glass lid. Aunt Deb and I stared down at the two dark, oblong pieces of meat floating in the muddy-colored stew. "Hmm. Maybe I cooked them too long? They've shriveled to half their size." I handed a plate to Aunt Deb. "But what they lack in presentation, they're sure to make up for in flavor."

Aunt Deb's mouth hung open. "I would love some, but... unfortunately I have to stick to my diet."

"Diet? Since when are you on a diet?" Carmella asked. Not only was Aunt Deb a small-business owner, she also headed up the town's hiking club and somehow convinced several dozen women to join her five days a week for early-morning treks along Bonn Creek, or Bone Creek as locals called it. At fifty-five, she had better legs than most twenty-somethings.

Aunt Deb pulled out a chair and sat across the table from Carmella. "It's one of those eight-hour liquid diets to detox my body." She eyed the glass in Carmella's hand. "Is that a mojito? Those are on my diet, thank goodness."

Grinning, Carmella poured the rest of the pitcher into an empty glass and gave it to Aunt Deb.

"Thank you, Carmella. You are an angel." She took a long sip, then closed her eyes and leaned back in the chair. "Hadley, hon, you'd better find yourself a thirsty man. Not hungry, you hear me? Thirsty."

I slid into the chair next to Carmella and waved off my aunt's backhanded compliment. "Or, how about I shoot for the stars and find a man who's both?"

She seemed to consider that idea. "Very well, but I want you to swear to me on your grandmother's *Joy of Cooking* cookbook that you will never make that"—she shook a passionate finger at my slow cooker—"dish for a man until he's put a ring on your finger."

Carmella swung her head toward me. "And while you're busy swearing, you need to swear to me you won't go snooping around on Vincent's behalf. It's too dangerous. Must I remind you what happened the last time you got caught up in a murder investigation?"

"Sorry, but I can't make that promise."

Aunt Deb sighed. "Carmella, don't even bother trying to talk her out of this one. Hadley told me about Vincent's request when I came by earlier today, and if I know my niece, she's already trying to piece it together. Hadley's just like her dad—my late husband's brother. Neither of them can let go of something once they fix their mind to it, God bless them." She took another sip of mojito, turning her eyes on me. "Just make sure you don't tell your parents about any of this. Your dad will worry himself back to Virginia and we don't want to do anything to jeopardize his retirement plans."

"Good point," I said. My parents were less than two years away from moving to a small retirement beach-town community in Nags Head, North Carolina. They had daydreamed about it for years. But my dad was indeed a worrier. He'd been so paranoid about me living by myself after I graduated college that he gave me a nine-millimeter pistol, which still lay in a mini safe in the depths of my closet because I couldn't stand to even look at a gun.

I couldn't imagine what he would do if he found out there had been two homicides recently in Darlington Hills, the last occurring at my place of employment, and that my boss had asked me to "irritate a confession" out of someone. He'd probably fly to Virginia, stuff me inside his suitcase, and smuggle me back to Japan.

A whoosh of fur swept across my leg. I reached under the table and picked up my cat, Razzy. I had adopted her from Whisks and Whiskers, the local cat café, immediately after I learned I got the job at Walnut Ridge and would be moving to Darlington Hills. She was a Siamese-tabby mix with stunning blue eyes and white fur with dark gray stripes around her eyes, cheeks and legs. She was as spunky as she was sassy, and at two years old, was deep in the throes of her angsty adolescent years. Some days she seemed to crave my attention, but most of the time I was sure she'd be quite pleased if she were the only living creature roaming the earth.

I held Razzy in my arms and scratched her between her ears. "I don't think Willy was a victim of a random robbery. Nothing was stolen, and a robber would have known the house wasn't empty, with all of the cars out front and with so many people in and around the house." Either the killer knew Willy was momentarily alone, or he despised him so much he was willing to risk being seen.

I lifted Razzy's chin and tickled her tiny white whiskers. "That kind of anger would be hard to keep a secret. Wouldn't it? Someone in this town must know something."

# CHAPTER FOUR

Two kittens slept in a tiny heap of cuddles near the cash register in the Whisks and Whiskers Cat Café. It was Saturday morning and the line to order was almost out the door. It had been two days since I found Willy's body, and I'd barely slept since. The puny liquid fuel I'd brewed at home failed to drag me out of the half-awake haze I'd been in since yesterday morning. I needed something stronger. The dense aroma of hazelnut coffee and buttercream icing drifting through the café reassured me the long line was worth the wait.

Vincent had sent a text yesterday saying his house was still off-limits and we wouldn't be able to resume working until early next week. Less than ten minutes after his text, Reid had texted and asked if I could stage his house this weekend. We planned to meet at Whisks and Whiskers at nine o'clock and then walk to his house. But it was five after nine now, with no sign of Reid.

A smiling young couple, each carrying a large coffee cup and a white bag of bakery treats, pushed through the door to the street. A wave of chilly April air sailed into the restaurant, blowing a small clump of fur across the floor. I shivered, despite the jeans and lightweight sweater I was wearing. In a rare fit of indecisiveness this morning, I'd tried on five different outfits—shorts with a quarter-sleeve top, three knee-length summer dresses, and yoga pants with a tank top—before I settled on jeans. I put more effort into getting ready than I normally would on a Saturday morning, and the more I reminded myself Reid would be moving soon, the more times I swept my mascara wand against my lashes.

An orange and white tabby cat pressed its face against my leg, then looked up at me expectantly. It was King Oliver, the personal pet of Erin Blakeley, who was not only the owner of Whisks and Whiskers, but also one of my good friends. King Oliver was the only rescue cat in the restaurant that wasn't available for adoption. While the other cats lounged on the elaborate carpet-covered towers, King Oliver paraded through the café demanding attention and respect. He knew he was royalty.

I leaned over and petted King Oliver, careful not to let my tote bag swing down and hit him. At five years old, he was twice the size of the other cats. I suspected Erin, the owner of Whisks and Whiskers, gave him more than his fair share of treats. Satisfied with my chin-tickling efforts, King Oliver strode to the next customer in line and commanded their attention with an authoritative meow.

A second barista stepped up to the coffee bar, hastily tying his apron behind his back. The line to the counter split in two and I was now only minutes away from the divine jolt of caffeine and sugar.

A woman with a smooth, silver bob left the counter carrying a stack of three white boxes. Instead of walking toward the door, she headed in my direction, her eyes on my tote bag. "Excuse me, dear. Do you work at Walnut Ridge?" She motioned to the company's logo on my canvas bag. A thick layer of brown, shimmery eyeshadow surrounded her red, watery eyes.

I nodded. "Can I help you with something?"

"I'm Regina Ellsworth; Gigi to everyone except my mother.

My husband was…" she started, then pressed her lips together and looked away.

My stomach spun. She was Willy's widow. "I'm so sorry for your loss. I can't imagine how devastated you and your family must be."

She returned her watery eyes to mine. "Were you there, at the house when it happened?"

"Yes, I was upstairs at the time." I glanced at her stack of boxes and held out my arms. "Here, why don't you let me hold those while we talk? They look heavy."

Gigi carefully transferred them to me. "Thank you, dear. I have a lot of hungry tummies to feed this week. The whole family is staying with us—with me—right now because Willy's funeral is in a couple of days." She adjusted the strap of the leather Gucci purse hanging from her shoulder. "Did you notice anything unusual the morning Willy was..." She trailed off again, but this time kept her eyes fixed on mine.

Without knowing how much the police had told her, I gave her an abridged version of what happened, leaving out any gory details that might upset her. She must have known Willy had gone to Vincent's house to deliver the cease and desist letter because she didn't seem surprised when I mentioned the disagreement between the two men.

"Ah, yes. Vincent Weatherford. What can I say? Willy had a habit of pestering people," Gigi said, keeping her voice low. "Vincent was the latest North Hills resident Willy hounded. I never did understand why those blasted homeowner's association covenants were so important to him. After Willy retired early from the banking industry, he became a realtor. You'd think he would try to please potential clients, but with each cease and desist letter he gave to our neighbors, our dinner parties grew smaller and smaller. I'm sad to say there are plenty of people in this town who disliked him."

"But Willy was president of the homeowner's association. I'd think he would've needed plenty of friends to earn that position."

Gigi gave a small laugh. "That isn't how it works in my neighborhood. Willy could be rather intimidating at times." She took a step closer to me, glancing at the people on either side of us who were busy tapping on their phones. "The other homeowner's association board members were keen to replace him. You know, after all those rumors started about Willy and the neighborhood funds."

"I don't live in North Hills," I said. "I live on the south side of town, so I haven't heard the rumors."

Gigi lowered her chin and lifted her eyes, as though she were used to peering over reading glasses. "I thought everyone had heard the rumors. How long have you lived in Darlington Hills?"

"About a month. Vincent hired me to stage the rooms in his home for his new catalog."

"You're an interior designer?" Gigi said, lifting her brows. "I've been wanting to update some rooms in my home, but Willy wouldn't agree to it. He never could handle change. I tried updating the furniture in our game room not too long ago, and that didn't go over well." She tilted her head and studied me intently. "Do you do design work on the side or do you work exclusively for Walnut Ridge?"

Wow. Gigi's husband had been dead less for less than three days and she wanted to redecorate now that he wasn't around to complain about it. Either she wasn't the sentimental type or she had an accelerated mourning timeline. But business was business, and I wasn't about to turn down a potential job. I shifted her boxes to my left arm and dug through my tote bag with my other hand. I pulled out a business card and gave it to her. "I'd be happy to work for you. My website is listed here at the bottom; you'll be able to see photos of past client projects."

Gigi slid my card into her Gucci bag and reached for her

boxes. “Thank you, dear. I’ll be in touch.” She turned and started for the exit, her heels clipping against the smooth tile of the café.

“Next,” the man behind the counter called out. I was happy to see Erin had hired another employee to help manage the weekend crowd. As much as I loved the café’s food, coffee, and feline company, I didn’t enjoy the slow service on weekends.

I glanced at the new guy’s nametag. “Morning, Timmy. I’d like a vanilla latte with a double shot of espresso, a blueberry—”

“Hey,” said a voice next to me. It was Reid, whose eyes were as watery as Gigi’s had been. “Sorry I’m late. I worked late last night and I’m embarrassed to say I hit snooze a few too many times this morning.” He reached for my hand and once again wrapped it in an electric handshake.

“No worries. All you missed was standing in a long line.” I gave Reid a quick smile, then returned my focus to Timmy. “—a blueberry muffin, and a small bag of fur-rocious fish niblets.”

Reid scrunched his nose. “Fish niblets?”

“They’re treats for my cat, Razzy, whom I absolutely love to spoil. I adopted her from Whisks and Whiskers about a month ago.” I nodded toward the table in the corner by the window where a volunteer with the Darlington Hills Animal Shelter sat talking to an older man with a rescue kitten on his lap.

“Can’t say I’ve ever heard of a cat named Razzy.”

“It’s short for raspberry. I was eating brownie raspberry cheesecake at that booth over there when I fell in love with her.”

Reid stared at the baggie of brown pellets Timmy placed on the counter. “Well, the fish niblets look delicious. Excellent choice. If I were a cat, I’d give up my tail for a bag of these.” He reached into his back pocket, flipped out a thick leather wallet, and handed Timmy a twenty-dollar bill.

I started to protest, but Reid assured me it was the least he could do for being so late.

"Thank you," I said as Timmy handed Reid his change. "Aren't you getting something?"

Reid shook his head. "I've already had a cup of coffee and I don't have a cat, so I won't be needing any fish niblets, thank you very much."

Timmy pointed to the table in the corner. "You could adopt one."

"Nope. Don't like cats," Reid said in the same irreverent tone Vincent used frequently.

I took a step back. What kind of person says they don't like cats while they're in the middle of a cat café? I scolded myself for wasting so much mascara this morning. "I wouldn't say that too loudly in here. They can hear you," I whispered, motioning to a green-eyed calico kitten staring at us from a nearby bench.

Timmy nodded. "It's heresy, dude." Watching Reid from the side of his eyes, Timmy handed me the vanilla latte and a small paper bag holding my muffin.

Outside, Darlington Hills was waking up. Leaves were swept against sides of buildings by a breeze as energetic as the children running around the large water fountain. The stone-paved town square sat at the intersection of two narrow perpendicular streets lined with boutiques and cafés. Shopkeepers raised window shades while waitstaff set up bistro tables and chairs outside their restaurants. It was the perfect morning to sit outside and enjoy breakfast.

"I'm on Drayerson Street, four blocks east of the square," Reid said, turning to the right. "Thanks for helping out this morning. I know it's been a rough week for you."

"Don't mind a bit. I understand you're in a hurry to sell." I paused to sip my coffee. "Have you already closed on another home?" That was usually the reason people were in a rush to sell.

"Not yet."

"Are you moving very far?" I didn't want to pry, but I needed details before my heart got its hopes up.

"Far enough from this town but close enough to the river." He motioned southwardly, and I assumed he meant the James River. "It's time for a change of scenery." He lifted the bottom of his light-blue T-shirt and rubbed his watery eyes.

I succeeded in keeping my gaze above his stomach, but my suddenly acute peripheral vision told me he had abs made of sit-ups and planks. "How's Vincent doing?"

Reid raised his palms. "Don't know. I haven't spoken with him since Thursday when I went to his house." His tone made it clear he didn't want to talk about his brother.

"So I met Willy's widow just now while I was in line," I said, changing the subject. "Poor woman has to bury her husband this week. It's heartbreaking."

He frowned. "Heartbreaking? Huh."

I took another sip of my latte. "What do you mean, 'huh'?" I felt like I had to pull the words out of him. Unlike his brother, who held back nothing, Reid seemed more guarded, more careful with the words he chose.

Reid rubbed his eyes again, this time with the back of his fingers. "Gigi Ellsworth returned to Darlington Hills a couple of months ago. She'd been visiting her sister somewhere in upstate New York for the past eighteen months."

"Eighteen months?" I repeated. "They were estranged?"

"So says the rumor."

I recalled Gigi's eagerness to redecorate and her less-than-kind words about her late husband. "Speaking of rumors, Gigi mentioned one about Willy and his use of his neighborhood's homeowner's association funds."

"Misuse is more like it," Reid responded.

"How did he supposedly misuse the funds? I haven't lived here long enough to catch up on all the rumors."

He smiled down at me. "You'll catch up soon enough. I moved

here seven years ago, but it only took a few months to learn about everyone's business. As for Willy, people complained he was spending an excessive amount of the neighborhood's money on attorney fees to make residents comply with HOA rules. Some say he got personal kickbacks from the attorney whom he paid with neighborhood funds."

"Do you know who the attorney was?"

"The same attorney half the town uses—Chuck Littenthorpe. His office is in the new, trendy section of town just off the highway. He may not have heard about Willy's death yet; he's been on a month-long cruise in the Mediterranean with his wife."

Gigi's comment about people in the town disliking Willy made more sense now, but I wondered why she would mention it to me—a stranger—only days after his death. Did she still resent him for whatever reasons had made her stay with her sister for more than a year? Was it possible she despised her husband so much she killed him? That scenario seemed unlikely, but I supposed it was plausible. Detective Sanders had certainly questioned Gigi, and he would do more digging if he thought there was any reason to suspect her.

As we neared Reid's street, shops and restaurants gave way to well-established Darlington Oak trees, their wide branches intertwined overhead. The steady morning breeze rattled the fresh spring leaves, challenging them to hold fast to their branches. I closed my eyes for a moment to enjoy the delicious blend of cool breeze and warm sun, which had now risen above rooftops and trees.

Reid pulled his keys from his pocket and led me up the sidewalk to his home. It was a large two-story brick house, although not as big as Vincent's. A sweet-smelling cloud of cinnamon and vanilla greeted me the moment he opened the front door.

"Air fresheners?" I asked. "Or do you run a home bakery?"

The corner of Reid's mouth turned upward. "Is it too much? I was trying to freshen things up a bit, make it more welcoming."

I surveyed his entryway, counting three electrical outlets and three plug-in air fresheners. "I suggest dialing back on the air freshener. A subtle whiff is always nice, but you don't want buyers to think you're trying to hide an unpleasant odor." I slipped off my shoes and studied a large, framed black and white photo on the wall to the right of the door. It was an old-time riverboat that looked like something Huck Finn and Jim would have seen while they floated down the Mississippi River.

"Nice boat," I said. I loved the simplicity of the photo and its thin, silver frame. It added character to his entryway without detracting from the open, airy feel of the space.

"You're looking at the *Sutherland*," Reid explained. "She's an old paddlewheeler that cruises up and down the James River several times a day, mostly for historic dinner cruises, weddings, and sometimes corporate events. Although last night, she hosted more than seventy-five children and their parents for a ten-year-old's birthday party."

I recalled Vincent's comment about Reid puttering down the river. "Oh, so you work on the *Sutherland*?"

"Yes ma'am."

"Are you the captain?"

He smiled. "No, I'm the owner. But I do play host at a fair number of the cruises and give guided history tours. My parents would be proud I'm actually putting my history degree to good use." He led me into his family room and gave me a coaster for my latte. "I'm going to leave you here for a moment. I gotta get these contacts out of my eyes. Feel free to start looking around and rearrange anything you need to. You're the boss." Rubbing his eyes again, he started toward a hallway near the kitchen.

Reid was a history buff? The idea intrigued me enough to make up for his dislike of cats. I had always loved history, especially as it related to this region of Virginia, with the colonial romanticism of Jamestown, Yorktown, and Williamsburg—an area known to locals as the Historic Triangle.

I took several steps back to get a wide-angle view of the family room. I had staged a number of homes in New Orleans and most of the time, I was able to get them ready for the market with minimal intervention. Sometimes I recommended changing wall colors to more neutral hues, but usually all it took was decluttering and rearranging the furniture and decorations they already had. After numerous bargain-hunting trips to flea markets and garage sales, I had accumulated an assortment of decorations, which I loaned to clients while their house was on the market. I kept my stash of lamps, rugs, throw pillows, and other decor in my so-called design studio, which was nothing more than a ten- by fifteen-foot unit at Aunt Deb's self-storage facility, Darlington Mini Storage.

Reid's family room was clean and tidy with minimal personal items like picture frames. These were a no-no when selling a home because it's easier for buyers to imagine themselves living in the home if there aren't photos of its current residents.

Moving to his fireplace mantel, I gathered his vast collection of small ceramic ducks, then put them in a pile on his coffee table for storage-bound clutter. I relocated a tall glass vase from his end table to the mantle, just to the right of a large rectangular mirror. Now the mantel held only the mirror, vase, and a fancy wooden clock that looked like an antique.

I pulled my notebook and pen from my tote bag and started a list of items to collect from my studio. At the top of the list was the bunch of dried cotton stems for his empty vase, as well as a pair of teal-striped throw pillows to jazz up his beige couch.

Moving throughout the family room, I continued decluttering and adding items to the discard pile on the coffee table. I scooted his sofa and recliner closer together, then repositioned the coffee table.

There. Now the room looked cozier and larger. I started toward the end table, then stopped abruptly. None of the furniture or decorations in the family room were from Walnut Ridge. Very odd.

A phone rang in the kitchen area. Wearing rectangular tortoiseshell glasses, Reid emerged from the hallway and retrieved his phone from the table he'd set it on before he went into his bedroom.

"Hang on a sec, Hadley," he said. In half a dozen large steps, Reid made it to a framed glass door that led to a covered patio. He brought the phone to his ear as he closed the door behind himself.

Immediately, Reid's voice penetrated through the glass. I couldn't make out what he was saying, but it sounded like he was repeating the same five words, as if the person on the other end wasn't acknowledging them.

The same Reid who had so kindly paid for my breakfast and who'd been full of casual smiles was now jabbing a pointed finger in the air as he paced and hollered. Seeing his scrunched-up red face through the window was all I needed to finish staging his home without entertaining any more fantasies of a paddle-wheeler cruise along the James River with a handsome man as my guide.

# CHAPTER FIVE

After I left Reid's home, I walked to my storage unit to hunt for some items to add a bit of flair to his family room and kitchen. I stopped by Aunt Deb's office to say hi, but she was talking with a customer. Once inside the gate, I headed to my unit in the far back corner of the facility. It was a hike, but I had insisted that Aunt Deb give me the least desirable location since she insisted on not charging me for my unit.

I gathered the decorative pillows, dried cotton stems, some decorative serving bowls, and a table lamp from the tiered shelves in my studio, then placed them in the corner next to my desk. Reid would have to wait on the decor. I needed some time to get his angry face out of my mind and he needed time to cool off. He had been in attack mode, and I was certain if the other person on phone had been there in person, Reid's back patio would have become a wrestling ring. I wondered if he was easy to anger or if someone had done something extreme to spark that level of anger.

"Knock, knock," Aunt Deb sang as she neared my unit. "It's too gorgeous of a day to hang out inside this metal cage." She slipped off her sandals before she stepped onto my studio's white shag area rug, which I had splurged on when I found out I'd gotten the job at Walnut Ridge.

"Sorry I couldn't chat when you swung by just now," she said. "I was trying to convince Mrs. Little she needs to rent a third storage unit now that her son is moving back home and she needs to make space for his belongings. But she kept talking nonsense, saying she needs to abandon her packrat ways and do some spring cleaning."

I laughed. "Don't give up on her. Once a packrat, always a packrat. I give her two days of spring cleaning before you hand her another set of keys." I hoped I was right. Aunt Deb's storage facility had been losing money since last fall, and there were more vacant units than ever. She and her late husband, my Uncle Bill, had bought the facility twenty-five years ago and Aunt Deb had done minimal repairs since his death five years ago.

Recently, customers began complaining about the rusty doors, mediocre security—there had been two break-ins in the past year—and worst of all, roof leaks. Three units on the west side had received water damage during a tropical storm last summer. She had the roof fixed, but the damage had already been done to the reputation of her facility. If she didn't lease more storage units soon, she would have to sell her business. If that happened, she would likely move to Chicago to live near her son, Michael.

My phone rang, and I scurried to retrieve it from my tote bag. I didn't recognize the number, but I relaxed when I saw it wasn't Reid. I wasn't ready to talk to him.

"Good morning, this is Hadley," I said, trying to sound professional in case it was Gigi Ellsworth calling to schedule a consultation.

"Dennis Appley here. Just wanted to check in and see how everything's going."

"Hi, Dennis—I mean, Officer Appley. Everything's good. I haven't gone back to work at Vincent's home yet"—I swished a hand to fend off Aunt Deb, whose man-radar had activated the moment I'd said 'Dennis'—"but you probably already know that, don't you?"

"That's right, we've been really busy out at Mr. Weatherford's home the past couple of days. Detective Sanders and I are working several leads, so I don't want you worrying about your safety. You just moved here and we'd like to keep you a while longer."

"The length of my stay here hinges on whether I have a job when all of this is over." I hoped he would understand the subtext of my response. If Vincent had killed Willy, I'd be saying sayonara to Darlington Hills.

"Ah, yes. I guess that makes sense." He sounded disappointed.

I frowned. Was Dennis calling to ask me more questions for the investigation or was this a social call? I'd never heard of the police giving courtesy calls to reassure citizens of their safety. "What leads are you working on? Are there any that don't involve my boss? Or should I start looking for another job?"

Dennis was silent for a moment. "You know, I heard the quilting supplies store on Sixth Avenue is hiring right now. It might not be a bad idea to go apply there. Today."

Yikes. Bad news for Vincent, bad news for my job. "Thanks for the advice, but quilting isn't my bailiwick." Though it might be a good idea for me to learn, in case Vincent went to jail and I couldn't get out of my apartment lease.

"I can't say anything one way or the other about your boss and our investigation, but be sure to check the classifieds in tomorrow's newspaper. And you have my number now, so please call me if you ever need anything."

"Actually, I do have something for you," I said. "I'm sure you've heard the same rumors I have, but it's worth mentioning that Willy's widow, Gigi, recently came back to Darlington Hills after staying with her sister for more than a year."

Dennis laughed. "Rumors aren't very helpful in my line of

work. I usually learn more about the person spreading the rumor than anyone else. Do you know Gigi well, or did someone else share the details of her personal life with you?"

I started to respond, but there was a strange bleating noise on Dennis' end of the phone, followed by the unmistakable sound of him covering his phone's mouthpiece and telling someone or something to hush.

He uncovered his phone's mic. "Sorry about that."

"Is that a…goat?" I couldn't think of anything else that would make such a noise.

"Yep. My Sadie is telling me it's time for lunch." The bleating resumed, this time louder. "Hey, I'll catch up with you later."

Aunt Deb raised her eyebrows as soon as I turned my phone off. "Who's Dennis?"

"Just a cop who's helping to investigate Willy's death."

"Is he available?"

"For you?" I said, throwing the question back to her.

She started coughing, as she usually did whenever I alluded to her dating again. "Goodness, no, dear. I've had my go-round with love and it ended when your uncle passed. We were still deeply in love with each other after twenty-five years of marriage."

The keyword being 'ended.' Aunt Deb was as kindhearted as she was beautiful, and I knew she could have another loving relationship if she wanted.

Aunt Deb reclined in my oversized bean bag chair, her long wispy skirt billowing around her. "I'm only saying you should consider going out with him if he asks." She wiggled her brows up and down several times. "Maybe he's looking for a lady's vase to place his flowers."

I laughed. The annual Spring Flower Festival was turning Aunt Deb into Cupid's sidekick. I'd never been in town during the event, but after living in Darlington Hills for one month, I'd learned everything I ever wanted to know about the festival, which had taken place once a year for the past ninety-five years.

Women would place a water-filled vase tagged with their name onto a long table in the town square. Throughout the festival, men placed flowers in the vase of any woman or women they're sweet on—sometimes anonymously but usually with an accompanying note. And businesses, of course, used the festival to showcase their offerings and generate income. I hadn't lived in Darlington Hills more than a week before Carmella convinced me to make flower wreaths to sell at the festival to raise money for cat adoptions at Whisks and Whiskers.

"Is he your age? Because this conversation is pointless if he's fixin' to retire."

I recalled Dennis' shaggy, boy-band hairstyle. "I'm at least five years older, probably more."

Aunt Deb clasped her hands together. "That's perfect."

"He isn't interested in me. That call was strictly business," I lied.

She sighed. "Well don't be surprised if you find a flower in your vase. I promise I won't say I told you so."

"He has a pet *goat,* Aunt Deb. A goat named Sadie." Mic drop. End of conversation.

She shook her head. "Never judge a man by how many horns his pets have, hon. I'm surprised your mama never taught you that."

# CHAPTER SIX

My stomach rumbled, announcing its extreme displeasure with me for waiting so long to eat dinner. It was almost eight o'clock and I was still working at Vincent's house.

Terence eyed my belly as he dragged a wicker sofa across the sunroom's terra-cotta tiles. "You think Vincent would mind if we finish this room tomorrow morning? I have a Psych exam to study for tonight and you need to get some dinner."

"Why don't you head home?" I suggested, then glanced at Josh, who was installing a rustic chandelier in the center of the room. "Josh and I should be able to finish up in the next twenty minutes."

Josh gave a non-committal grunt from the top of the ladder. I gave a thumbs-up to Terence, who collected the painting supplies he'd used to change the room from pastel yellow to a light minty green. His shoulders, like mine, drooped from a long day of scurrying around trying to make up for not working the past week. We had finished staging and shooting two bedroom sets, the new line of office furniture, and three casual family room arrangements before lunch.

The afternoon was just as crazy, beginning with photos in the most dreaded room of all—the kitchen. An electrician had come out earlier in the week to rewire an old circuit, so the lights were working once again. Although the kitchen's spotless wood floor bore no evidence of last week's tragedy, the mood was tense. Words were not spoken; they were whispered. No amount of bleach and scrubbing could change what had happened in the sunshiny-white kitchen. The room was like a graveyard, heavy with gloom and death.

But the mood didn't stifle Vincent's outbursts. In the midst of a looming murder investigation and local media coverage of the stabbing at Walnut Ridge, his deadline for photos was shrinking. He expected time to slow down and productivity to speed up, and he lashed out when neither happened.

Everyone seemed extra amenable to Vincent's demands today. I guessed it had more to do with suspicions of his involvement in Willy's death and less to do with empathy for him during a stressful time. Even Sonya's protesting seemed muted, perhaps because none of her Forest Action League buddies had joined her.

Terence looked at me, jingling his car keys. "You sure you don't want me to stick around and give you a ride home? It's already dark out and I'm not sure it's safe for you to walk home by yourself."

"Thanks, but I don't want to keep you waiting. You have a test to ace, mister. And it's only a ten-minute walk. The streets are well lit and if I need anything, I'm never far from a nice neighbor." Except for the short trek over the Bonn Creek footbridge. Maybe I'd jog that stretch of my walk tonight.

"Don't you have a car?" Josh asked. "Might not be a bad idea to drive to work for the time being."

I nodded. "But it's pointless to drive when I can just as easily walk. I enjoy the exercise. And a violent crime every now and then doesn't make Darlington Hills unsafe."

Terence's tired eyes grew serious. "I grew up here, and I can tell you this town isn't what it used to be. Ten years ago, ninety percent of folks living here had great-great grandparents who had also grown up in Darlington Hills. But then some tourists came along who snapped some photos of the Ladyvale Manor, posted them on Instagram, and the photos went viral. Then Darlington Hills became one of the top tourist destinations in Virginia, and a good number of those tourists decided they'd like to move here. Those people brought money with them and the money brought problems."

Aunt Deb had told me the story. The Ladyvale Manor became famous overnight, enchanting everyone with its ivy-wrapped facade and labyrinth-like hedges. The new wave of people moving to Darlington Hills gradually drove up home prices, which made property taxes shoot up so high some residents could no longer afford to live here.

I moved toward the family room. "Come on, I'll walk with you to the door. I need to grab a pitcher and glasses from the storage bin near the office."

"Darlington Hills isn't the same place you used to come visit as a child," Terence said, following me. "Look at our man Vincent. He came to town dangling his wallet in front of the old woman who used to own this house and she sold it to him. No telling how long she and her family had lived here."

"Don't worry about me. I've lived in cities with a murder rate a gazillion times higher than here."

Terence didn't look convinced by my reasoning. "Okay, but call me if you need anything." He stepped outside and his car beeped twice as he pressed the unlock button on his key.

I rummaged through the storage bin and found some glasses and a pitcher for the coffee table in the sunroom. It wasn't part of a new collection, but the rustic vibes of the hammered copper pitcher meshed well with the wicker furniture. I started back toward the sunroom, but paused when Rachael's chipper voice drifted in from the dining room.

Setting down the pitcher and glasses, I headed toward her. She was talking to Silent Kyle and Harry the Hummer, telling them to arrive early tomorrow to set up extra lighting in the dim mud room before the photo shoot. I approached her when she finished talking.

"Hey, Rachael. You have a minute?"

She gave a warm smile. "Sure. What's up?"

"Do you have a flash drive or memory stick with all of the photos you've taken so far? I'd like to look through them and flag my favorites for Vincent." Technically, it wasn't my job to help select the photos for the catalog, but I wanted to look through them from the morning of Willy's death and see if anything seemed off.

Kyle grunted. "We've taken more than three thousand photos so far. No way would they fit on a flash drive."

"I can give you access to our cloud photo storage website," Rachael said, laughing. "I'll text you the login info tonight."

I blushed. "Right. The cloud. Of course." At least I hadn't asked her to save them to a floppy disk.

After a long day on my feet, my fuzzy pink memory foam slippers were the next best thing to a long foot massage. Sitting at my table with a plate of chicken tikka masala and biryani rice, I propped up my happy feet on the chair across from me—one of the few benefits of eating by myself.

I had thrown all of the ingredients into the slow cooker this morning and scheduled it to cook on low for eight hours. Had I known my chicken would cook for nearly twelve hours, I would have planned on something else for dinner. Usually when I overcooked chicken it was charred and rubbery. But the amazing smell that greeted me when I came home confirmed my faith in the power of the slow cooker, which automatically switched to the warm setting after eight hours passed.

If only Aunt Deb could witness this dinner victory. I decided I'd put some in a storage container for her and drop it off before work tomorrow. It would make a nice lunch.

The rich, flavorful aroma circulating through my kitchen helped to make my tiny apartment feel more like home, adding another dimension of coziness and comfort. Still, I couldn't help but wonder what it would be like to cook such a meal in a kitchen with endless countertops like Vincent's. I would need numerous clients before I could ever afford a kitchen like his. And I'd need to keep my job at Walnut Ridge, which meant I needed to prove Vincent was innocent—if he truly was.

I flipped open my laptop and typed in the web address Rachael had texted me, along with her team's username and password. More than a dozen folders popped up, categorized by date. I took another bite of rice, then clicked on last Thursday's folder. Rows and rows of thumbnail-sized photos appeared, some loading more slowly than others.

This would take a while. I sat up straight and folded my legs under me, which Razzy took as an invitation to jump onto my lap. The pink flannel pajama pants I'd slipped into when I got home were her favorite.

The thumbnail photos were too small to see any level of detail, so I double clicked on the first photo and waited several seconds for the full image to load. For the next thirty minutes I scrolled through photos of the entry hall. Close-ups, wide-angles, bird's-eye and worm's-eye views—they had photographed the room and all its Walnut Ridge decor from every angle possible.

Photos of the entry hall's large floral rug, walnut bench, oval mirror, and white-washed teak console table were interspersed with photos of a gray card. I had learned the cards help them fine-tune their white balance setting so everything is true to color.

One of the photographers who was shooting the entry hall from inside the adjacent dining room must have gotten sidetracked because he or she took dozens of close-ups of the ceramic vase and peony floral arrangement on the dining room table.

I yawned and checked the clock on my microwave. It was ten o'clock and I'd only made it through half of the photos from Thursday. Scratching Razzy's chin with one hand, I clicked my mouse with the other, zipping through photo after photo of the peonies. There was another photo of a gray card; this time it was tilted against the side of the ceramic vase. In the background, the wide-arched doorway revealed the breakfast room where Vincent was standing with his back to the dining room.

He had been arguing with Willy when this photo was taken. My heart accelerated at this realization, and I punched the mouse button to advance to the next image. I couldn't bear to look at photos of Vincent yelling at a man who was killed less than an hour later. What a sad, sad way to spend his final minutes on earth.

More peony photos followed, but from a different angle that seemed to catch the light from the window better. If Vincent had known the photographer had veered from the itinerary and shot photos of the dining room during the entry hall photo shoot, perhaps he would have berated the photographer instead of Willy.

An image of Vincent yelling at Willy flashed through my mind. I froze as I forced myself to revisit the ugly memory. I had been standing between the two men while they argued in the breakfast room. Vincent had stood to my left with his back to his kitchen.

That meant the man in the photo with his back to the camera had been Willy, not Vincent.

I moved my mouse slowly to the left until the arrow on my screen hovered over the back button. I didn't want to see a photo of Willy standing on his two feet, unaware he'd soon be dead on his stomach.

But I clicked the back button anyway. The photo of the gray card popped up and I sighed with relief. It wasn't Willy with his back to the camera; it was Vincent in his blue shirt.

I gasped, then clicked the zoom button furiously. Although the enlarged photo was heavily pixelated, it was clear enough to show the man with his back to the camera was wearing a blue, long-sleeve shirt and khaki pants.

Vincent never wore khakis. He abhorred them.

My eyes had tricked me, but my memory of the argument was correct: Vincent had stood to my left and Willy to my right, but at the time I hadn't noticed that when Willy removed his raincoat, he was wearing a long-sleeve blue shirt similar to Vincent's.

My pulse quickened. What if I wasn't the only one who'd thought Willy was Vincent?

I narrowed my eyes and studied the photo. Willy had gray hair and a slender frame. From behind, he looked just like Vincent. Could someone have stabbed Willy in the back accidentally? The similarities between the two men had been enough to fool me, and it was reasonable to think they could have fooled anyone else. Maybe the killer hadn't seen Willy's face before killing him.

Maybe Vincent was the target.

I snatched my phone from the table and dialed Vincent. After the fourth ring it went to voicemail, and I asked him to call me as soon as he got my message.

I continued scrolling through the photos on my laptop, looking for anything that seemed out of place. Between each photo, my eyes traveled to the clock in the corner of my computer screen to check how much time had elapsed since I'd called Vincent. Two minutes. Two minutes and fifteen seconds. Three minutes. My mind raced as time putted along. If someone had accidentally killed Willy instead of Vincent, would they try again?

I pried Razzy from my lap, set her on the chair next to me, and retrieved my Walnut Ridge tote bag from the kitchen counter. Detective Sander's business card was wedged between my design inspiration notebook and some magazines.

I started to enter his number into my phone but hesitated before I tapped on the green 'call' button. I didn't have any valid reasons for disturbing him at this late hour; I was overreacting.

Detective Sanders would probably be irritated if I called to tell him Vincent and Willy were wearing the same shirt. Surely he had already made the same observation; he was the pro. And he would have let Vincent know if they thought he was in any danger.

But I wanted to make sure Vincent knew. With the tap of a few buttons, I found his number and dialed again.

Voicemail. Instead of leaving another message, I texted him.

HADLEY

Call me when you get this. It's urgent.

"He's probably in the shower," I informed Razzy. "Or he's turned his music up so loud he can't hear his phone ringing."

Razzy gave me the classic cat stare that told me she had zero interest in my opinions.

"I can wait until tomorrow to talk to Vincent. This isn't urgent and I do not need to drive to his house right this minute to show him the photos."

My computer screen dimmed after several minutes of inactivity. I jiggled my mouse and the screen brightened, illuminating the photo of Vincent's backside look-alike.

I closed my laptop and stuffed it in my tote bag, then pulled my car keys from the junk drawer next to the refrigerator. "Be right back, Razzy girl." I ran outside to the parking lot and scrambled inside my little blue Ford Focus. The seats were cool, and my breath immediately fogged up the windshield. I put the car in reverse and pressed the gas pedal.

During the day, Darlington Hills was a kaleidoscope of vivid colors, with green trees, red-brick homes and yellow, pink, and purple flowers. At night, it was a city of shadows. The dim gas street lamps illuminated small circles beneath them, casting everything else into blackness. I hadn't minded walking home earlier this evening, but I was thankful I was in my car now.

I turned left onto Picket Lane, the main road connecting the north and south sides of Darlington Hills. While there were two footbridges across Bonn Creek—one on the west side and one on the east—there was only one bridge for vehicles. I flashed my high beams as I approached the narrow bridge, which was more like a tunnel because it was enclosed on all sides with heavy red timber to protect the bridge from the rain and ice.

At the next stop sign, I checked my phone to see if Vincent had returned my text. He was usually so quick to respond.

I sighed. Nothing.

He's probably in the shower. Or maybe he's already asleep. I slowed my car and put on my blinker, ready to turn around and wait until tomorrow to show Vincent the photos. It wasn't likely someone had accidentally killed Willy, but a faint tug in my stomach, a flutter of nerves, told me I needed to let Vincent know tonight. I flipped the blinker off and drove the rest of the way to his house.

Vincent's convertible was parked with its roof down in his driveway. Walking up the sidewalk toward his front door, I rang his doorbell then took a step back and stared down at my feet. Dim light shone from the downstairs windows.

Rats. I was in my pajama pants and fuzzy pink slippers.

I'd been in such a hurry to leave that I hadn't changed my shoes or grabbed a jacket to cover my thin tank top. I glanced back at my car, tempted to run from his house so he wouldn't see me. But if he caught me doing a ring and run, he'd think I was more of a nut than if I greeted him at the door in my PJs.

I peeped through the narrow window next to the door. The entry hall and family room were empty, and the lights were off in the office and dining room.

Something moved above me. I shifted my eyes upstairs in time to see a shadow slip along the far wall at the top of the stairs.

I punched the doorbell again. Was Vincent avoiding me? There was no way he hadn't heard the doorbell. It was loud enough for me to hear outside on his front porch. How rude.

I tossed up my hands and looked back at my car. It was late and I wanted to return to the warmth of my apartment. I pulled my phone from my pocket and dialed his number again. One more time, and then I was going home.

The ringing that sounded through my phone's earpiece was followed by a faint echo. I lowered my phone and listened. No, it wasn't an echo; it was Vincent's ringtone. I pressed my ear against the window. It wasn't coming from inside the house.

I backed away from the window and listened. Following the sound, I crossed Vincent's driveway and walked around the side of the house, which was lined with tall hedges. Vincent must have left his phone outside. That would explain why he hadn't answered my calls.

The ringing stopped, and I paused before I rounded the corner to his backyard. Something wasn't right. Vincent always kept his phone in his pocket. Rarely did an evening pass where he didn't send multiple texts to us through his team's group chat. And he wasn't asleep; I'd just seen him moving around upstairs.

I called Vincent's phone again and continued to follow its ringtone. With only dim exterior lighting in the backyard, I had to squint to see. The ringing grew louder, but I didn't see the light from a screen.

The low-hanging clouds separated, and the weak glow of the slivered moon helped me navigate past his multi-level stone patio. A dark heap on the ground near the far corner of the house caught my eye. It was too large to be a neighbor's dog, unless it was a Great Dane. I tiptoed toward it, my legs ready to run in the opposite direction if it was indeed an animal.

His ringtone grew louder as I approached and the dark form took shape: arms, legs, head, neck.

My phone fell from my hands. It was a body—Vincent's body—his phone ringing excitedly from the side pocket of his pajama pants.

# CHAPTER SEVEN

"Is he alive?" Dennis asked me the moment I called and told him what happened.

"He has a pulse, but I can't wake him up," I shrieked.

"Have you called an ambulance?" Dennis' voice was calm, unlike the shrill, panicky mumbo jumbo coming from my mouth.

"I called 9-1-1. They're sending an ambulance now. I didn't have Detective Sanders' number handy, but I had saved yours after you called me last weekend. I thought you'd want to know what happened in case this has anything to do with the murder investigation."

"Oh, you saved my number?"

"Yes…" I said, suddenly aware he sounded far more interested in being added to my list of contacts than in the murder case he was working. "I wanted to have your number handy in case I came across anything that could help you with Willy's case." I didn't tell him Aunt Deb had guilted me into saving his contact info.

"Oh, right. The case." I practically heard his heart sinking with disappointment. "Well listen, this is probably a medical issue—heart attack, stroke—something like that. But I'll call Sanders and we'll be there in less than ten minutes. Don't try to move him. Wouldn't be good if he has any sort of neck or back injury. And try not to touch anything in the area in case it is a crime scene."

I found a deep shadow against the back of the house not too far from Vincent, and sat in the grass while I waited. My gut told me this wasn't a medical issue. It was too coincidental. Willy was stabbed in Vincent's kitchen. Willy looked just like Vincent from behind. And now, Vincent was unresponsive in his backyard a week later.

I frowned. I had seen Vincent moving around upstairs only minutes ago when I looked through the window. So how did he get to his backyard without coming down the stairs? I would have seen him.

Unless the shadow hadn't belonged to Vincent.

I turned around and lifted my eyes to the second story of the mammoth home. Vincent's balcony, which extended from his private bedroom, was directly above where he lay in the grass. A new wave of dread struck me. He had either fallen, jumped or been pushed. My bets were on the latter scenario.

A door closed somewhere nearby, then moments later feet crunched on grass—slow at first, then more rapidly. Something or someone was running, but not towards me. Maybe a neighbor had let a dog outside to do its business before bed, or someone was going for a late-night jog.

Or someone who wasn't supposed to be at Vincent's house was leaving.

I wrapped my arms around my legs and pulled them close to my chest. The footsteps vanished and the night returned to stillness. Aside from the swishing leaves overhead, the neighborhood was quiet.

I rubbed my forehead. Had someone pushed Vincent over the balcony tonight? If so, what awful thing could he have done to make someone try to kill him? It wasn't difficult to think of people who disliked Vincent—Sonya and her Forest Action

League friends, the North Hills homeowners association, Vincent's neighbors, and probably half of his own Walnut Ridge crew. I'd even sensed tension between Vincent and his own brother.

I gasped. Reid! I hadn't called to tell him about Vincent. Even if they weren't the best of friends, he'd still want to know what happened. I scrolled to his number and called him. After one ring, it went to voicemail.

"Hi, Reid, it's Hadley. Please call me as soon as you get this. It's about Vincent. Thanks." I lowered the phone to hang up, then added, "It's an emergency."

Despite the gravity of the present situation, I couldn't help but wonder if Reid had saved my number in his phone's contacts list. We had exchanged a handful of texts in the past several days, but they were all about getting his home ready to sell. And even though his texts were strictly business, each time my phone had dinged and I saw his name, my stomach rippled with excitement.

The sky lit up with swirling red and yellow lights. Paramedics and police officers streamed into the yard, their flashlights racing across the grass. I ran over to Detective Sanders and Dennis as soon as they rounded the corner of the house.

"I think someone pushed him over his balcony," I said, walking alongside them as they approached Vincent. "Look at him. Vincent is lying directly under his balcony."

Detective Sanders held up his hand. "Whoa, whoa, Miss Sutton. Let's take it from the top. "First of all, kindly tell me what you're doing here this hour of the night." His eyes shifted to my pajama pants and slippers.

I cringed, imagining what he was thinking. Vincent was in pajamas, I was in pajamas—it didn't look good. I folded my arms across my thin tank top. "Vincent wasn't answering my calls or texts tonight, so I drove over here to talk to him. I thought I saw him through his window, but when Vincent didn't answer his door, I called him again and heard his phone ringing in the backyard. That's when I found him on the ground."

Detective Sanders glanced at Vincent, the balcony, and then me. "And what, may I ask, did you need to tell him that was so important? It's past eleven o'clock." His slow, deep voice was as serious as the two squinted eyes he set in my direction. Dennis, who was standing to Detective Sanders' right, looked like he was fighting a smile.

"I thought he was in danger," I said, then told them about the photo I'd come across and my theory about Willy as the accidental victim.

After studying me for a moment, Detective Sanders called out to a paramedic with a militaristic buzz cut. "Billy, what's the word? Is this looking like a health case or something else?"

Billy didn't look up as he took Vincent's vitals. "Definitely a fall, Detective. Broken leg—just look at the angle of his left one—and possible fractures elsewhere. Probably has a concussion as well. We're taking him to the hospital as soon as we can get a neck brace on him and put him on the stretcher."

Detective Sanders returned his attention to me. "I've got some work to do here, but I'll need to see that photo of yours."

"So you think the person who killed Willy could have pushed Vincent tonight?" I asked.

"I don't play guessing games," Detective Sanders said. "I gather evidence and I analyze it. I've worked in law enforcement for thirty-seven years, miss. I spent most of that time in Dallas, Texas, which has a much higher crime rate that this little town. I can tell you this: when a person of interest in a murder case ends up flattened on the ground under their window, roof, or balcony, it's usually one of two things—either their conscience got the better of them or they'd rather die than go to prison."

I digested his words. "You think Vincent jumped?" I shook my head. "I don't think that's what happened. When I rang his doorbell earlier and looked in his window, I saw the shadow of someone moving upstairs. I think it belonged to whoever pushed Vincent. He wouldn't have jumped; he cares too much about his company."

Detective Sanders chuckled. "Don't worry, I'm going to do a full sweep of Mr. Weatherford's home—just like the one I did last week. If I see any suspicious shadows, I'll be sure to let you know."

He started walking toward Vincent, pulling a small camera from his pocket. He looked back at me and chuckled again. "But I have to warn you, it's mighty hard to ID a shadow in a police lineup."

Detective Sanders nodded at Dennis. "Officer Appley, please make sure we get a copy of that photo from our honorary police trainee."

Dennis turned to me, releasing a smile. "You know, there's a good reason I gave you my card last time we met. It's so you can call me if you have something pertaining to our investigation." Dennis' authoritative, professional voice didn't seem to match his shaggy blonde hair and smooth complexion.

My cheeks warmed. "I guess I can't get away with claiming I didn't have your number handy, can I?"

"No ma'am. I haven't forgotten that I officially made it into your list of contacts," he said, his cop tone turning slightly flirtatious. "Be sure to make good use of your brand-new phone contact. Call me if you have anything related to this case to share. Or unrelated. I'd welcome that kind of call as well."

Razzy greeted me with an impatient meow when I returned to my apartment. Usually at this time of the night, she was curled up next to me on my bed, using my legs as her personal heating pad.

I locked the door, then refilled her water bowl. "Sorry, sweetie. Tonight's going to be a late night." It was almost midnight but my mind was spinning with too many questions to sleep.

After filling a glass of water for myself, I sank into a chair at my table and rubbed my temples. The three scenarios that could explain what had happened to Vincent cycled through my mind like a frantic merry-go-round. Jumped, fell, pushed. Jumped, fell, pushed.

I was pretty sure he hadn't fallen. He wouldn't have been on the roof fixing anything because he never did his own home repairs. And if he had stumbled on his balcony, the waist-high railing would have protected him.

That left two possibilities with vastly different implications for Vincent, one in which he was likely guilty of murder, and another in which he was a victim. Sanders implied Vincent had likely jumped. Hopefully Vincent would remember what happened if and when he regained consciousness.

No wonder Vincent had asked me to do some sleuthing on his behalf. As ridiculous as his request had seemed at the time, maybe Vincent truly did need someone with a different perspective looking into Willy's murder—someone who wouldn't laugh at a shadow.

I knew what I'd seen when I looked through Vincent's window. He didn't have any pets, which meant someone had been walking around upstairs. And that someone didn't want to answer the doorbell. If the shadow belonged to Vincent, he would have fallen or jumped while I was at the front door. Maybe he didn't know it was me at the door, and he was trying to get away from whomever he thought it was. If that were the case, wouldn't I have heard him fall? Surely he would have yelled when he fell, whether he did it intentionally or not.

That left one logical explanation: someone pushed Vincent before I rang the doorbell—possibly moments before I had arrived—and was still upstairs when I peeked through the window.

I sucked in a quick breath as a new thought zipped through my mind. If I had indeed seen the shadow of the person who pushed Vincent, they probably would have seen me or noticed my car out front.

Footsteps thumped overhead, making me jump. I grabbed my phone and dialed Carmella. She picked up after one ring.

"Sorry to call so late, but I know I'm not waking you up because I hear you walking in your kitchen," I said, looking up at my ceiling. "Do you have a minute to talk?"

"How do you know I wasn't sleepwalking?"

"Because sleepwalkers don't walk through the kitchen, then dispense ice and water from the refrigerator."

"The walls in this place are too thin." She laughed, not sounding the least bit tired. "I just got off the phone with Neil, so I'm free to talk now." Neil was Carmella's on-again, off-again long-distance boyfriend. They met in Oregon, where Carmella was born and raised, shortly before she took the position as principal of Darlington Hills Middle School three years ago. Neil was still in Oregon, finishing his last year of law school. "What's up? Everything okay?"

"Vincent's in critical condition at Southwest Regional. He somehow fell off his second-story balcony tonight."

"He fell?" Carmella repeated.

"Not sure. Most likely he jumped or was pushed. Detective Sanders seems to think he jumped, but I saw something at his house tonight that makes me think he was pushed."

"What were you doing at Vincent's house?" she demanded. "Never mind, I'm coming over. I'll be down in two minutes."

As soon as Carmella hung up, Reid beeped in.

"Reid! Thank goodness you got my message. There's been an accident, and Vincent—"

"Yeah, I know. I'm heading to the hospital now. Billy, one of the paramedics who worked on Vinn, is a friend of mine. He called me on my way home."

"Late night at work?" I asked.

"No, I had…I was just out." Reid sounded distracted, but perhaps it was because he was worried about his brother. Although he didn't sound that worried.

"I don't want to keep you, but please let me know if there's anything I can do."

"Thanks, Hadley. I'll let you know."

I hung up with Reid, then opened my door for Carmella, who was wearing a plush violet robe over her silk pajamas. She picked up Razzy, then settled into a chair at my table.

"Okay, you were about to explain to me why you were at Vincent's house tonight. And please don't tell me it had anything to do with the homicide investigation. I'd rather hear you were there working late or even paying a social visit to Vincent."

"Ew," I said, wrinkling my nose at the thought of getting romantically involved with Vincent. "Definitely not a social visit." I told her about the photo of Vincent and Willy, my numerous calls to Vincent, and what happened when I'd arrived at his house. I kept the scary details, like the odd angle of Vincent's leg, to myself. Carmella couldn't watch a scary movie without having nightmares, so I didn't want to traumatize her right before she went to sleep.

Carmella listened to my story intently, then let out a low whistle. "Here's what I want to know: why did you go to Vincent's house by yourself, in the dark, when there's a solid chance he stabbed that man in the back last week."

I shrugged. "Because I think there's a 'solid' chance he didn't kill Willy. And I'm fairly certain someone else was in his house tonight. While I was waiting for the police, I heard someone open and close a door somewhere nearby and then run away. I don't think it was a neighbor going for a midnight stroll, Carmella. I think it was whomever was inside Vincent's house."

"It makes more sense you saw Vincent's shadow and he didn't want to open the door. Listen, before you make any more solo trips to his house, you need to be certain your boss isn't the killer."

Maybe Carmella was right. I had only worked for Vincent for a handful of weeks, so there was a lot about him I didn't know. Maybe my desire to keep my paychecks coming influenced my reasoning.

I pulled my laptop from my tote bag and powered it on. "Let's see what good 'ol Google has to say about Vincent." I had researched his company before my interview, but it was mostly to learn about the products he offered so I could better explain why my design style and vision would match well with his company.

Starting broad, I typed 'Vincent Weatherford Walnut Ridge' into the search box. "Only two million, four hundred results to sort through," I informed Carmella.

Carmella yawned. "You're going to need some coffee. I might as well, too. How about I brew us a couple of cups?"

"Thanks, hon. You're the best." I returned my focus to the screen. The official Walnut Ridge Furniture and Decor Company website appeared at the top of the search results page. The rest of the results were links to mentions of Walnut Ridge on websites like Pinterest, Instagram, and the style sections of small-town magazines. I clicked on the images tab at the top of the results page, which led to photo after photo of Walnut Ridge furniture and Vincent himself, usually wearing blue jeans and a button-up dress shirt.

After scrolling through the photos on the first page, I clicked the link to show more results. Three rows down, there was an image of a very bent Walnut Ridge floor lamp from the Charmed Harvest collection. The link under the photo was walnutridge-junk.com.

"It is not junk," I said defensively.

Carmella, standing next to my coffeepot, raised an eyebrow.

"Someone created a website dedicated to bashing Walnut

Ridge." I clicked on the link under the thumbnail photo of the bent lamp. The web site loaded. A large image of a Walnut Ridge Lazy Breezes upholstered sofa flashed on the screen. The sofa was white, but two of the seat cushions featured giant brown splotches. In bold, red letters overlaying the image, it read "Got Junk?"

"Someone wasn't very happy with their purchase," I said, letting out a whistle. "But creating an entire website to voice their complaints? Seems rather extreme, doesn't it?"

Carmella leaned over my shoulder and looked at the screen. "Probably an unhappy customer with way too much time on their hands."

I read the caption under the photo of the sofa: "Walnut Ridge's so-called stain-proof designer fabric couldn't stand up to one spilled cup of coffee. This couch is the disappointment of a lifetime."

"Ouch," Carmella said.

I cringed. "Let's hope this website doesn't get a lot of visitors." Scrolling further down the page, I scanned half a dozen photos of other items from Walnut Ridge: lopsided shelves on a mango wood bookcase, the bent lamp I'd seen on the Google image results page, and four poorly sewn decorative pillows that looked more like rhombuses than squares. It was hard to believe one person had received so many defective products. "This website is new. All of the items are from Vincent's recent collections."

"Doesn't Walnut Ridge have a refund policy?" Carmella asked.

"It has a no-questions-asked refund policy. I don't understand why the owner of this website didn't call customer service. They would have replaced everything."

Carmella laughed as she moved over to the coffeepot, which was now full of my favorite brew, roasted hazelnut. "Vincent needs to do a better job of marketing his refund policy."

I frowned. "But it's printed on every box the company sends. You can't miss it. It says something like, 'If you're not happy, we're not happy. Satisfaction guaranteed.' And then it lists the customer service phone number."

"Oh. Well then, that is odd." Carmella filled two mugs with coffee and brought them to the table.

I returned to the top of the webpage and read the list of links along the horizontal navigation bar:

- The Truth about Walnut Ridge Furniture
- An Unresponsible Neighbor
- Killing Trees for Profit
- Petition: Take Action Now

Carmella groaned. "*Unresponsible* neighbor? You've got to be kidding me. It's irresponsible, people! Not unresponsible." Not only was Carmella a middle school principal and former English teacher, she was also a steadfast member of the Grammar Police.

Giggling, I clicked on the Unresponsible Neighbor link. "Why don't you leave a comment on the page and correct them?"

Carmella stole my mouse and slid my laptop closer to her. "You're darn right I'm gonna correct this irresponsible unresponsible nonsense." She scrolled past the image at the top of the page and past a lengthy block of text toward the section that encouraged site visitors to leave a comment.

"Hang on, go back up," I said. "Look at the photo at the top."

She slid her finger along the mouse's scroll wheel until she reached the top. The banner image showed a wide-angle view of the front of the Walnut Ridge home with dozens of cars and the large moving van parked out front.

"This is a recent photo," I said. "Look, there's Terence's car in front of the moving van. How did this website's owner get a hold of this?" I took a slow sip of hot coffee. Why would a website decrying Walnut Ridge's poor craftsmanship also criticize the company for being a bad neighbor?

Carmella shook her head, her sleek bob swinging energetically. "I don't know...maybe one of Vincent's competitors set this site up."

I skimmed the text under the photo of the house and cars. Among dozens of complaints, it mentioned unreasonable levels of noise, garbage in the front yard, and the inability of the school bus to maneuver past all the cars on the street.

At the bottom of the page was a comment from another angry customer:

**@Noodles7839:** Worst company ever. Someone needs to get rid of its owner, take him out to the trash with his furniture.

"Eesh, people can be so awful online," Carmella said.

I nodded. "I'm thinking one of Vincent's neighbors made the website. Let's see if we can find out." I reclaimed my mouse and laptop, then opened another window and navigated to a domain name registrant directory.

After college when I bought the domain name for my budding interior design business, I debated on whether to pay extra to keep my name, email, phone number and address private. Although I'd doubted anyone would search the online directory for my information, my customer service rep convinced me to invest in my privacy so I wouldn't get additional spam.

I typed walnutridgejunk.com into the search box in the registrant directory. The results loaded and I read through the information. "Let's see...the site was created about a month ago, on March fifteenth, and the registrant name is—" I sighed. "Rats. The website owner bought the privacy protection plan."

Carmella pointed to another line on the screen. "This says the owner registered the site from Virginia. Maybe this site does belong to an angry neighbor."

"Or the protestors could have set it up. They may have the resources to do this sort of thing, and they definitely have the motive. They hate Vincent."

If Sonya and her friends were ruthless enough to throw mud balls at Vincent's window, they were ruthless enough to bash his company online.

I returned to the homepage of walnutridgejunk.com and clicked on the image of the bent lamp. It took me to another page with a larger photo of the lamp, followed by a four-paragraph rant about the damaged product.

"Not everyone thinks Walnut Ridge sells junk," Carmella said as I finished reading the last paragraph. She pointed to a single comment at the bottom of the page:

**@Bluezmozart:** Lamps don't bend like this during delivery, you idiot. This is a phony website with phony reviews. Walnut Ridge offers only the finest furniture and decor. No one believes this ridiculousness. Nice try.

"Bluezmozart isn't some random commenter," I said. "It's Vincent. He uses the same name for his home Wi-Fi network. Looks like he found this website before we did."

# CHAPTER EIGHT

With paint color swatches, fabric samples, magazine pages, and colored pencils scattered across the table in my design studio, I brainstormed ideas for a summer-themed fireplace mantel. My apartment didn't have a fireplace, but Aunt Deb was happy to let me decorate hers. I wanted to snap some photos and upload them to my website and Instagram account to promote my Hadley Home Design business. We were already halfway through spring, and now was a good time to showcase my style of summer.

The hallway outside my studio was quiet. Saturday evening wasn't a high-traffic time at Darlington Mini Storage. Most people were likely eating dinner with their family or enjoying an evening out. After a hectic day of staging rooms for photo shoots, a dose of solitude and the soft, soothing scratches of my pencil against the paper was exactly what I needed to unwind.

Vincent was conscious now, but remained in the hospital because he'd had surgery on his broken leg. Terence had a key to Vincent's home, so we were able to continue staging and shooting photos. Vincent didn't want anything stalling his catalog; not even his own near-death experience.

A page I'd torn from a fashion magazine featured a lithe

woman at the helm of a sailboat wearing a white designer sundress splashed with turquoise and bright yellow tulips. Using that photo for color inspiration, I sketched a fireplace mantel featuring a large white vase with a sheer yellow ribbon tied around its neck, holding a dozen white tulips. I drew a round mirror with a wide light-oak frame next to the vase, along with an assortment of turquoise painted jars and a vintage aluminum watering can.

The shelves in my design studio held most of the items I needed to stage the photo—mirror, vase, jars, watering can—but I would need to buy the tulips and yellow ribbon. I scanned my shelves for any additional decorations to add. A worn wooden stool on the top shelf caught my eye. I added it to my sketch, placing it on the floor to the left of the fireplace. I would put Aunt Deb's potted ivy on top of it, and I'd drag one of her larger houseplants to sit on the opposite side of the fireplace.

My phone rang. I was so wrapped up in my sketches that I considered letting it go to voicemail. But after the fourth ring, I glanced at the caller ID. It was Reid.

My stomach swirled with nerves and excitement. It had been two days since Vincent's fall. Reid and I had exchanged a few texts about his brother's status but hadn't spoken.

I pressed the green icon on my phone to answer the call. "Hi, Reid. How's it going? Vincent doing any better today?"

"Actually he is," he said, his voice upbeat. "He's in a lot of pain, but his doc expects him to go home in less than a week."

"Thank heavens," I said. "That's wonderful news." Vincent had suffered a concussion, along with a broken leg and significant bruising.

"Does he remember anything about the night he fell?" I asked.

Reid paused long enough for me to worry I had overstepped the boundaries of my role as his brother's employee. "He does, but I'm not sure how clear his memory is. Vinn says someone pushed him, although he didn't see or hear anyone in the house before his fall."

My heart accelerated as I processed the implications of Reid's statement. If Vincent was indeed pushed, there was a good chance he didn't stab Willy. I recalled Detective Sanders' initial skepticism about the idea of someone pushing Vincent. Did he still think Vincent jumped?

Uncertain of how comfortable Reid was with discussing his brother's accident, I changed the subject. "And how have you been? Getting any sleep? I know you've been up at the hospital quite a bit the last couple of days."

"I'm okay, thanks for asking." I could almost hear a smile in his voice.

"Any bites on your house?"

"I just hired a new realtor and she reshot the photos of my home after you made it look so nice. I've had two showings in the past four days. One of those families is returning for a second showing tomorrow. So keep your fingers crossed for me."

I absolutely would not keep my fingers crossed. Maybe I shouldn't have helped him stage his home.

"Anyway, I'm on my way back from the hospital now and I was wondering if you've eaten dinner yet."

More stomach swirling. Was he asking me to dinner? "I grabbed a bite earlier, but if you'd like some company while you eat then I'd be happy to join you. I'm just hanging out in my design studio working on some fireplace sketches."

"My fireplace? I like what you already did. I wouldn't change a thing."

I laughed. "No, it's for photos I'm taking to promote my design business."

"You work for my crazy brother and you still have energy at the end of the day to run your own business?"

"At this point it's more of a slow crawl than a run, but I'm trying to revive the business I started in New Orleans."

"You won't have any trouble finding clients," he said, his voice deep and confident. "After the influx of new homeowners moved to Darlington Hills, they spent the last several years renovating their homes' exteriors. Soon they'll be itching to change things inside. The timing of your arrival couldn't have been better."

I smiled at his encouraging words. "Thanks. I hope you're right." Especially if his older brother stabbed a man and I lose my job.

"And more important than your timing—you're good at what you do," he said. "I can't believe how much better my place looks after you fixed it up."

"Oh! That reminds me. I have a few more decorations I'd like to loan you until your house sells." I glanced at the pillows, bowls, lamp, and dried cotton stems piled up in the corner.

"I'd appreciate all the help I can get. Tell you what, how about I pick up a burger and then pop by your studio to eat and visit. I promise to share some fries. And then I can load everything for you into my truck and bring it back to my house."

My heart drummed faster as I stared at the cotton stems. Looking at them triggered a flashback of the last time I was alone with Reid, and his pinched red face when he yelled into the phone on his patio. Now he wanted to come over, and I was alone in the storage facility. Not even Aunt Deb was around; she was out with a friend tonight.

Then I remembered his warm handshake and even warmer smile. Forget about listening to my gut; I wanted some fries and company. "I'm in unit ninety-nine at Darlington Mini Storage. When you come to the gate, the passcode to open it is thirty-seven, forty-eight, ninety-two."

Ten minutes later, Reid stepped into my studio, scanning the room with wide eyes. "This is the nicest storage unit I've ever seen." He looked up at the glowing strings of globe lights criss-crossing the ceiling. "How'd you get a unit wired with electricity?"

"My aunt owns this facility," I explained. "She hooked me up with an extension cord patched into an electrical outlet outside."

He grinned when his eyes fell on my oversized bean bag chair. "I used to have one of these in middle school. My parents gave one to both Vinn and me for Christmas." He kicked off his shoes, walked across the rug, sank into the chair, then dug into a brown paper bag and pulled out a burger.

I sat on the rug, stretching my legs out in front of me as he ate. "How are your parents taking the news about Vincent? Will they be able to visit him?"

His eyes shifted down to the floor. "No…they would if they could—God knows they'd be here in a heartbeat—but they've been gone for about seven years now. It was a car crash on a rainy evening."

"I'm so sorry," I said, regretting I had assumed they were alive and well. "I had no idea. Vincent never mentioned their passing."

Reid took another big bite of his burger, looking thoughtful as he chewed. "I'm not surprised. He doesn't like to talk about it; it's too painful for him." He gave a small smile. "He's not all angry outbursts and bad moods, you know. He has a sensitive side, too."

I raised my eyebrows. "Oh?"

"I'm serious," he said, laughing. He extended his container of fries toward me, and I pulled several long ones from the box. "That side of Vinn is hard to find, but it's somewhere beneath his rough shell. After our parents passed, we inherited a lot…well, we inherited their entire estate. Hence, Vinn's company and my paddlewheeler boat."

The natural blush of Reid's cheeks deepened, as if he were embarrassed to talk about money. "I still remember the day Vinn called me and told me his plans to start a home furnishing company. He was so excited, especially when he told me the name of his company. He named it after the walnut tree in our backyard we climbed every day when we were boys. It had the best climbing branches."

"What about your boat?" I asked. "Any significance of its name?"

"Sutherland was my mom's maiden name. I couldn't think of a better way to honor her life." Reid gave me a quick wink, then stood. Crumpling the empty wrapper of his burger, he tossed it into the paper bag along with the empty fries container and stuffed it under his arm. He moved to the corner and lifted one of the throw pillows I was loaning him. "And how did the amazing Hadley Sutton end up in a small town like Darlington Hills?"

My cheeks warmed. "Vincent hasn't told you anything about me?"

He reached down and lifted the lamp and another pillow. "He said you're talkative and sassy. But Vinn and I don't talk much, so you're going to have to tell me your story."

I shrugged. "There's not much to tell. I left New Orleans after my boyfriend left me and I moved to the happiest place from my childhood." I gathered the remaining items from the corner.

"I've had my share of breakups, and it's never pretty. You'll have to get busy making more happy memories here. And you're not off to a very good start, with the homicide and now Vinn's accident."

"Any suggestions on where to start?" I asked.

He smiled mischievously. "There's an amazing paddlewheeler dinner cruise along the James River that people rave about around town. It tops the charts of the happy memory-makers. How about Tuesday evening, seven o'clock?"

"Tuesday sounds great. I'd love to see your boat."

His honey-brown eyes met mine. "I can't shake the feeling I know you from somewhere, like we met at some point before Vincent introduced us."

I returned his smile, but my heart sank. "I get that a lot. I have a familiar face."

His gaze swept across my face, settling on my lips. "Nah. Not a familiar face. A friendly face. Those dimples of yours suck people in like a black hole. You make people feel comfortable, which makes them think they already know you."

I bit my bottom lip as I fought a smile. "I like that explanation."

"I'll bet my potted petunias that Hal Stenner puts flowers in Shirley Decker's vase at the Flower Festival," Aunt Deb told her friend, Patty Aberdeen.

"And I'll raise you two pots of snapdragons that Hal gives his flowers to Gigi Ellsworth," Patty said, reaching across our table to shake on their wager. Thirty minutes after church and my aunt and her friend were gossiping about friends and making bets. "Mark my words, Debra, next Saturday Gigi's vase will be overflowing with pink roses. That's what he gave to Edith last year, remember? Twenty-four long-stem pink roses. Of course we all know how their relationship ended, what with the banana pie in Hal's face."

Aunt Deb stuck her fork into a heap of frizzled egg and grits, Whisks and Whisker's signature brunch dish. "Gigi's husband hasn't been dead more than two weeks. Hal wouldn't be so tactless."

"Debra, we're talking about Hal," Patty said, her mouth agape. "Hal Stenner, the man who joined that dating website a month after his sweet Cathy passed. Don't tell me he won't make a move on Gigi. She's quite a catch and she's newly single."

Hal Stenner was the over-sixty equivalent of a high school prom king, with his gemstone green eyes and square jaw. He was the only male member of Aunt Deb's hiking club, and I suspected he was the reason the club had such a committed group of female hikers.

Patty poured a packet of sugar into her iced tea and swirled a spoon through the glass. Two calico kittens sitting on a nearby cat tree swiveled their heads toward the clinking sound, then blinked and looked away. "I didn't say this, but I don't reckon Gigi was devastated by Willy's passing. She spent so long at her sister's house that I had assumed they secretly divorced." Patty looked at me. "So imagine my surprise when she came home to him a couple of months ago."

I glanced at the spot near the café's counter where I'd spoken with Gigi two days after Willy was killed. Her watery red eyes had seemed incongruous with her eagerness to redecorate her house. And I'd been surprised by her less-than-kind comments about her late husband.

"I hear there were plenty of people in Darlington Hills who disliked Willy," I said, recalling Gigi's words.

"Oh, honey. 'Dislike' doesn't begin to describe the way people felt about him." Patty peeked over her shoulder at the family with small children behind her. "I don't like to use the 'H' word, but I dare say there were people in this town who hated Willy."

"Because he had a habit of sending cease and desist letters to neighbors?"

Aunt Deb laughed. "Because he was an angry, angry man. Sure, the letters had something to do with it, but he liked to have things go his way and when they didn't, he would buddy-up with that lawyer friend of his and take them to court. Other than his lawyer, I don't think he had too many friends in this town."

"And I heard a rumor that Willy may have been misusing funds from his neighborhood homeowner's association," I said. "Do either of you know anything about that?"

The lines around Patty's lips grew deeper as she pressed them together in a show of disapproval. "It's not a rumor; it's the truth. That man was as crooked as they come."

"And yet people hired him as their realtor?" I asked.

Patty nodded. "I suspect he pestered most of his clients into hiring him. 'Cause like your aunt said, he didn't handle himself well when things didn't go his way. You should have seen him when Geraldine decided to sell her home without hiring a realtor. He badmouthed her until the day he died."

I raised my brows. "Who's Geraldine?"

"Geraldine Henkle, hon," Aunt Deb said. "She's the lady who sold her home to your new boss. Apparently she had a verbal agreement with Willy to sell her home to your boss, but then she decided to sell it directly to him."

"I'm surprised Willy didn't burn that house down, he was so angry," Patty said.

I lifted a bite of eggs Benedict into my mouth. Maybe Willy had been the target the morning he was killed. It sounded like there were plenty of people who disliked—or even despised—him. Still, it didn't make sense that he could have been elected to the HOA and have a thriving real estate business while he was disliked by so many.

Patty straightened her back and looked at Aunt Deb triumphantly. "Like I said, Gigi likely wasn't too devastated by Willy's death. I know this and Hal knows it, which is why we're going to find Gigi's vase stuffed with roses. I'm going to win our little bet, so I'll swing by your place next Sunday to collect your petunias. In fact, I wouldn't be surprised it Hal and Gigi become an item."

Aunt Deb rolled her eyes over to me. "Would you like to get in on this wager? I wouldn't mind winning those potted succulents of yours."

I laughed. "I'm not risking any of my plants, thank you very much."

"I'll bet you're going to find some flowers in your vase," Aunt Deb said. "Perhaps from a certain animal-loving police officer?"

Patty swung her head toward me. "I didn't know you'd found yourself a man already."

I grunted. "I haven't. He's just someone who—"

The door to the café swung open and Josh Finney walked inside. I was tempted to go say hi to him to escape the conversation about my non-existent boyfriend, but I waved at him instead.

Aunt Deb followed my gaze towards the door, then faced Patty. "Now you see, she hasn't found one man, she's found two. No wonder she's been so shy to talk about men. She hasn't made up her mind yet. This one looks nice. What's his name, hon?"

"Josh. He works for Vincent, too."

Patty looked toward the door, waved, then returned her focus to me. "Josh is a good catch," she said matter-of-factly. "I approve."

Of course she knew him. Patty knew everyone. "He's done some work for you?" I asked, stealing a quick glance at him. Instead of his typical paint-covered jeans and cotton T-shirt, he wore golf shorts with a trendy polo shirt. And no 1980s glasses.

"I hired him for the first time this season. He's based in Richmond, but well worth the drive. He's a quirky man alright, but this is the first year in decades I've gotten a refund, so I overlook his oddities."

I frowned. "A refund? On your paint?"

Patty mirrored my puzzled expression. "I don't think paint had anything to do with my refund." She turned around again and waved Josh over. He approached reluctantly, his cheeks growing red.

"Mrs. Aberdeen," he said, shaking Patty's hand. "Good to see you."

"You too. I was just telling Hadley this is my first year in quite some time to get a refund on my taxes. I don't know how you—"

"Taxes?" I swung my gaze from Patty to Josh. "You worked on Patty's taxes?"

Patty swished a hand at me. "Of course he did my taxes, he's my accountant. CPA to be more precise. What do you think he does for Vincent, sweep the floors?"

I stared at her, unsure of how to answer her sarcastic question. She wasn't too far off-base. "Josh is a man of all trades, but I didn't know accounting was one of them. He's one of Vincent's handymen; he does an amazing job of painting, wallpapering, and getting the house perfect for photo shoots."

"What business does a CPA have painting walls?" Patty demanded. "You couldn't be making much more than minimum wage over there, right?"

Aunt Deb placed a hand on Patty's shoulder. "Why don't you say what you really think?" she joked. "Try to be more blunt so we don't have to wonder what's going on in your mind."

Curious to know the answer to Patty's question, I raised my brows at Josh. His eyes met mine for a brief second, then skittered around the room.

"I'm working temporarily for Vincent to help my mother pay off her substantial medical debt." He gave a small smile to Patty. "And I make significantly more than minimum wage, ma'am."

Patty clasped her hands together. "I knew I liked you. Working an extra job—manual labor, no less—to help pay off your mother's debt. She must be so proud to have a son with such a strong work ethic."

"I'm sure she is, but this is the least I can do for her. I'd work three jobs if I needed to." He glanced at me and smiled. "See you tomorrow, Hadley."

Josh turned toward the coffee counter. Aunt Deb waited three entire seconds before she squealed and started doing soft happy claps. "Two men, Hadley. Two men in the four weeks you've lived here. A police officer and a CPA/handyman. Imagine that!" She leaned over and hugged me.

I hugged her back, grateful to have an aunt who cared so much about my happiness. But there was no way I would tell her about my upcoming date with Reid on his paddlewheeler. She'd start making a guest list for my wedding.

# CHAPTER NINE

Terence's phone dinged for the third time in the past sixty seconds. It was Vincent, texting from his hospital bed, giving instructions on where he wanted each piece of furniture to go, even though it was stated clearly in our daily itinerary.

Terence and three other guys had just finishing moving sections of an enormous entryway storage bench with shelves and cubbies from the moving truck into the mudroom, which sat between the kitchen and garage. He was now installing the hooks into the unit's beadboard paneling.

"Make sure you install the chrome drum pendant light in the mudroom, not the copper one," Terence read. "Then please install the matching chrome curtain rod over the window."

I unrolled a yellow and green floral area rug and positioned it next to the entry cabinet. "He said please? Seriously?"

Terence laughed. "He must have hit his head pretty hard." His phone dinged two more times, back-to-back. "Would it be wrong to ask his nurse to slip some sleepy-time medicine into his IV so I can get my work done? These rapid-fire texts are killing me. I can't even reply before he sends another one."

"Sounds like Vincent has made a full recovery—at least

mentally." It would be a while before his broken leg healed, but his doctors were planning to release him this week.

My phone buzzed with a text from Vincent reminding me to hang the Pottery Barn backpacks I'd ordered on the hooks Terence was installing. I had already retrieved them from the bin and carried them into the mudroom, so I was one step ahead of him.

Monday mornings were usually chaotic, with Vincent in peak-stress mode and everyone else still waking up from the weekend. Today seemed to be no different, except the morning hullabaloo consisted of beeps, buzzes, and ringtones instead of shouting. Even though Vincent's calls and texts were nonstop, his tone was softer than I'd ever seen. Maybe it was whatever meds he was taking, or perhaps his fall helped to put things in perspective.

Sonya and one of her activist friends were in the backyard, adding to the chaos with their screeching bullhorns. Instead of posters, they held large Styrofoam cutouts of tombstones inscribed with the word 'trees.' The tombstones, as macabre as they were, looked like they might fare better than posters if it rained. The dark, low-lying clouds hanging over us this morning told me there was a good chance it would storm.

Josh popped his head around the door to the mudroom. "Hey, Terr. Got an extra tape measure on you? One of the guys ran off with mine. Can't find it anywhere." He glanced at me and smiled. "Mornin', Hadley."

I returned his greeting with a wave. Gone were his straight-off-the-golf-course plaid shorts and polo shirt, replaced by baggy jeans, white cotton tee, and the 1980s glasses smudged with dried paint.

Terence nodded. "It's in my kit. On the sofa in the family room."

Josh thanked him before turning to leave.

I waited until Josh rounded the corner to the family room,

then took a step closer to Terence. "Just curious, did you know Josh is a CPA?"

He looked toward the family room and pointed. "That Josh?"

"Yep."

"CPA, as in Certified Public Accountant?"

"That's right," I said, keeping my voice low. I told him about running into Josh at Whisks and Whiskers yesterday.

Terence continued looking in Josh's direction, rubbing the back of his neck as he stared. Finally, he turned to me and shrugged. "I never would have pegged him for a numbers guy."

"Do you think it's odd he never mentioned it to you?"

Terence lifted a braid that had fallen from his hair tie and slid it back under the band. "Not really. Maybe he isn't paying off his mother's debt. It could be his own debt and he's too embarrassed to say so." A slight grin crossed his face. "I don't imagine it would be good for business if his clients thought he couldn't manage his own money."

"Good point. And my aunt's friend is one of his clients, so he could have been trying to save face in front of her."

Terence's phone dinged again, but he left it in his pocket and resumed tightening a screw on a coat hook. "Have you heard whether the cops have questioned Vincent now that he's awake?" he asked. He had likely heard all of the speculation about whether Vincent had jumped, fallen, or been pushed.

"His brother told me Vincent said someone pushed him, although he didn't see who did it."

"That figures. I bet he doesn't recall seeing anything unusual the morning of the stabbing either." Terence's tone was thick with sarcasm.

I lifted the three backpacks, then placed the blue one with surfboards on the right hook and the pink one with unicorns on the middle hook. I held a larger, more mature-looking backpack while Terence installed the final hook. "It is hard to imagine Vincent not getting at least a glimpse of his assaulter. Do you think it's possible he doesn't remember who pushed him? Maybe selective amnesia from his concussion?"

He kept his eyes on the screw and hook. "I'd call it serendipitous amnesia, if you catch my drift."

"Ah. You think Vincent is lying?"

"That type of selective amnesia can happen, but statistically it happens to those prone to anxiety and fear. Not someone like Vincent."

Terence finished screwing the hook into the beadboard, then took the third backpack from me and hung it to the left of the other two. He sighed. "And you know as well as I do Vincent has a short temper. The man physically cannot handle when something doesn't go his way. He blows up. Aside from his temper, there's too much evidence against him for it *not* to be him. Vincent got into an argument with Willy that morning. He went downstairs right before the man was stabbed. And no one was around to witness what Vincent was doing downstairs because he'd sent almost my entire crew to Richmond to exchange a load of furniture at the warehouse. They weren't supposed to do the warehouse run until later that afternoon, but Vincent texted me shortly after he argued with Willy and told me to have my guys leave for Richmond right away."

I frowned. "That is strange. It was pouring, so it wouldn't have been the best time to unload and load furniture."

"And Vincent never veers from his daily itinerary, if he can help it. So what made him change his mind that morning?"

"Maybe the weather was supposed to get worse later in the day," I guessed.

Folding his arms, Terence leaned his shoulder against the edge of the entryway cabinet. "Don't you think Vincent killed Willy?"

"Not necessarily. I've looked through the photos from the day Willy was killed and realized both he and Vincent were—"

A loud thud sounded above us, making me jump. I looked

toward the ceiling. Had a tree fallen on the roof? The thud came again. It sounded as if someone were doing construction work upstairs, but no one was scheduled to come out today.

Another thud, followed by some yelling in the backyard. Terence and I rushed to the mudroom's window. Josh and two other handymen were looking up at the house, yelling into cupped hands. Josh yanked the bullhorn from the hands of Sonya's friend and held it in front of his mouth.

"Get down right now," he yelled.

"Ah, man," Terence groaned. "I don't like the sound of that."

Terence and I ran through the kitchen and out the back door. His entire crew, along with Rachael, Kyle, and Harry, were outside looking up at the back of the house. I followed their gazes toward the roof, where Sonya was standing. She was holding a large can of paint over her head.

"Get off the roof, lady," Josh shouted into the bullhorn. "You're going to fall."

Sonya slammed the paint can into the roof, swore loudly, then raised it above her arms again.

I ran over to the other Forest Action League activist in the backyard, who was staring at Sonya with an open mouth. "How'd she get up there?"

"She climbed that tree..." Without moving his eyes from Sonya, the young man gestured toward a tall oak tree near the house, whose branches seemed to touch the far side of the balcony from which Vincent had fallen. She must have stood on the railing and pulled herself onto the roof. Impressive, but crazy. I hoped I'd be agile enough to climb roofs when I was in my sixties.

Sonya smashed the paint can against the roof shingles again. Terence grabbed the bullhorn from Josh.

"Come on, Sonya," Terence said. "We don't want you getting hurt. We'll listen to everything you have to say as soon as you get down."

Sonya peered at Terence. For a moment I thought she was going to put the can back in the backpack she wore and come down, but she turned around and climbed higher up the steep roof.

"What's with the paint can?" I asked the man. "Why's she banging it against the roof?"

"She doesn't have the lid opener." He patted his front pocket. "I forgot to give it to her."

"Lid opener," I shrieked. "Why does she want to open the paint?"

Sonya hurled the can against the roof, but this time her left foot slid out from under her and she waved her arms to her side.

My stomach felt like it dropped to my knees as I watched her fight to regain her balance. My arms instinctively flew above my head, as if I'd be able to catch her if she fell. The paint can flew from her hands and hit a metal vent cap on the roof. The lid popped off, splattering ketchup-red paint down the side of the roof.

Vincent was going to blow an artery when he saw the mess.

For a moment, the chorus of yelling in the backyard stopped as we watched the paint roll down the roof, over the side of the rain gutters and onto the balcony beneath it. Sonya retrieved the paint can and poured the rest of it over the top of her head. To my right, her buddy was recording a video with his phone.

"Our fearless leader succeeded in showing the world how serious we are about defending Mother Earth, he said to the camera. "My friends, today we have achieved a victory for our friendly forests. Stop the madness and insanity; kill the catalog, not the trees!" He pointed the lens of his phone toward the tombstone in his other hand, then flipped the phone to record himself as he spoke. "Please consider supporting our cause today. Donate to the Forest Action League, and if you haven't already, don't forget to subscribe to our account."

Terence brought the bullhorn to his mouth. "Sonya, I want you to get down right now. You've pulled your stunt and now we need you to get off the roof. We don't want you getting hurt."

Sonya took several hesitant steps toward the edge of the roof, then froze.

"Come on, Sonya, you can do it," Terence said. "Come back down the same way you got up there."

Fixing her eyes on all of us below her, she shook her head. She was saying something, but I couldn't hear her.

"What's that?" Terence said.

Her long dreadlocks dripping with paint, Sonya backed away from the edge. She started to cry. "I said, I don't think I can. It was easier climbing up."

"Ah, man," Terence said, looking at me with a 'what now?' expression.

I whipped my phone out of my pocket. "I'm calling the police." I found Dennis' name in my list of recent calls and tapped the phone symbol next to his name.

The man from the Forest Action League ran to the side of the house and grabbed his water bottle. "Sorry, Sonya," he yelled. "Gotta go. I can't have another arrest on my record."

"Hey, Hadley. How's it going?" Dennis' chipper voice filled my ear. A bleating noise—his goat, I presumed, sounded in the background.

"We have a minor emergency this morning. One of the activists who's been protesting out here decided to climb Vincent's roof. Now she can't get back down."

"Ten-four, Miss Hadley," he said. "We'll get an officer out there along with a fire truck and ladder. I took the morning off to run a personal errand, but I'll swing by as soon as I can."

# CHAPTER TEN

Thirty minutes later, Sonya's red feet were planted firmly on the ground as she spoke with Dennis and two other officers. Four firefighters carried a collapsible stretch ladder they had leaned against the side of the house to help Sonya get down. The smallest of the four, a pretty woman with a paint-streaked ponytail sticking out the back of her helmet, scowled as she tromped through the yard.

Terence had decided it was best to wait until the paint dried before cleaning it up. Spraying it with water now would likely cause a bigger mess, and he didn't want to risk spreading it to the side of the house. Most likely, Vincent would need to replace that section of shingles on his roof.

I had tried calling Vincent's mobile phone several times, but hadn't been able to reach him. Reid wasn't picking up his phone either. He told me yesterday he was planning to swing by Vincent's house later today to check on things. I didn't know if Vincent had asked him to or if Reid felt like it was the brotherly thing to do, and I wouldn't ask. I still sensed tension in Reid's voice whenever I mentioned Vincent.

Dennis thanked the other two officers, then jogged over to me. "Have you reached Mr. Weatherford yet?"

"Not yet," I said. Which was odd, considering how many texts Vincent sent less than an hour ago.

He let out a low whistle. "I tell you what, Sonya Bean is in a heap of trouble. Penalties for criminal mischief are harsh around here, so I hope her little stunt was worth it. She's looking at fines, restitution for property damages... She'd better have a good attorney." In black athletic shorts, T-shirt, and running shoes, Dennis looked like he'd just come from the gym. I was surprised at how thick his arms looked when they weren't hiding under his dense polyester uniform.

"What about jail time? Is that a possibility?" As annoying as her chanting was, I hated to think Sonya would have to spend time behind bars.

"Maybe, but it wouldn't be a long sentence," he said, seeming to sense my concern. "Although she does have"—he glanced over his shoulder, then took a step closer to me—"two prior convictions. So she may face more jail time than someone without a criminal record."

"Criminal record?" I whispered. It was hard to imagine Sonya, the wiry woman who'd been crying on the roof half an hour ago, in a prison uniform behind bars. "Why was she convicted?"

Dennis checked his watch. "Listen, I can't hang around here much longer. I need to be at the station by noon and I'd like to grab a sandwich first. Want to join me?"

I looked at my phone. Ten forty-five. I had finished staging the mud room, and now I needed to tackle the bedroom upstairs before its two o-clock photo shoot. I had already sketched out how I wanted the room to look, so it wouldn't take more than two hours to transform it into a child's dream bedroom, using Walnut Ridge's adorable Apple Rose furniture set. Easy peasy.

"I understand if today isn't a good day," he added, then frowned with mock disappointment.

I grinned. Most people took themselves too seriously and it was refreshing to be around someone who didn't. And I really wanted to find out about Sonya's prior convictions. "Sure, I'll grab my bag. Be right back." On my way into the house, I told Terence I was taking an early lunch break. He said he'd tell his crew to break early too, since, with all the commotion, they weren't getting anything done anyway.

Stepping into the kitchen, I grabbed my tote bag from the counter near the microwave, which was the designated junk space for personal items we didn't want to carry while we worked. Amid the collection of car keys and empty coffee mugs was a small framed photo of the *Sutherland Paddlewheeler*. I had seen the photo before, but had never paid much attention to it since the space wasn't one we included in our photo shoots.

Slinging the straps of my bag over my shoulder, I turned hesitantly away from the photo. Vincent wouldn't mind if I grabbed an early lunch with Dennis. I'd be doing him a favor by asking a police officer questions about Willy's death. But Reid? I hadn't considered how he would feel if I went to lunch with Dennis. It wasn't like Reid and I were officially dating, but he was planning to take me to dinner on his boat tomorrow night.

I fixed my eyes on the door to the backyard and inched toward it. I had to get the scoop on Sonya. Dennis said she had two prior convictions. Had she done anything violent in the past? Were the police eyeing her as a suspect? She had, after all, been hanging around Vincent's house the day Willy was killed.

Turning the doorknob, I stepped on the back patio and headed toward a grinning Dennis. *This is not a date*, I told myself. *This is not a date.*

Dennis scooted closer to me on the tailgate of his old Chevy truck, grazing my elbow with his. "That shade of purple sure does look nice on you, Miss Hadley."

Uh-oh. This was starting to feel like a date. I had worn my ruffled, purple blouse—one of the newer tops in my closet—because Reid had told me he was dropping by the house today. And here I was in the back of a truck with another man and his noisy but somewhat adorable pet goat that he had taken to the vet earlier this morning. But I had to admit, Dennis was a cutie with his shaggy hair and wide grin.

I smiled at him. "*Miss* Hadley? You make me feel like an old woman when you call me 'miss.'"

He peeled back the paper wrapping on his turkey hoagie. "Then I guess that makes me an old man, because I'm thirty-one. One year your senior."

I almost choked on my bite of chicken salad sandwich. Thirty-one? "I thought—" I closed my mouth, deciding not to tell him I thought he was much younger. "Wait. How do you know my age?"

"I've seen your file."

"I have a file? Since when?"

Dennis chuckled, and Sadie bleated. He pulled a chunk of lettuce from his sandwich and fed her through the metal travel cage. "Since the first time I met you."

"Wow. Less than a month in Darlington Hills and I have a file. With the *police*."

"Yup. You'd better be on your best behavior from here on out."

I stopped chewing and stared at him.

His laughter shook the tailgate. "I'm kidding. I just wanted to see that expression of yours again, where your eyes get really big. It reminds me of those little Beanie Boo stuffed animals with the glitter eyes that I give my niece whenever she comes to town."

"Awesome. I've always wanted to look like a Beanie Boo." Still, it was better than the typical you-look-like-someone-I-know comment. My phone buzzed, and I glanced at the notification on my lock screen.

VINCENT

Saw you called. Spoke to Terence and he filled me in. Thanks.

Wow. He said thanks. I slid off my pointy-toe flats and let them fall to the dirt ground. We were in the parking lot behind the sandwich shop, which was two blocks north of the town square. The midday sun wove through the dense leaves of the trees, warming small patches on my face and arms.

I set my sandwich next to me and leaned back on my hands. "Speaking of police files, you said Sonya has a criminal record. With two convictions?"

Dennis nodded. "That's right, two misdemeanor convictions. Five years ago, she vandalized a logging company's fleet of trucks. Slashed some tires and released a bunch of termites onto the logs stacked on the trucks. She cost the company tens of thousands of dollars."

"How's that possible? It's not like you can go to a local pet store and buy a bag of termites."

"No idea. She might not look formidable, but she isn't one to be underestimated. Fifteen years before the logging fleet incident, she was convicted of simple assault. Punched some guy and broke his nose."

So she was capable of violence. "Any idea why she punched him?"

"He was an exec at a paper mill company. She testified she did it because he was a serial tree killer, but some witnesses claimed she'd had a previous romantic relationship with the man." He shrugged. "Her motivations couldn't be proven, but your boss would probably find it in his best interest to refrain from spraying her with any more water hoses."

I pulled my chin back. "What? When was that?"

"Three Sundays ago, when Sonya first showed up at Vincent's house with her signs and chanting. He tried to run her off with his high-pressure garden hose, but she didn't budge. She called the police claiming Vincent was attacking her while she was protesting peacefully. My buddy Stevens, who was on duty that day, responded. It was a bunch of nonsense and a waste of his time, but he said both Sonya and Vincent were livid."

I swung my legs, relishing the cool breeze on my bare feet. I was surprised I hadn't heard about the water hose incident. But no one worked at Vincent's on Sundays, so it was possible none of his staff knew about it. "Is Sonya one of the suspects in Willy's case or is Vincent still your key person of interest?"

"Unless you want to join Darlington Hill's finest, I can't disclose those kinds of details about the investigation." He gave me a playful nudge. "You sure do ask a lot of questions."

I laughed. "Twenty questions has always been my favorite game."

"Mine too. My mama always said she saw question marks swirling above my head. Says she knew I'd become a detective. And I may not have gotten there yet, but Detective Sanders asked me to assist with this investigation."

"What made you want to become a police officer?"

He leaned back on a hand. "I started out in the army, spent several years in the military police before I decided I'm more of a small-town law enforcement kinda guy."

"You'll make a great detective," I told him. Dennis was so personable, he could probably get a door to talk.

"Thanks. I hope so. I'm fortunate Sanders is letting me help with this case. He preaches the importance of creativity in connecting the dots between various pieces of evidence." Dennis stuffed the rest of his sandwich into his mouth, looking thoughtful as he chewed. "Take the crime scene as an example. In the statement you gave us, you said the back door in the kitchen was open when you found Mr. Ellsworth."

"Right. And then I closed it because rain was blowing into the room."

"But then we found drops of Mr. Ellsworth's blood in the garage." He lowered his voice as his eyes shifted around the parking lot. "By the way, don't tell anyone I told you that."

"Promise."

"And why was there a broken glass bowl in the kitchen with no traces of blood on any shards of glass or no indication the victim was hit by the bowl?"

"Maybe Willy threw the bowl at his attacker and missed?" I suggested.

He shrugged. "Maybe. These are the dots we have to connect to form a complete picture, and it's never drawn in a straight line, so to speak."

"Because some of the dots—or evidence—are missing, right?"

"Or they look like dots and they turn out to be nothing." He folded his hands behind his head and stretched, his sleeves taut around his broad shoulders and well-defined biceps. "And it may sound crass, but this case is good experience. Before this homicide and the one last month, I was working on the string of bicycle thefts we've had this year. There have been four since January."

"It's not crass. This case is good résumé material," I said. "And speaking of the case, what if the killer thought Willy was Vincent? Did you or Detective Sanders look at the photo I sent you? You know, the one that shows Willy in the kitchen with his back to the camera. He looks just like Vincent from behind."

"It's a good observation, but it's not our number one theory."

"What about Willy's wife?" I pressed. "Don't you think it's odd she was visiting her sister for the past year and then she returns to Darlington Hills a couple of months before her husband is murdered?"

He pointed to my sandwich. "Eat up, Miss Hadley. I need to drop off Sadie and pick up my patrol car before I bring you back to work."

I picked up my sandwich, opened it, and removed a large piece of lettuce for Sadie. I turned around to feed it to her, but the lettuce slipped from my hands and landed on Dennis' shirt.

"Rats. Sorry about that." I peeled the lettuce off his shirt, revealing a large splotch of mayonnaise underneath. Grabbing my napkin, I swiped it off. "Good thing you're going home to change. It should come out; just put some dishwashing liquid on the stain and let it sit for a while before you wash it."

Dennis examined the greasy stain. "Aw, man. This was my favorite shirt."

His sea-blue eyes crinkled as he looked up at me. "I'm kidding. Seriously, I could care less about my clothes. You can stain them any time you like. Though I might have to buy some extra laundry soap if you're going to make a habit of it."

"Your next soap is—uh, your soap next time—" I paused to regroup so I could speak coherently. Why was I flustered? Maybe something to do with his breezy laugh and lopsided grin? I cleared my throat. "What I'm trying to say is, your next bottle of laundry soap is on me."

Dennis plucked the piece of lettuce from my fingers, tossed it in his mouth, then looked at Sadie. "Sorry, for stealing your treat. Don't hold it against me." Then, turning to face me, "And don't even think about buying me more soap." He hopped off his tailgate and reached for my hand. "Shall we get going? You can finish up your sandwich in the truck."

I took his hand and jumped off the tailgate. He let go when my feet hit the ground, but the feeling of his skin against mine lingered, as though my hand didn't want forget his.

Slipping into my shoes, I recalled Reid's electric handshake when we first met and then again at Whisks and Whiskers. The memory of meeting him at the café reminded me of staging his house, which brought back a crystal-clear replay of Reid yelling into his phone on the patio, jabbing his finger in the air as he spoke. It was an unsettling memory that didn't mesh with his warm hands and kind eyes. I was pretty sure I wanted to learn more about this man of mystery, but the slightest flutter of nerves stirred my stomach when I thought about joining him for dinner on his boat.

# CHAPTER ELEVEN

Dennis eased his patrol car alongside the curb of Vincent's house. The moving truck was in Richmond exchanging a load of furniture and decor we had already photographed for new sets.

"Thanks for joining me for lunch," he said, shifting the car into park. "I hope I didn't run you late by dropping off Sadie first."

"Nope. I'm good on time." Dennis' home wasn't much of a detour. He lived on the outskirts of Darlington Hills in a simple ranch-style home with a couple of acres of land in the back. I'd been curious about what kind of property a man with a goat would have, so I hadn't minded swinging by his place. "Of course not. And thanks for buying my sandwich..."

I trailed off as my attention shifted to the tall form moving toward Dennis' patrol car. Reid. His car was in the driveway, the driver's side door still open.

Dennis rolled down my window and waved. "Mr. Weatherford, good seeing you again."

It took me a moment to remember when the two had met. Dennis had taken his statement after Willy was killed.

Reid stuck his hand through the window, and, reaching over me, shook Dennis' hand. "Officer…Appleton?"

"Appley. Officer Dennis Appley," he clarified, his voice remarkably deeper than usual.

Turning his focus to me, Reid lifted his thick eyebrows and grinned. "Never thought I'd see you riding in a police car." Then turning to Dennis… "What kind of trouble has Hadley gotten herself into?"

"No trouble"—he glanced at me and smiled—"unless you count spilling mayonnaise on my shirt."

I closed my eyes for a beat. Oh brother. I was stuck in the middle of a show of male dominance. Both of them were laying it on thick. If they were bucks, they'd be locking antlers right now.

Reid's smile faded. "Ah."

I released my seatbelt and gathered my tote bag. "I grabbed lunch with Dennis—I mean, Officer Appley—so we could catch up on some things." Stepping out of his car, I gave Dennis a final wave before he pulled away.

I had enjoyed my lunch outing with Dennis more than I thought I would, and it was sweet of him to buy. Glancing at Reid, I tried to decipher the slightly quizzical expression he wore as he watched Dennis drive away. Was he jealous? Reid and I weren't dating and I didn't know if tomorrow night's dinner was an official date, or if it was just his way of thanking me for staging his house.

Most importantly, why was I obsessing over this? It was probably pointless to start something with Reid since he was moving soon.

"Nice guy, that police officer," I said, trying to sound chipper. "He was kind enough to answer most of my questions about the murder case."

Reid gave me a strange look.

"You know, for Vincent's sake." I hoped Vincent had told Reid he'd asked me to snoop around, but his scrunched brows told me he didn't know what I was talking about. "Your brother asked me to talk to folks in town about the homicide. He pointed out that since I'm prone to chit chatting, I might as well chit chat about who disliked Willy enough to… well, you know."

Reid's eyes bulged. "You're joking, right?"

"Nope. He asked me to irritate a confession out of someone." I slung my tote bag over my shoulder and walked alongside Reid toward his car, a black four-door Mercedes. I hadn't realized it before, but he was almost a head taller than me. And at five-six, I was slightly taller than average for a woman.

"Sounds like something he'd say," Reid murmured, shutting the driver's side door with more force than necessary. "I'd heard some buzz that you were asking questions about Willy's death, but I didn't believe any of it." Turning to me, he pressed his lips together and inhaled deeply through his nose, as though he were trying not to get upset. "Listen to me, Vinn never should have asked that of you. You're a designer, not a detective. We're talking about murder here, Hadley, and you don't need to get involved in figuring out the details of the crime. Leave it to the police."

"But there's a good chance the police think Vincent's the one who did it."

He shrugged. "They're good cops. They'll figure out who killed Willy." We were both silent, his words hanging between us. It was what Reid hadn't said that made the hairs on my arms stick up. He hadn't defended his brother. He said the cops would figure it out; he didn't say they would realize Vincent wasn't guilty of murder.

A red BMW SUV pulled in front of Vincent's house, stopping where Dennis had parked minutes before. A forty-ish woman with long, radiant brown hair worthy of a shampoo advertisement emerged from the driver's seat.

"Reid," she said, clipping her heels on the pavement as she walked toward us. "I'm glad I caught you out here today. I have some HOA matters to discuss with your brother. I understand he's still in the hospital but can you ask him to return my calls? You're in charge while he's away, I take it?"

He shook the lady's hand when she approached. "No, I'm only stopping by to check on things. It's been a crazy morning around here."

"Good grief, Reid. It's always crazy here. That's why half the neighborhood is complaining—daily, I might add—to the North Hills HOA."

Reid turned to me. "Hadley, this is Gayle Nuñez. She's a board member of this neighborhood's HOA—"

"Now, the acting president," she interrupted.

"—as well as an interior designer like you. Gayle, meet Hadley Sutton, my brother's designer for his upcoming print catalog."

Her eyes flicked toward me, then down to my blouse, skirt, and shoes. "Nice to meet you."

I scanned her face, outfit, and shoes in return. Perfect was the word that came to mind. Trim and trendy black slacks, snug white blouse, and silver strappy heels. She had sculpted brows and prominent cheekbones that shimmered not from caked-on makeup, but from the blend of whatever perfectly nutritious food she ingested.

Facing Reid again, she straightened her shoulders and lifted her chin. "We'll see about that new catalog of his. Do you know how many HOA rules he has broken since he moved in? Seven. And you know full well Willy hand-delivered Vincent a cease and desist letter the day he...passed." Closing her eyes, she sighed. "Look, I don't mean to take this out on you, Reid. But I need Vincent to address the issues surrounding his home business."

Reid dipped his head. "Absolutely. I'll make sure Vinn knows you came by."

"I'll be in touch," Gayle said. "I'm going to settle this with either you or your brother."

He turned away from her and took a step toward the house.

"Hadley?" he said, inviting me to escape the awkward conversation with Gayle.

"Actually, why don't you give Hadley and me a moment?" Gayle smiled, revealing porcelain-white teeth. "I'd like to get to know Darlington Hills' youngest interior designer."

The word 'youngest' had never sounded so condescending.

She whipped around to face me, her grin frozen in place. "So you're Vincent's home designer. Congratulations. It is a wonderful job for a newbie designer, and despite all of the mayhem surrounding Vincent at the moment, Walnut Ridge is an adorable little company. The furniture is...how shall I say...too basic for my clients' taste—most of whom live in North Hills neighborhood—but his collections are a good option for those with a more moderate budget." She did another head-to-toe sweep of my clothes and shoes. "But I can see you're well accustomed to making the most of bargain buys."

It took an extra dose of self-restraint to keep myself from getting defensive after her quick one-two punches to my ego. Newbie designer? And my clothes look cheap?

I returned her smile. "Actually, I've been in the business for almost four years, since graduating with a degree in interior design. Before I moved here, I worked in New Orleans for a custom homebuilder." I reached into my tote and fished around for a business card. "And I have my own company, Hadley Home Design."

Gayle laughed softly through her nose. "Of course you do. Who doesn't have their own interior design business these days?"

I stopped searching for my card and withdrew my hand from my bag. Clearly, Gayle wasn't interested in networking. She wanted to mark her territory.

Gayle sighed. "Unfortunately, you'll find there isn't much of a market in Darlington Hills for interior design services. Other than the residents of North Hills neighborhood, the people around here don't bother with what their homes look like on the inside."

I widened my smile. "I'm not worried. In my experience, if there isn't an existing demand for a service, you have to get out there and create it. Besides, I already have one client, as well as a prospect who lives in North Hills." Technically, Reid wasn't a paying client but he had bought me a coffee, so that should count for the purpose of the conversation.

Gayle tilted her head. "A prospect? In North Hills neighborhood? Who might that be?"

"Yes, in North Hills." No way was I telling her Gigi Ellsworth was looking to redesign her home.

Gayle waited for me to answer, then gave a dismissive wave. "Anyway, normally I would advise you to hang onto your full-time job at Walnut Ridge until you grow your client list—and believe me, that will take years—but the company's future doesn't look too promising, with Vincent having one foot in a jail cell." She brightened. "But I hear the quilting supplies store in town is hiring."

Oh, brother. I turned my feet toward the house. "It was nice meeting you, but I need to get back to work."

Gayle grabbed my arm, intensity flashing through her eyes. "You watch out for those Weatherford men. There's a lot of history between those two, and it's not a pretty story."

The house was twenty, maybe thirty steps away from the driveway, from this ridiculous conversation. I shook my arm free from Gayle and moved toward the front door. One step, two steps, three—

I stopped. Like a never-ending merry-go-round, the memory of red-faced Reid yelling into the phone circled back into my mind.

I turned to face Gayle. "What history?"

"You know why Reid is moving, don't you?" A subtle note of triumph hung on her words. I had taken the gossip bait.

"Change of scenery," I said, repeating Reid's explanation.

She gave a harsh laugh. "Not exactly. Vincent threatened to report the *Sutherland* to the local port authority for maintenance issues and safety risks if Reid doesn't leave town."

"I can't imagine Vincent trying to put his own brother out of business. He wouldn't do such a thing."

Lifting her eyebrows, Gayle nodded toward the house. "Of course he would. Reid stole his fiancée."

"*What*? Vincent had a fiancée?"

"Yes, who left Vincent for Reid. Soon after Vincent moved to town, his fiancée—Claudia, I think was her name—met Reid, the two hit it off and then she left her ring on his kitchen counter and headed for Reid's arms."

I shook my head. "How do you know all this?"

"Everyone knows. Reid is Darlington Hills' biggest heartthrob and most eligible bachelor."

"But Reid doesn't have a girlfriend now."

"Oh?"

"I don't think he does. Maybe they broke up?"

She shrugged. "I'm not so sure about that. I've never met the woman and she doesn't live here anymore, but I hear she and Reid are still an item." Gayle jingled the keys in her hand, signaling the end of her gossip download. "Just watch your step around the Weatherford men. There's an ugly feud going on between those two and you need to make sure you don't get caught in the crossfire."

"Why would he invite me to dinner if he's involved with another woman?" I asked Carmella. We were in my kitchen making wreaths for the Spring Flower Festival on Saturday. "Maybe it's not a date. Maybe I misinterpreted it."

Carmella clucked her tongue. "Don't start doubting him before you even go out with him. Why else would he have invited you to dinner on his boat? To discuss gardening?"

"It could be a thank-you dinner for staging his house."

Carmella nudged the pitcher of iced mint tea closer to me. "Drink up and quit your crazy talk."

"But Gayle said—"

"Gayle Nuñez is a hurricane with all the hot air she blows. She's the PTA president at Darlington Hills Elementary and, *whoa*, you should hear the teachers complain about her. That school is drowning in her gossip and negativity. Unfortunately, my middle school is in the path of Hurricane Gayle, so I'm bracing myself for when her son moves up to sixth grade in September."

"Yikes. That's something to look forward to." Shuffling to my refrigerator, I added more ice to the pitcher, then refilled Carmella's and my empty glasses. I didn't usually drink caffeine in the evening, but it was going to be a late night. Carmella and I had told Erin at Whisks and Whiskers we would donate the time and materials needed to make twenty flower wreaths to sell at the festival, and so far we'd only made eleven. She wouldn't be upset if we made less, but the money was going towards cat adoptions, so I wanted to follow through on our commitment.

Thunder rattled above us and rain agitated the wind chime outside my door. Razzy, who usually demanded my attention when it was storming, lay quietly by my feet, seeming to understand I was helping her fellow felines.

Lifting the wreath in front of me, I trimmed the end of a tulip stem protruding from the side of the wreath. "Twelve," I proclaimed, setting it in our pile of completed wreaths. "Now only eight more."

Carmella groaned, but continued making a large bow. We had bought pre-made twig wreaths, but it still took a long time to decorate them. Each wreath had a large, double-layer bow—a thinner white one over a wider burlap one—and two dozen tulips splayed out whimsically from either side of the bow. So far, we had two yellow wreaths, three red ones, and three yellow and orange ones.

I scanned the pile of artificial tulips on the table, then gathered an armful of pink ones. "But what if Gayle is right?" I mused. "What if Reid and Vincent are in the feud of all feuds?"

She swished a hand at me. "So what? Lots of families have arguments. It has nothing to do with you. I say go out with Reid tomorrow night—there's no harm in having dinner with him—and slip in a question about Vincent's ex-fiancée."

I tried to imagine a subtle way of asking if he had stolen his brother's fiancée and was still involved with her. As important as it was to find out, it seemed like lousy date-night conversation material.

"I'll casually ask if he's seeing anyone else, but I'm not bringing up Vincent's ex," I said. "Reid gets weird when I mention his brother. He gets quiet and broody, changes the subject." Except for the evening he stopped by my design studio when he had reminisced about climbing trees with "Vinn," as he called him, when they were boys. That memory still had the power to light his eyes with a smile. And he must care about Vincent enough to visit him in the hospital and check on progress at the house in the afternoon.

"Broody, huh?" Carmella looked up from the ribbon and wire entwined around her fingers. "Maybe this man isn't worth your time. Next thing you're going to tell me, he's like his brother, patronizing and—"

"He's nothing like Vincent."

"—and blows up at people when they aggravate him."

I closed my mouth. Okay, so maybe he was a little like Vincent.

"Actually, Reid did yell at someone once," I admitted. "It was the day I helped him stage his home." I told her the rest of the story, sinking into my chair when I was done. "Maybe he was on the phone with Vincent, if the two of them truly are at each other's throats these days. Who else could have made Reid so furious?"

"It depends on how easily angered he is," Carmella said. "If he's anything like Vincent, then he could have been yelling at a plumber who was running fifteen minutes late."

I shook my head, thinking again of Reid's red face. "No, it was something more personal than a tardy plumber." Pinching a tulip's stem between my fingers, I slid it into the wreath, then twirled wire around the stem and twigs. "I want to know what's going on between those two brothers. Exactly *how* angry is Reid at Vincent?" Angry enough to push him off the balcony? Or worse? "I need to find out if Reid called his brother that day. Maybe if Vincent has a recent phone bill..."

"Don't even think about it." Carmella set her half-finished bow on the table. "I know where you're going with this, and you are not going to snoop through Vincent's personal belongings. Your boss is hot tempered and quite possibly a killer. If he found out, there's no telling what he would do."

"He won't know; he's still in the hospital," I reassured her. "It's been about a week and a half since I staged Reid's house, so it's possible Vincent has gotten a phone bill since then, depending on what his billing cycle is."

"Not a good idea," Carmella sang, her expression in full middle school principal mode.

"Before I go out with Reid tomorrow night, I have to know if he was on the phone with Vincent. Reid's either a nice guy...or he isn't." Was he the kind-eyed Reid who visited his brother in the hospital and looked after his house, or the red-faced Reid who stole his brother's fiancée and yelled at him on the phone? Maybe it was fatigue setting in, but my excitement about our impending dinner was dwindling. I had always loved boats and the open river, but I couldn't shake the feeling that dark clouds loomed on the horizon, threatening to rile the waters.

We worked on the wreaths for another hour, then called it quits at ten o'clock. Even though we had drunk an entire pitcher of tea, it was taking me twice as long to make a wreath as when we'd started. Between each flower I inserted I yawned, listened to the rain hammering against my windows, had a sip of tea, then stared into nothingness while I waited for more energy to arrive. Fortunately, we'd had a productive session and only had four wreaths left to make.

Carmella stood, then transferred the unused tulips to the plastic bag from the craft store. She looked as tired as I felt.

"Please don't worry about cleaning up," I said. "I'll take care of it tomorrow."

"Thanks, Hadley. See you tomorrow, hon. It shouldn't take us long to finish." She slipped into her rain jacket, which she'd hung over the back of her chair, and headed for the door.

I carried the pitcher to the sink and rinsed it with water. "Have a good night," I called over my shoulder.

She opened the door just as a gust of wind sent my outdoor wind chime into hysteria. "Don't forget to lock the door after I—" Carmella's words slid into a scream, rising above the clanging chimes and pounding rain.

# CHAPTER TWELVE

The knock on my door was soft. "Dennis, here," said the voice on the other side.

Staying as close as possible to the wall—and as far away from the window on the other side of my door—I looked through the peep hole.

"It's Dennis," I whispered to Carmella, who was pressed against the wall next to me. I cracked the door and looked around, then opened it wider to allow Dennis to come through.

He closed the door behind himself, wiping his wet sneakers against my mat. "It's a sad day for your boots." With a gloved hand, he held up a clear plastic bag holding two glossy yellow rain boots. A steel kitchen knife with a red handle pierced the toe of the right one, pinning a torn piece of paper to the boot.

"Those are Carmella's," I told him, then introduced the two of them.

"*Were* Carmella's," she clarified. "Past tense. They won't do me much good now." Her voice was still trembling, along with both of her hands. I suspected the caffeine from the tea wasn't helping her calm down.

Dennis switched on the hall light and studied the contents of the bag. I took a hesitant step closer to look.

"Oh!" I gasped. "That knife…I've seen it before." I squeezed my eyes closed, racing through memory after memory of kitchens and knives, trying to remember where I'd seen knives with red handles. Reid's kitchen? No. Vincent's? No, the knives in his kitchen were a different brand and had white handles.

Dennis read the note pinned to the boot. "Stop asking questions. Mind your own business." He shifted his eyes to Carmella. "Do you know what this is about?"

"Don't look at me," she said, thrusting her thumb in my direction. "I guarantee you this wasn't left for me. There are some crazy parents at my school, but not this crazy. Whoever did this thought they were Hadley's. She's the one who's been talking to people about the homicide."

Dennis turned hard, serious eyes on me. "I know you've had some questions for me lately, but is there anything else I should know?"

I turned my palms up. "The whole town is talking about his death. I'm not the only one."

Carmella cleared her throat. "Seeing my shiny new boots with a knife in them tells me you're asking the wrong people the wrong questions. Or the right questions, and you're making someone nervous."

I cringed. "Sorry about your boots. I'll buy you a new pair."

"You buying me a new pair requires you to live long enough for the store to restock them. I bought the last pair in my size on Saturday."

Dennis shook the bag. "This is a threat, Hadley. Aimed at *you*." His tone was harsh. He was no longer the carefree guy swinging his legs off the back of his tailgate. Dennis was in cop mode now. "Who all have you been talking to?"

"The storage bin," I blurted, remembering where I'd seen the knife with the red handle. "The knife in Carmella's boot looks just like the set in one of the plastic bins at Vincent's house."

Dennis frowned. "He keeps his knives in a bin?"

"No, he keeps a set of knives like this one"—I motioned to the one sliced through the boot—"in storage to use for photo shoots in the kitchen. In case we go with a red theme that day. I haven't used them for any photo shoots yet, but I have seen them in one of Vincent's bins."

"Who has access to the bins?" he asked.

I shrugged. "Anyone who's in the house. The bins are always out when we're working, usually with their lids off."

"I'll need to confirm whether this knife is from the set at Vincent's," Dennis said. "I'll go by his house after I drop this bag off at the station. I doubt we'll find any prints on them, but we'll run them anyway."

"Vincent is still in the hospital, so no one's going to be there at this hour," I warned. "Although Terence will be there at eight tomorrow morning, and he has a key."

Dennis nodded, but I could tell his mind was elsewhere. "Who have you talked to about the circumstances of the homicide?"

"I've had a lot of conversations about Willy in the last week and a half. Too many to count." I paused, thinking maybe Vincent had been right about my chattiness. "It's on everyone's mind these days. A better question is, who haven't I talked to?"

Carmella let out a low grumble. "You see, Hadley? This is what happens when you go snooping around in other people's business. I told you it was dangerous." Throwing her arms up, she marched between my sofa and coffee table and retrieved her glass from the kitchen table. She swallowed the last drop, then refilled it with water from the faucet. "Not just anyone's business, mind you, but someone who has a track record of stabbing people they don't agree with. You're lucky you got a warning. Poor Willy Ellsworth wasn't so lucky."

I didn't want to put myself in any danger, but the knife in the boots told me I was, like Carmella said, asking the right people the right questions. I was getting close.

"Do you remember who you've spoken with about the homicide?" Dennis pressed. "Is it only with people at work, or are there others?"

"Both," I confessed. "In fact, after we had lunch today, Reid told me he had heard some 'buzz' around town that I've been asking questions about Willy."

The swish of Carmella's hand drew my attention to the kitchen. She was giving me a look that demanded an explanation for failing to mention my lunch with Dennis.

"Reid said that today?" Dennis confirmed. I could see him making a mental note, although I didn't know if he filed it in the 'male competition' or 'homicide investigation notes' category.

"Yes. We talked for a moment after you dropped me off." I held back a smile as I tried not to look at Carmella, who was now several feet behind Dennis, overtly taking stock of the attractive man in lightweight knit pants—pajamas?—and navy blue sweatshirt.

Dennis looked at the boots in the bag. "Do you have any thoughts on who would have done this? Any conversations you had that rubbed you the wrong way?"

"No, but whoever did this must know me well enough to know where I live." That was a disturbing thought.

"Not necessarily," he said. "There are numerous ways to find an address. All someone needs is your license plate and a subscription to an online database that stores public records."

I cringed. That was even more disturbing.

"Have you lost your wallet recently? Had anything stolen from your purse or car?"

I glanced at my tote bag. "Nothing's been stolen, but I usually leave my bag on the counter in Vincent's kitchen while I work."

Carmella puckered her lips at Dennis from behind, clearly

trying to make me laugh. I prayed he wouldn't turn around and see her.

He sighed. "Listen, I'm generally an optimist, but I don't like seeing this kind of a threat after you've been asking questions about an open homicide case. I am worried about your safety, Hadley. Do you use protection?"

Carmella coughed violently, choking on water and laughter.

"Protection? I—uh..." I blinked hard, forcing myself not to look at Carmella. One look, I knew, would send me into a fit of giggles alongside her.

"Yes, ma'am," he said nonchalantly, as if he didn't know he'd just sent both Carmella's and my mind into the gutter. "Do you have anything to protect yourself? Stun gun, security alarm, baseball bat?"

"Oh." I pressed my hands against my cheeks, which were searing from the supreme awkwardness of the moment. "I have a handgun."

He looked impressed. "You know how to use it?"

"Absolutely not. I will never use that thing."

He lifted the corner of his mouth. "Then why do you have it?"

"My dad gave it to me and made me promise not to throw it away. It was his when he was younger and apparently it's sentimental. Don't ask me how a machine of death can be sentimental, but I can't get rid of it, so it's hiding in the far corner of my bedroom closet." I shuddered, thinking about the small metal safe under my pile of winter blankets.

He cleared his throat. "Okay, do you have any forms of protection that aren't completely inaccessible?"

I brightened. "Pepper spray." Opening the coat closet by the door to my apartment, I rummaged through an open box I hadn't unpacked yet. The pepper spray was wedged between an old pair of headphones and a tape measure. "Spray and Run," I said, reading the name on the side of the canister. I handed it to Dennis. "It's brand new, never been used."

He rolled the tiny pink canister between his thumb and fingers. "This is the most intimidating personal protection device I have ever laid eyes on. The mere sight of this thing will terrify even the most hardened criminal."

"Very funny," I said, holding out my palm.

He returned the pepper spray, then checked his watch. "I need to drop this bag off at the station now, but please call if anything else comes up."

Carmella stepped between Dennis and the door. "I'm not walking home by myself tonight." She nodded toward the knife in her boots. "Not after that. It's a thirty-second trek from Hadley's place to mine. That's thirty seconds of opportunity for someone to jump out and attack me."

He dipped his head in a nod. "I'd be happy to walk you home." Then, turning to me, he pointed to the pepper spray in my hand. "Don't forget to put that on your keychain. You take care of yourself, Miss Hadley."

"Miss Hadley?" Carmella mouthed behind him, fluttering her long lashes.

Rolling my eyes, I waved goodbye. No way was she letting me live this down.

Forty seconds after I closed and locked the door behind Carmella and Dennis, my phone dinged. I moseyed over to my breakfast table and checked my message.

CARMELLA

You had a lunch date with that fine young man today?!? And you somehow forgot to mention this??

I picked up my phone and carried it with me to the front window. Pressing down on one of the wooden blinds, I peeked outside as Dennis stepped into his patrol car. He was talking into his phone, likely telling Detective Sanders about the threatening note. After he drove away, I sank into my sofa, propped my feet on the coffee table, and responded to Carmella.

HADLEY

Wasn't a date. Though he did buy my sandwich.

He bought your lunch?! You can bet your bouncy little ponytail it was a date.

No it wasn't, LOL. My real date is tomorrow with Reid.

Maybe you should cancel since Reid yells on phones and Dennis is a cutie.

??

I yanked the yellow linen throw pillow from the end of the sofa, held it over my face and groaned. Why did dating have to be so difficult? It should be simple: meet nice man, go on date. It shouldn't be complicated by mysterious red-faced phone conversations, ex-fiancées, and shaggy but attractive cops who buy me lunch.

I tapped on my phone again, this time telling Carmella I was going to dinner with Reid, period. I'd find out soon enough if he was temperamental like his brother, but I wouldn't know unless I took the time to get to know him better.

Fluffing my throw pillow and returning it to its proper place, I headed to my room for a shower. I hoped the hot water would calm my nerves and allow me to get some sleep.

Twenty minutes later, I pulled back my sheets and crawled into bed. The rain had dwindled to a drizzle, and I was suddenly aware of how quiet it was in my apartment.

"Razzy," I whispered, then followed up with a two-note whistle.

A few seconds later, the soft tapping of her feet on the carpet in the hallway told me she was coming to snuggle. She hopped on the bed and pressed her head against mine, asking me to scratch her ears.

As soon as Razzy lay down next to me, my phone beeped in the kitchen and she jumped off the bed.

"Come back," I pleaded, but she was already sprinting back down the hallway toward the kitchen. Razzy was as ferocious as my pink canister of pepper spray, but it was still comforting to have her by my side.

I slid out of bed and padded along after her. She was sitting near her food bowl, looking up expectantly.

"Silly girl," I cooed. "Just because I got out of bed doesn't mean it's time for breakfast."

I reached down to pick her up, but the latest text notification on my phone's bright screen stopped me midway. It was a message from Dennis asking if there was any chance I could skip work tomorrow.

Skip work? What was he talking about? I flopped down into a chair and replied.

HADLEY

I can't skip work. Why?

Just stopped by Vincent's home. His brother was there and let me look around inside. Knife was missing from the set in the storage bin.

You know who didn't stab the boot tonight? Vincent.

Yes, but don't read too much into it.

I worked my thumbs across my phone's screen, asking Dennis why Reid was at Vincent's house. Reid had left around two o'clock for the *Sutherland* because he had a couple of tours lined up in the afternoon. I tapped the send message button and my phone dinged immediately.

This time, the message was from Reid, asking what I was up to. My heart flip-flopped. Wouldn't he assume I was asleep? Or did he know about the knife-in-the-boot incident?

Swiping back to the text thread with Dennis, I waited for him to respond to my question about why Reid was at the house so late.

A new message flashed across my screen.

DENNIS

Don't know. He was upstairs when I rang the doorbell. He came out of the room at the top of the stairs.

The room on the left or the right?

Left.

I stared at the screen. Vincent's room was on the left at the top of the stairs. Why was Reid in his room?

HADLEY

Did you tell Reid why you were looking through the storage bins?

No. I suggest you don't mention it to him.

Why?

I waited a minute for Dennis to respond, then returned to my text conversation with Reid.

HADLEY

You're a night owl?

Not usually. I'm tired but can't sleep.

Sorry to hear. I can't sleep either.

Unfortunately, I might fall asleep in my soup at dinner tomorrow.

Me too, though I prefer to sleep atop my dessert. Why can't you sleep? Too much on your mind?

I had a long day. Just got home from work and I can't unwind.

My stomach rolled. Why didn't he tell me he'd stopped by his brother's house? It shouldn't be a secret—unless he was doing something he shouldn't have.

Dennis had said Reid was upstairs when he arrived at Vincent's. I imagined Dennis looking through the window next to the door as I had done less than a week ago.

My phone became slick in my hands as I recalled the night Vincent was pushed: Moving shadow upstairs, Vincent on the ground, footsteps running away. I had zero explanations for the disturbing chain of events, but one burning question: Had the owner of that shadow seen me? The kitchen knife in the boot and threatening note on my doorstep told me they probably had.

My screen showed Reid was typing a message, but I preempted whatever he would say next by telling him I was shutting off my phone to try to sleep.

Another ding sounded, followed by a notification at the top of my screen. I straightened my back, eager to read Dennis' response to why I shouldn't tell Reid about the threat.

DENNIS

Just because. And it's an active investigation. Try to get some sleep.

I looked at the ceiling, listening for any signs that Carmella may still be awake. A lot had changed since the last text I sent her, and I wanted to talk about it. My excitement about dinner with Reid was fizzling. Visions of a gently swaying boat, clinking wineglasses, and soft background music were gone, replaced by the echo of warnings I'd received today from Gayle, Carmella, and now Dennis.

Opening my phone app, I scrolled down to find my most recent phone call with Carmella. My thumb hovered over her name as I continued to listen for movement above me. Sighing, I turned off my phone and set it on the table. It could wait. If she was asleep, I didn't want to wake her.

# CHAPTER THIRTEEN

I slipped away from the Walnut Ridge kitchen, which bustled with creative energy as Rachael, Kyle, and Harry bounded from corner to corner taking photos of the Indonesian-inspired teak barstools from every angle possible.

The family room was empty. Terence's crew was divided between the warehouse in Richmond and the storage sheds in the backyard, where they were returning tools and supplies they had used during the workday.

It was four o'clock in the afternoon, and we were nearly done staging and shooting all the rooms on the day's itinerary. After Rachael's and Terence's crews wrapped up, we could go home. Even Sonya, who had arrived with her sign and bullhorn at noon, had already called it quits.

Any other day, I would have been thrilled to cut out early from work and have more time in the afternoon. But not today. As the hour hand climbed around my watch, my sighs grew heavier. It was getting closer to my date with Reid and I hadn't decided whether I wanted to go.

I still needed to locate several antique-looking accessories for tomorrow's photo shoot of the rustic Wimberley bedroom set. I had already searched the plastic bins and the storage shed in the backyard with no luck. Vincent had told me there were boxes of the previous homeowner's 'junk' in the attic, so I was planning to head up there before I left for the day.

But first, I wanted to search for some answers while the house was quiet.

I slipped through the family room, into the entry hall, and through the double French doors leading to Vincent's office. A large mahogany desk sat in the center of the room, its surface void of papers or clutter. Although Terence's crew sometimes swapped this desk for other office furniture before photos, they always returned this piece to the room. There was a good chance this was Vincent's personal desk.

I studied the brass pull handles. Which one to open first? There was one large drawer in the middle of the desk, flanked by four smaller ones on either side. I started with the middle drawer because if I had a desk this size, that's where I would keep my mail. I pulled on the handle, opening it swiftly, then closing it as quietly as possible. It was empty.

I glanced around me, making sure no one was around. Rachael laughed in the kitchen, but it didn't sound like she was coming any closer. The wood shutters in the office were perched open wide enough to see a partial glimpse of the front yard, but it was unlikely anyone outside would be able to see in. If anyone did ask why I was rummaging through the desk, I'd say I was looking for a pen. Seemed like a logical response.

I opened the other six drawers; they were also empty. Apparently Vincent didn't actually use this office. Apart from his personal living space upstairs, this beautiful, enormous home was just for show. It was a business, not a warm, inviting place to kick your shoes off at the end of the day.

I looked up. Vincent's personal bedroom was directly above the office. I had gotten a glimpse of his room my first day on the job, when he'd taken me on a tour and opened his door for a fraction of a second and told me his space was off-limits. I was fairly certain there was a small desk on the same wall as his bed. He had to keep all of his papers and mail somewhere, so if it wasn't in the office, the next logical place was Vincent's room.

Closing the double glass doors behind me, I climbed the stairs. Halfway up, I spun around and looked out the narrow window next to the front door—the same window I peeked through the night Vincent fell from his balcony.

During the day, it would be easy to see someone on the other side of the window. I guessed it would be just as easy at night when the porch light was on, like it had been the night I was here. More likely than not, whoever had been inside the house last week saw me.

I turned back toward the top of the stairs and nearly collided with Wes, a tall man with a buzz cut who worked for Terence. He was carrying a rolled-up drop cloth covered in blue paint.

I slapped my hand against my chest. "Sorry, Wes. Didn't see you there."

He chuckled. "It's alright. Need help with anything? We're wrapping things up, gonna get outta here early. I might even make it to my son's t-ball game this evening."

"Then don't let me hold you up. I know your son will be thrilled to see you in the stands."

He smiled appreciatively, then descended the remaining steps two at a time. I waited on the stairs until he closed the front door behind himself.

With the entry hall still empty, I jogged up the rest of the stairs and pressed the lever handle on Vincent's door. It was unlocked.

After one more quick glance over my shoulder, I slid into Vincent's room. On the left was an arched doorway leading to his bathroom. To the right was his bedroom, which was large enough to fit a king-size bed, a bookshelf filled with books, treadmill, two dressers, and a small desk. Sunlight poured through the sliding glass doors that opened to his private balcony, making the room warmer than the rest of his house.

I moved quickly toward the desk, looking briefly at the balcony from which Vincent had fallen. Two wicker chairs from an older Walnut Ridge patio collection were arranged around a matching table with a glass top. Nothing seemed out of place—no overturned plants, broken glass, or signs of struggle.

Vincent's desk was old, possibly an antique, and it was covered with loose sheets of paper and notepads. His mail was in a neat stack next to an empty coffee mug branded with the Walnut Ridge logo.

I lifted the pile of mail, careful not to move the other papers on his desk. The envelope on top was postmarked after Vincent's fall, telling me someone had been checking his mail and bringing it to his room. Reid? That would explain why he was in here when Dennis came by last night.

All of the envelopes had been opened, even the ones postmarked within the last couple of days. I thumbed through his mail: credit card bill, municipal water utility bill, an advertisement from a local landscaping company, phone bill.

Bingo.

The postmark date was last Tuesday, and the bill half-protruded from the envelope. I set the rest of the mail on his desk and pulled the phone bill from its envelope. Vincent's mobile phone number was printed at the top, along with the dates included in the billing cycle. March 15 through April 14.

My eyes raced across the call history section, looking for calls made on April 12, the date I'd gone over to Reid's house. Near the bottom of the second page, I spotted the date. Vincent had made dozens of calls that day to local and out-of-town numbers.

I slid my finger across the page to find the calls he'd made in the morning. I'd met up with Reid at Whisks and Whiskers shortly after 9:00 a.m., which would have placed me at his house around 9:30.

I flipped to the third page of his phone bill, then froze when my eyes hit the third line from the top.

Outgoing call on Saturday, April 12 at nine forty-two a.m., duration: four minutes and seventeen seconds. Holding my breath, I swept my gaze to the right side of the page. It was Reid's mobile number, the same one I had saved in my phone's contacts.

I stared at the page so long it blurred. All of Reid's anger, his scrunched up red face and jabbing finger *had* been aimed at his brother. What could Vincent have said or done to make Reid so angry? Based on the conversation I'd had with Gayle, I guessed it had something to do with either Vincent's ex-fiancée—Claudia—or Vincent's threat of reporting of the *Sutherland* for maintenance issues.

I whipped my phone from my pocket and took a photo of the call details, then flipped through the rest of the bill to look for other calls with Reid. After skimming the rest of page three and then page four, I returned to the second page.

There, towards the top, was Reid's number again. I traced my finger down the row to the left column and read the date. April 10, 10:40 a.m. Call duration, twenty-one seconds.

Reid had called Vincent less than an hour before Willy was killed.

The front door opened and two deep voices mumbled in the entryway. I started toward the other side of Vincent's bed, planning to duck down and hide if the voices grew louder.

But the two voices met up with another low-talker and moved into another room downstairs. I returned to the desk, then closed my eyes and replayed in my mind the events of that dreaded morning. Where was I at 10:40 a.m.? Staging the bedroom upstairs? Maybe, but Vincent hadn't been on his phone while we were in the room.

I shook my head. I had been walking up the stairs, asking Vincent if I could look for books in his personal bedroom when his phone rang. He had a brief conversation, and then he was in a particularly sour mood after he got off the phone.

I scrunched my eyes tighter, trying to remember what Vincent said on the phone. He hadn't yelled, but he was impatient.

I gasped, the pages of the phone bill falling from my hands onto the floor. Vincent had told Reid to 'take care of it this morning.'

Take care of what? Or whom?

I frantically collected the fallen pages and located the fifty-three-second call with Reid. I snapped a photo of it, then texted both phone bill images to Dennis.

HADLEY

Can't talk now. Tell u about these later.

Dennis wouldn't like that I was searching through Vincent's mail. He didn't even want me to go to work today, much less snoop around. Were he and Detective Sanders close to making an arrest? They must have solid evidence against someone if Dennis was nervous enough to suggest I miss work.

Before returning my phone to my pocket, I texted Carmella.

HADLEY

I am NOT going out with Reid tonight. I need an excuse to tell him. Help!

On call with angry parent. Talk later.

Something creaked in the hallway, making me whirl around. I kept the phone bill hidden behind my back. No one was there, but the door was cracked open wide enough for a face to fit through.

I returned the bill to its envelope, then slipped it in the middle of the stack, sliding the mail back to the open space by the desk lamp.

With a thudding heart, I inched toward the door. Had I shut it on my way in? Surely I would have; I'd been sneaking into Vincent's room.

I shook my head. No, I must not have shut it because I would have heard if someone opened it. I paused, considering the chances someone had seen me going through Vincent's mail. Someone had been in the hallway—floorboards didn't creak on their own—but it was possible it was one of Terence's guys making another trip from the staged bedroom on the other side of the house to the storage shed.

I took a deep breath, then continued toward the door. If someone saw me coming from his room, I would say I was looking for a book with a blue spine. It was half-true, since I'd wanted to look for such a book a couple of weeks ago.

No one was in the hallway when I stepped out of Vincent's room. This time I made sure to close the door. The mumbling of voices I'd heard earlier had multiplied, and as I walked down the stairs, they grew louder and clearer. One voice rose above the others: Reid's.

On the bottom step, I checked my phone, hoping Carmella had texted me a brilliant excuse for backing out of my dinner plans. I needed something good. Something that wouldn't anger a potentially dangerous mysterious man whose brother had asked him to 'come take of something' less than an hour before Willy was killed, and who'd had a fiery argument with Vincent the same week he mysteriously 'fell' from his balcony.

I wandered toward the voices in the kitchen, taking the long way through the family room to give me extra time to think of an excuse. Normally, I preferred sticking to the truth, but there was no way to tell him delicately that he made me feel uneasy.

Now there was only one voice—Reid's—in the kitchen. I slipped into the room and stood behind two of Terence's tallest guys. From what I could tell, the entire crew was in here. Most of them looked annoyed, probably because he was preventing them from cutting out early.

"Ah, Hadley!" Reid called out over the crowd. "You're just in time. I was about to share some exciting news. Vinn has made remarkable progress, and is coming home from the hospital tomorrow." He paused, as if waiting for everyone to whoop and cheer, then continued talking. "The hospital is supposed to discharge him around noon, and he will need the afternoon to get situated at home. He would like everyone to work tomorrow morning as planned, but leave by noon."

Now came the clapping and cheering, mostly from Terence's crew. Reid joined in with the clapping, his eyes alight with enthusiasm. Was he really excited about Vincent's release, or was this an act?

"To celebrate Vinn and his recovery, I am hosting a dinner for him this coming Sunday on my riverboat. Bring a guest and a big appetite. Drinks and dinner will be on the house. I'll send details in a few days."

The room erupted with chatter, but Reid's voice rose above it. "But before we celebrate his return, we have some work to do. Terence, tomorrow morning I'd like your guys to remove the furniture from the office and replace it with Vinn's bed and dresser," he said. "With his leg the way it is, it would be unresponsible for him to climb those stairs."

I gawked at Reid. Unresponsible? It was the non-word Carmella had thrown a fit over when we looked at the walnutridgejunk.com website. I looked down at my phone and panic-texted Carmella.

HADLEY

OMG, Reid just—

"Hadley?" Reid called out.

My head shot up. "Huh?"

"I was asking if a seven o'clock start time tomorrow is okay with everyone. I know it's early, but we want to get as much done as possible before Vinn comes home."

"Oh. Um…yeah. That's fine." I held his gaze for a long beat. Who was this man? Was he the mystery owner of the website? The photo on the "unresponsible neighbor" page had been taken recently, and it seemed like too much of a coincidence that both Reid and the website owner used the same non-word and lived close enough to Vincent's house to take the photo.

"Great. Then seven o'clock it is." Reid thanked us, then wished us a good evening. As everyone turned to leave the kitchen, he signaled me with a two-fingered wave. "Hey. You mind sticking around for a minute?"

I nodded, placing a hand on my stomach to quiet the sudden onset of fluttering nerves. Had he seen me going through Vincent's mail?

My phone dinged, making me jump. I turned the phone in my hands so I could read the screen.

DENNIS

We've already pulled Vincent's phone records. Please do not go through his personal belongings if that's what u did. Too risky. Don't want you getting hurt.

Duh. Of course they would have pulled his phone records. And of course he wouldn't have told me what he found. Why should he? It was an open homicide case.

The kitchen had cleared out, and I suspected everyone would head home soon. I spun around and eyed the door to the family room—my escape route—but turned to face Reid instead. If I was going to cancel our dinner plans, now was the time.

"Everything okay?" he asked, keeping his voice low. He crossed the kitchen and joined me on the other side of the island. "You seem jumpy."

I feigned a smile. "Who, me? I'm fine."

"Well, I'm looking forward to tonight. I need your address so I can pick you up. The *Sutherland* leaves at seven sharp, so if I come by at 6:30 we'll have plenty of time to get there."

I studied his eyes, trying to decipher whether he really needed my address. Carmella's mutilated rain boots told me someone around here already knew where I lived, even though I'd never shared my address. "Reid…about dinner..." My eyes darted around the kitchen as I raced through potential excuses for canceling.

"Are you worried about a late night and early start time tomorrow? I shouldn't have kept you up last night texting. And I know I just asked everyone to come at seven, but Vinn probably wouldn't mind if you came later."

I gave a small laugh. "Yes, he would."

He dipped his head in agreement. "Okay, so he would. But who's going to tell him?"

Unable to look him in the eyes, I continued scanning the room. My eyes landed on a white vase filled with yellow roses. Flowers. Of course.

"Actually, I'm going to have to take a raincheck on dinner tonight. I was really looking forward to it, but I have to make tulip wreaths for the Spring Flower Festival this weekend." I winced, realizing how ridiculous my excuse sounded. Why hadn't I just said I had a scratchy throat? "Carmella and I…you see…the two of us—uh—we volunteered to make wreaths to raise money for kitten adoptions. I still have a lot to make before Saturday."

The more I talked, the lower his brows hung over his eyes. "Kittens, huh?"

"Yep," I squeaked.

He gave a tight smile. "It's okay, I get it. Maybe another time."

I turned my foot toward the family room. "Well, I should get going. I have one more thing I need to do before I leave."

"Would you mind locking up when you're done? I'm heading home now, but there's a spare key to the back door in the pot of marigolds out there." He motioned to the patio in the backyard. "You'll find it. It isn't buried too deep."

"Absolutely. And I won't be here too long. I need to get home."

"Right. To make wreaths." His light eyes carried a fleck of a smile, telling me he hadn't bought a single word of my excuse.

# CHAPTER FOURTEEN

As lavish as the Walnut Ridge house was, its attic was like any other attic—musty, damp, and dark. It was the perfect place for me to mope and indulge in self-pity.

Darlington Hill's so-called heartthrob had asked me to dinner, and I had just canceled on him. Despite the fact he was potentially involved in a recent homicide, he was gorgeous nonetheless. Every two minutes, my hand wandered to my pocket as I considered calling him to say something along the lines of, 'Goodness, what was I thinking? I can make wreaths another night.'

But then I would imagine him arriving at my doorstep looking exquisite in a trendy sports jacket with pockets that may or may not be filled with sharp objects.

I sat crisscrossed in the far corner of the attic, which had been finished out with sheets of thick plywood, yielding lots of storage space. The entire perimeter of the attic was consumed with shoulder-high stacks of brown boxes, most of which were moldy and looked like some critter had gnawed on them. None of the boxes were Vincent's. All of them, labeled with elegant cursive handwriting, belonged to the previous homeowner, Geraldine Henkle.

After going through a dozen boxes, I learned Geraldine was a big fan of the Boston Red Sox, liked to play Mahjong, and had cross-stitched tapestries for every major holiday. It wasn't until box number fourteen that I found anything antique-looking I could place on the Wimberley dresser or nightstand.

The box was marked 'keep,' which was ironic since she hadn't taken it with her when she moved. Inside were a pair of bifocal glasses from the early 1900s, a tarnished silver hairbrush engraved with the initials S.L., several tall stacks of hand-addressed letters, and a broken wooden picture frame with a faded photo of a middle-aged woman and two children.

I laid the frame, hairbrush, and glasses on the attic floor and squinted to study them. Light from the bulb that hung in the middle of the attic didn't reach to the far corner where I was. From what I could see, the items from the boxes were in decent shape. I wanted rustic but not tacky.

The picture frame would need some wood glue, but it was exactly what I had in mind to accompany the Wimberley set. It would be worth the extra effort to run over to my studio this evening and fix it.

I checked the time on my phone. Six o'clock. What I'd thought would be a quick, fifteen-minute trip to the attic had turned into an hour-plus scavenger hunt through the boxes.

Sliding the items carefully into my tote bag, I turned off the light and stepped into the game room, then closed the door behind me. There was no telling what kind of critters would crawl out from the attic if given the opportunity. I stopped off in the front guest bedroom and arranged the brush and glasses on the dresser in a mirrored tray with brass edges.

Out again in the hallway, the only sound was the soft crunch of my shoes on the new carpet. The house was never this quiet.

Everyone was likely at home, out eating dinner, or like Wes, at their kids' sports games.

I reached the bottom of the stairs, checked the locks on the front door, then headed for the back of the house. Rounding the corner to the kitchen, I quickened my pace. Reid had left the kitchen light on for me, but I didn't want to be alone in the room where Willy died. It was disturbing enough being there during the workday with other people around, much less in the evening by myself.

The spare key was exactly where Reid said it would be. I didn't have to dig through the plant to retrieve it, since the metal keychain was sticking halfway out of the dirt.

I locked the back door and jogged around the side of the house to the well-lighted street. The sun wouldn't set for another couple of hours, but the dense, low-level clouds made it seem like the sun was giving up early today. The light-sensitive street lamps had begun to flicker on, and the trees overhead were already alive with the evening songs of insects and birds.

I headed west on Vincent's street, then turned south on a paved walking path that led to the Bonn Creek footbridge. Six o'clock was a popular time for evening walkers and joggers, most of whom smiled and waved as they passed me. The large grey silhouettes of homes in North Hills faded behind me as the path wound through Darlington Park, which was dotted with oak trees, park benches, birdbaths, and small ponds.

Two squirrels ran along the top of a wooden sign explaining the legend of Bonn Creek. I smiled. My cousin Michael, who was one year older than me, used to try to scare me with stories of 'Bone Creek' when I came to visit. The town of Darlington Hills, which was settled in 1715, was originally named Bonnville in honor of Charles Bonn, a prominent colonist who emigrated from London with his extended family—fifty in all. There weren't any official accounts of what happened, but the legend said that in 1730, Bonn and forty-eight of his relatives drowned in the creek, leaving only one surviving member of the family.

Some townspeople believed descendants of the sole survivor still lived in the town. If the legend were true, I doubted those people would confess to their family heritage. The Bonn family was said to be cursed, and years after the unexplained tragedy, Bonnville officially changed its name to Darlington Hills, after the Darlington Oak trees that blanketed the town's gently sloping hills. As for the creek, someone along the way officially named it Bonn Creek in deference to the eighteenth-century tragedy that allegedly occurred.

Whether or not the legend was true, it was good fodder for spooky ghost stories. One Christmas evening when I was eleven, Michael shared the horrific tale when we were skipping rocks along the creek's bank while our parents visited back at Michael's house. As any twelve-year-old boy would likely do, he embellished the story with gory details and claims of ghost sightings near the creek. I begged him to go home, but he insisted we stay until nightfall so we could see the Bonn Creek ghosts. Less than ten seconds later, I found a large, smooth, white rock half-buried in the creek's muddy bank. Seizing the opportunity for revenge, I told him it was a skull.

I had never heard anyone scream as loud as he did that evening. We sprinted back to the house, Michael far more spooked than I had been. Aunt Deb claims Michael never returned to Bonn Creek, even though I'd long since confessed to him it was only a rock.

I wondered if Michael would have been spooked in the Walnut Ridge's attic this evening. I stopped and pulled the picture frame from my tote bag. The photo was old and faded, and judging from the woman's plaid overcoat and poufy hairdo, I guessed it was taken in the nineties. The child on the woman's right, a seven or eight-year-old boy in blue jeans and tucked-in flannel shirt, made a goofy face at the camera. The other child, a scrawny toddler in overalls and light blue T-shirt, had bangs that were obviously the handiwork of a scissor-happy child.

I wondered if the blonde woman in the middle was Geraldine Henkle. Maybe Aunt Deb would know who she was. I'd ask her on my way in to my studio. It was possible Michael had been friends with these children.

The path wound gradually to the left, and I fixed my eyes on the footbridge in the distance. The trees grew denser and the number of joggers on the path thinned out. Off the path to my right, a hooded figure sat on a park bench at the far end of a small field. Underneath the jungle-like canopy of interlaced branches, the figure was as dim and formless as a shadow.

But I could feel its eyes on me.

Stuffing the frame back into my bag, I quickened my pace, ready to run if necessary. The figure stood, but did not move toward me. Only fifty or so more steps to the footbridge. Then I'd cut over to a more populated street to walk the remaining two blocks to Darlington Mini Storage.

I kept my head pointed straight ahead, but shifted my eyes toward the figure. It was still standing, the opening of the yellow raincoat pulled tightly across its face as if were pouring. Its eyes were hidden in blackness, but the hood's opening was undoubtedly aimed in my direction. Maybe it was an innocent onlooker and I was being hyper-paranoid.

Or not. I sprinted until I reached the end of the Bonn Creek footbridge, periodically checking behind me, then slowed to a jog until I reached the gate of Darlington Mini Storage. My shoes held up and didn't rub any blisters, delivering through on their 'comfy chic' advertising slogan.

I looked over my shoulder once again. All clear. I entered my passcode. Waiting for the gate to open, I considered calling Dennis about the hooded figure in the park. But the person hadn't done anything wrong—hadn't chased me or threatened me. And it wasn't illegal to wear a raincoat when it wasn't raining.

The lights were out in the Darlington Mini Storage leasing office, which was attached to Aunt Deb's two-story house. Technically, the office was the home's garage, but it had been so long since my uncle transformed it into the leasing office that it was hard to imagine it as a garage. He had replaced the wide automatic garage door with sliding glass doors, finished the space out with hardwood floors and new paint, and added heating and air-conditioning.

The small parking lot just inside the gate, where Aunt Deb kept her car, was empty. I'd have to show her the photo later. I hustled to my design studio and quickly located the wood glue in my bin of hardware goodies.

I cleared some space on my work table, relocating my four-inch, three-ring binder to the floor. The binder was like my real-time Pinterest account, filled with inspirational pages from magazines and photos from home tours I'd attended. It had started as a project in a senior-year college course and grown in the years since.

I laid my tote bag on the table and removed the frame. It was filthy. It would need more than a dab of wood glue to restore it to its former glory. Flipping it over, I lifted the prongs holding the cardboard backing to the frame. I was worried the photo would have adhered to the glass as old photos sometimes do, but it slid out easily.

The children in the photo looked vaguely familiar. Something about their eyes. And I recognized the three-panel bay window as the same one in Vincent's breakfast room. On the back of the photo, in the same loopy handwriting used on the boxes in the attic, was the caption 'Christmas 1991.' If Geraldine Henkle was still alive, I would make sure she was reunited with this frame and her other personal items in the attic. Vincent would probably know her whereabouts.

I cleaned both sides of the glass, then repositioned the photo in the frame and glued the broken corner.

My phone rang. It was a local number I didn't recognize. "Hello, this is Hadley."

"Good evening, Hadley. Gigi Ellsworth here. May I borrow a minute of your time…must be busy…would like to…"

I checked the signal status on my phone. Only one bar. Rats. The metal walls and roof of the storage facility were infamous for sucking the soul out of my phone signal.

"Hi Gigi, it's great to hear from you," I said.

"What's that? You…and…didn't catch…"

"Can you hold on for one second, please?" I switched off the desk lamp on my work table, grabbed my keys, and left the studio. "Sorry about that. I had to move to a spot with better phone reception. Anyway, it's good to hear from you. How can I help?" I locked the thick padlock to my unit and left the building. I would grab the frame on my way to work in the morning.

"Ah, yes, that's much better," she sang. "Anyhoo, as I mentioned to you when we met in the coffee shop after my dear Willy passed, I would like to make some changes—rather soon, I might add—to the first floor of my home. The second story will come later, but I first must focus on the areas where I entertain guests. I'll need new furniture, paint, accessories, drapes, rugs, and maybe new countertops in my kitchen and bathrooms. I've seen photos of your work on your website, and I would love to schedule a consultation with you to discuss this project. Do you have time this weekend?"

Wow. This wasn't a small refresh project. This was a complete redesign that could breathe fresh life—and revenue—into my Hadley Home Design business. All new furniture? New countertops? Feeling like I couldn't breathe, I somehow managed to squeeze out a few words between my ear-to-ear grin.

"Absolutely, I would be happy to meet with you. I'm volunteering at the Flower Festival on Saturday, but I'm free on Sunday." Reid's dinner party for Vincent was Sunday evening, but I was pretty sure I wouldn't go.

"Wonderful. How about one o'clock? I have to tie up some loose ends with my attorney Sunday morning. He's been out of town on a cruise for the past month and his schedule is booked for the next three weeks. I don't want to have to reschedule."

"Sunday at one is perfect. If you have any photos of rooms you like, we can look at those when I come. They'll give us a good starting point." I thanked Gigi and hung up, then ran all the way back to my apartment, this time not from fear but from the pure exhilaration.

# CHAPTER FIFTEEN

This morning I drove to work. My feet were tired and I was running late. I remembered our seven o'clock start time when I was only two sips into my morning cup of coffee at six-thirty. Although I was usually out of bed by six, I had slept twenty minutes later because last night I guilted myself into finishing the four remaining wreaths for the Flower Festival. Since I had told Reid I had to make wreaths, it felt like a little less of a lie if I actually worked on them.

The Wimberley set and coordinating Walnut Ridge accessories looked amazing during their photo shoot. The silver hairbrush and wire reading glasses added rustic authenticity to the bedroom set, but I hadn't had time to run by my studio for the wooden frame.

Rachael flitted about the room while Kyle moped along behind her. Harry and I stood on opposite sides of the bed, fluffing the duvet cover every thirty seconds to make it look plusher than it actually was.

"Alright, gang," Rachael chirped, moving to a different vantage point. "One more fluff and then we'll be good on photos of the bed."

Humming a *Mary Poppins* tune, Harry strode toward his side of the bed. I adored *Mary Poppins,* but "Spoonful of Sugar" made me think of coffee, which I desperately needed. Taking a deep breath, I summoned an extra dose of energy and grabbed the edge of the duvet cover.

"One, two, three—lift!" I called out.

My cell phone vibrated in my back pocket, but I ignored it. It was probably my parents calling. Wednesdays and Fridays at 7:30 a.m. were our typical times to catch up, since they were getting ready for bed in Japan and I was usually enjoying a cup of coffee before work.

"Let's try it again," I said. "It still looks flat." We fluffed the covers again, then stepped aside so Rachael and Kyle could snap more photos.

My phone buzzed again. Retrieving it from my pocket, I stepped into the hallway. It must be important; this was the second time in one minute they had called.

Just outside the room, I stopped short. It was Aunt Deb. She never called this early in the morning on a weekday.

"Aunt Deb?" I answered.

"Hadley!" she shrieked. "Thank heavens you're okay."

"What's going on? Are you okay?"

"I'm fine, but someone broke into my office last night while I was asleep. Chip yapped his little head off at two in the morning, but I gave him some treats and made him calm down. I never imagined he was yapping because of an intruder. They did a real number on the window frame and even dumped the contents of my file cabinet. There are papers everywhere."

My pulse hammered in my ears. "What about your home? Is anything missing?" My aunt usually kept the door between the leasing office and her private residence unlocked, and her China cabinet held all of the crystal bowls and miniature figurines my uncle had given her.

"No, nothing was taken from the house that I'm aware of."

There was something she wasn't saying. "And your leasing office?" I pressed. "Did they steal anything?"

"Don't worry, I've called the police and they are on their way. As soon as I mentioned your name, they said they would send a detective along."

"My name? What does the break-in have to do with me?"

"Oh, Hadley, hon, I'm so sorry. I should have installed an alarm system like folks have been telling me to do." Her words were garbled with sobs. "The intruder took the spare set of keys to your unit. I had them in my desk drawer."

Eight minutes later, I pulled into a customer parking spot next to Aunt Deb's leasing office. Detective Sanders was stepping out of the passenger side of a squad car in the space to my left. Hoping Dennis was the officer behind the steering wheel, I peered through the squad car's open door.

He greeted me with a wave and pleasant smile when he saw me. I let out a sigh of relief. With several decades of experience, Detective Sanders was the more experienced of the two, but it was comforting to see the face of a friend.

"Mornin', Hadley," Detective Sanders said. "Although evidently it's not a good one, considering the mess we have in front of us." He motioned to the shattered window of the leasing office.

"I've had better," I agreed.

Aunt Deb flung open the office door and ran outside wearing her typical hiking attire—sleeveless cotton shirt and khaki shorts. The only things missing were her hiking boots. Chip, the poufy white Bichon dog she recently adopted after fostering for several weeks, trailed her closely, yapping ferociously at Dennis and Detective Sanders.

Detective Sanders looked at Aunt Deb's bare feet. "Careful, ma'am. I don't want you cutting yourself on all this glass."

Without acknowledging Detective Sanders, Aunt Deb rushed toward me, opened her arms and threw them around me. "I'm so sorry, hon. I never should have kept your key in an unlocked drawer. When I realized it was missing, I thought I would die I was so worried about you."

I hugged her back, then pulled away and looked in her eyes. "Please don't worry about it. Now's not the time to second guess everything. Darlington Hills is a safe community, and I'm sure you're not the only one without an alarm."

Detective Sanders took a step in our direction and held out his hand toward Aunt Deb. "Detective Roy Sanders, ma'am. I recognize you from the ten o'clock Sunday service, though I can't claim I go every week."

Aunt Deb raised an eyebrow as she shook his hand. "Deb Sutton. Nice to meet you, Detective."

"Please, call me Roy."

Aunt Deb leaned over and picked up Chip, bringing him into her arms. "How have we never met? I generally make it my business to know everyone in town."

Detective Sanders chuckled. "I live on the outskirts of Darlington Hills and don't venture into town too often when I'm off-duty. Except for Sunday service occasionally." Detective Sanders introduced Aunt Deb to Dennis, then pulled a notebook and pen from his pocket. "Now listen here. Officer Appley and I are going to ask you some questions and look around your office. Have you gone out to Hadley's unit yet to see if anything's missing?"

Aunt Deb shook her head. "I didn't feel safe going out there by myself. I wanted to wait for the police."

"You're a smart woman," he said, one side of his lips curving into a smile. "We'll take a look when we finish up in here."

Inside the leasing office, we stood amid a sea of loose paper from the emptied four-drawer file cabinet. Dennis took photos of the mess while Aunt Deb showed Detective Sanders the drawer where she kept the spare key to my unit.

"Do you keep spare keys for all of your tenants?" he asked.

"No, only Hadley's. In case she lost hers or if I needed to go in there."

He nodded. "Was anything else stolen?"

"In this drawer"—she pointed to the one under her desktop computer—"I kept a floor plan of my facility. I used it to keep track of which units were rented. It's missing too."

Detective Sanders tapped his pen to his white beard. "Did your floor plan show the names of your tenants?"

Aunt Deb cringed. "Yes. I never thought anyone would break in and steal it."

"How about security cameras? Any on the property?"

"No, I'm afraid I don't," she said quietly, looking at the floor. "Until recently, there's never been much crime here. I never saw the need."

"Don't worry, ma'am, I'm not here to judge. What about your access gate?" Detective Sanders asked. "Do you know if it's damaged?"

"No damage. If the intruder did venture into the storage facility, they either climbed over the gate or they knew the code. For all I know, the intruder was a tenant."

Detective Sanders turned his gray eyes on me. "Do you keep the gate code in your purse?"

"No."

He nodded. "Good. Because Officer Appley told me someone may have browsed through your purse to find your home address before they left the"—he shifted his eyes to Aunt Deb—"*surprise* on your doorstep."

"Surprise?" Aunt Deb asked.

"I'll tell you later," I told her. Now wasn't the time to worry her even more with the knife-in-the-boot story.

Detective Sanders and Dennis examined every inch of the leasing office and window, then asked Aunt Deb to open the access gate.

"I'd like you and Hadley to stay here while Officer Appley and I search the premises," he told Aunt Deb.

Twenty minutes later Detective Sanders and Dennis returned to the leasing office, both wearing stoic expressions that were impossible to read. They could have found a dead body or absolutely nothing.

"The grounds of your facility are clear, ma'am," Detective Sanders announced. "Hadley's unit is locked and appears untouched."

Aunt Deb placed her hand over her chest. "Oh, thank heavens. And thanks to you both for checking things out in there."

"My pleasure," he said, bowing his head.

"But the intruder had my key," I blurted out. "They wouldn't have had to break into my unit with a key. Before you leave, can you check it out and make sure it's safe? Please?" I pulled my jumble of keys—car, apartment, storage unit—from my pocket and held them up.

Detective Sanders chuckled. "Intruders don't typically lock doors on their way out, but I'd be happy to go take a look. You're welcome to come with us."

After leaving Chip inside her house, Aunt Deb and I walked several steps behind Detective Sanders and Dennis to my unit. Standing in front of my metal roll-up door, I studied the lock. Not a scratch on it. I slid my key into the padlock and popped it open, then grabbed the metal handle at the bottom of the door and heaved it open.

A whoosh of air blasted us as the door rolled up, along with a wave of tiny white balls.

"What in the name of—" Aunt Deb said, swishing her hands around her face.

There was a blizzard of Styrofoam balls in my design studio.

My bean bag chair lay in a deflated heap in the middle of my studio, split open from top to bottom.

I let out a frustrated moan. The mess! How were there so many balls in one little bean bag chair? They were everywhere—on my storage shelves, worktable, inside the artificial ficus plant in the corner—and I couldn't even see the rug or concrete floor.

"This is quite a fancy storage unit you've got, Hadley," Detective Sanders said, looking up at the string of globe lights. "I've never seen anyone make one up like this before."

"It's her studio for her interior design business," Aunt Deb said proudly.

Dennis, his hand wrapped around his face, surveyed the room, clearly holding back a laugh. Rolling my eyes, I shuffled through the balls and joined him near my storage shelves.

"Why would someone make such a big mess?" I asked, keeping my voice low so Aunt Deb wouldn't hear. "You think the same person who stabbed Carmella's rain boots did this?"

He lowered his hand and cleared the smile from his face. "I think this is the biggest mess I've ever seen. And I don't have enough info at this point to say for certain, but it appears to be the work of the same person." He leaned closer to me. "By the way, I'm free tonight if you need help cleaning this up."

"Oh!" Aunt Deb clapped her hand over her mouth.

I spun around, prepared to bolt if she had discovered any bodies or body parts in my studio. "What's wrong?"

She aimed her gaze at Dennis. "You're the young man with a goat. The one who called not too long ago."

Dennis' cheek dimpled. "Yes ma'am, I'm the proud owner of a very opinionated, very needy goat. I inherited Sadie from my grandfather two years ago when he passed away."

"I'm sorry to hear that, but I'm sure she's in good hands now." Aunt Deb snapped her eyes to me and then back to Dennis. Uh-oh. She was now in full-on matchmaker mode. "This may seem a little…off topic, Dennis, but are you planning to attend this weekend's Flower Fes—"

"Aunt Deb, do you have a broom and dustpan I could borrow?" I gave myself a mental hand slap. Dustpan? Really? It was the best I could come up with in an attempt to dodge the impending matchmaking session.

She frowned. "For this mess, hon? I'm thinking more along the lines of an industrial size vacuum cleaner."

"Maybe, but a broom would help with an initial round of cleaning. Like on my workstation. I wouldn't want a vacuum to suck up all my…" I trailed off as I walked over to my table and brushed away the piles of Styrofoam balls.

"My bag!" I cried. "Look at what they did to my tote bag." I held it up. One of the handles was missing and there was a giant rip through the bottom, similar to the slash through my bean bag chair.

Similar to the slash in Carmella's boot.

I scanned the rest of my workstation area. My pens and fabric samples were still there; my design binder was still on the floor where I'd placed it—thank goodness!—and my bin of hardware was on the far side of the table, exactly where I left it.

My head snapped up. "The picture frame is missing. I had it right here." I tapped the middle of the table. "I brought it home yesterday from Vincent's so I could fix it. Why would they take the frame?"

"Is that the only thing missing?" Dennis asked. "Nothing else of more value?"

I walked around my studio doing a quick inventory. Shelves appeared fine, all of my home accessories were untouched, and nothing appeared sliced or diced like my bean bag chair and tote bag. My file cabinet was cracked open, but nothing was missing inside. It was very possible I had left it open.

I swept my foot through a particularly large pile of Styrofoam balls near the back leg of my workstation. Something glimmered below, reflecting the weak light from my desk lamp. I kicked the cluster of balls again.

"It's my scissors," I said. "Whoever broke in got these from the bin of office supplies I keep in my file cabinet. I bent over to pick them up.

"Whoa, whoa, hang on a second," Detective Sanders said. "Don't touch them. We'll see if we can get any prints off these since this may be connected to…" He trailed off, glancing at Aunt Deb.

Dennis donned a pair of gloves and removed a plastic bag from the front pocket of his uniform shirt. He lifted the scissors gingerly, grasping them by the tip of the blades, and slid them into the bag.

He looked up at me. "Tell me about the frame that was stolen."

"There wasn't anything special about it. The former homeowner left a bunch of boxes in the attic, and I went up there yesterday afternoon to look for some antique items to use in a photo shoot today. It was old and broken, so I brought it back here to fix it." I motioned to the wood glue on the table.

Detective Sanders rubbed his beard. "That is odd. Don't know why anyone would care about a frame."

"Maybe it was the photo they cared about," I mused. "It was a middle-aged woman with blonde poufy hair and two young kids. The back said Christmas 1991." I turned to Aunt Deb. "I was thinking the woman was the previous homeowner and her grandkids."

"No, Geraldine was a brunette," Aunt Deb said, twirling the ends of her auburn hair. "Like me, she never went through a blonde phase, even when it became the 'in' thing to do." Aunt Deb gazed at the ceiling with narrowed eyes. "Geraldine did have some grandkids who used to run around town for a week or two in the summer, but they stopped visiting years ago. Apparently she had a falling out with her daughter."

Dennis watched Aunt Deb intently as she spoke, nodding his head as though he were taking copious mental notes.

Aunt Deb shrugged. "I'm afraid I don't know much more about Geraldine. She was a kind woman, though I wouldn't say she was a friend. She always kept to herself."

I opened my mouth to tell them about the person on the park bench yesterday afternoon, but stopped myself. In light of everything going on, it was probably nothing—just me being paranoid.

Dennis's eyes sparked with curiosity. "Hadley?" he pressed. "Now's not the time to hold anything back."

I told them about the hooded person and how I checked to make sure I wasn't being followed once I neared the storage facility.

Detective Sanders listened attentively. "I'm pleased you're aware of your surroundings, but try not to worry yourself too much. When possible, walk with a friend and make sure you always have your cell phone on you."

"And your pepper spray." Dennis winked at me. "Wouldn't hurt to carry that around too."

Aunt Deb sighed as she gazed at the mess in my studio. "I'm so sorry, hon. I should have kept your key in a safer spot. And I should have invested in security cameras a long time ago."

I put my arm around her and gave her a hug. I didn't want to say so, but it was possibly a blessing that my key and the floor plan had been so accessible. If the intruder had been desperate to get into my unit, there was no telling what they would have done —or who they would have hurt—to get access.

"Actually, no. This is my fault," I said. "Someone's trying to intimidate me because I've struck a nerve and now you have a smashed window to deal with."

Not to mention all the questions she'd have to field from tenants. Aunt Deb's business was already struggling, and it pained me to think this incident could contribute to its reputation as a storage facility with sub-par security. She didn't need any more reasons to sell her business and move to Chicago.

"I'm going to pay for your window," I said. "It's the least I can do." The pinch pleated Walnut Ridge comforter I'd been saving for could wait. This was more important.

Aunt Deb held up her hand to object, but Detective Sanders stepped between us. "Why don't you let me come out here another day and do a security audit?" he asked her. "Free of charge, of course. I'll see if there's anything we can do to tighten your security—procedures, cameras, and the like. I know some first-rate technicians who can install cameras and I'll make sure they give you the Darlington Hills Police Department discount."

Aunt Deb beamed. "Thank you. I'd like that very much."

# CHAPTER SIXTEEN

Blooms in every color and variety filled the town square at the Spring Flower Festival. Fragrant garlands of jasmine and roses twined around lampposts, and giant arrangements of colorful blooms lined the stone-paved street. Young boys had single-flower boutonnières pinned to their shirts while girls had sprigs of pink and white daisies woven through their braided hair.

Even the birds, chirping louder than most days, seemed to know this was a special occasion.

Carmella and I sat at a portable table in front of Whisks and Whiskers Cat Café, selling the tulip wreaths we had made. I bopped my head to a lively tune from the community orchestra as I watched the bustling town square. I had never seen it so crowded. Vincent had given everyone the day off, and I had already seen two of Terence's guys with their families, as well as Kyle, who was walking around by himself snapping photos, looking as grumpy as ever.

Further down the road, on the other side of the large fountain in the center of the square, tables were lined end-to-end, holding vases placed there by women hoping to find them filled with flowers before the end of the day.

Carmella had insisted I put a vase on the table. "It's bad luck to break tradition," she had claimed. So I brought a simple glass vase, and Carmella tied several lacy ribbons around it. She added a heart-shaped paper tag to the bow and wrote my name written in her pretty handwriting.

Around ten o'clock, a short line formed in front of our table. I wrapped the purchased wreaths in tissue paper and stuffed them into paper bags while Carmella took care of the payment. King Oliver, Erin's pet tabby, watched us from his spot on his personal blanket, which we'd place on top of the table. As the other cats meowed from inside the café's windows, King Oliver seemed smug to have special privileges.

I rubbed King Oliver between his two ears. "Razzy would be jealous if she knew I was petting you," I told him. King Oliver looked up at me, his orange and white face now darkened by the shadow of our next customer.

"Mornin'," a familiar voice called out in front of me. Reid was holding a coffee cup in his hand with a fifty-dollar bill sticking out between two of his fingers. He wore the same lightweight charcoal-gray sweater he wore the day I first met him, the thin sleeves pulled mid-way up his tan forearms.

My heart pitter-pattered despite my resolution to not get involved with him. "Hey, Reid. Good morning."

Scanning the wreaths hanging from a rack behind us, his easy smile grew. "These are amazing, Hadley. They were definitely worth bailing on me for dinner."

"I have a very demanding boss"—I hooked my thumb toward King Oliver—"who wouldn't give me the night off."

Reid eyed King Oliver warily. "I hope he's more appreciative than he looks. You obviously put a lot of work into these."

"I can't take all the credit. Carmella made half of them." I put my hand on her shoulder. "Reid, meet Carmella, my friend and neighbor. When she's not making wreaths, she's the principal at Darlington Hills Middle School."

Reid held out his hand and introduced himself. Mid-handshake, Carmella shifted her eyes to me, giving me a brief, pointed look that told me I was crazy for canceling on him.

"Hadley, which wreath would look best on my front door?" he asked, looking over my shoulder at the selection.

I stood and scanned the remaining wreaths. We had sold seven in the last hour but we still had a nice variety left. I lifted one in the middle and brought it to the table. "I'd go with the all-white one. It'll contrast nicely against your black door and it'll be great for the summer months, too. Although I know you're hoping to sell your house before then."

"Actually, I have a contract on my house now. The offer came in on Wednesday, and I close in thirty days if all goes well."

"Congratulations," I said, feeling a weird combination of relief and disappointment. Despite all the giant red flags surrounding Reid, I didn't want him to move away. "Have you found a new home yet?"

"Nope, I'm still house-hunting. But thanks again for staging it. There wasn't much interest in it before you gave it a makeover, so I'm convinced that's what sold my house." Reid removed a leather wallet from his back pocket, opened it, and pulled out a check that had my name on it. "It's a little something for your troubles."

I waved a hand at him. "Put your check back, please. I refuse to charge my friends—right, Carmella?"

"That's right," she confirmed. "Hadley helped me pick out my new bedroom set and didn't charge me."

"Well then, I'd like to take you to dinner. Sometime when you don't have to make wreaths."

"Thank you." It was the most non-committal yet polite response I could think of. Until I was absolutely positive he wouldn't show up on my doorstep holding flowers in one hand and a knife in the other, I would have to take one raincheck after another.

He tucked his wallet back in his pocket. "Speaking of dinner, are you planning to come to Vinn's party tomorrow night?"

Turning my eyes to the wreath he was buying, I carefully wrapped several sheets of tissue paper around it. "I wish I could, but I already have plans." Plans that included not getting stabbed by whomever had mutilated Carmella's boots and wrecked my studio.

A spirited breeze blew a whiff of his cologne toward me, sending my senses into a tailspin. Musky and sweet, it evoked images of a sultry afternoon on the beach, iced cocktail in-hand. I took a deep breath. It was like inhaling tiny heart-shaped packets of sweet, rugged masculinity.

My eyes found his. "But there's a chance I might be able to get out of those plans." I could always bring my pepper spray, as Dennis had suggested.

"I'll give you a private tour of the *Sutherland*, since dinner didn't work out last week." His cheeks reddened. "Although it's just as well you didn't come. I've hired several of Vinn's handymen to do some maintenance work and they turned my small private banquet room—the one I had planned to take you to—into their supply storeroom. There are ladders, toolboxes, and paint buckets everywhere."

"A tour would be nice," I mused, trying to push away the heaps of doubts I had about him. I slipped his wrapped wreath into a paper bag and handed it to him.

"I know Vinn would love to see you there too. He probably hasn't told you this, but he really appreciates you driving to his house that night when he didn't answer your calls. Your instinct was right. I don't want to think about what would have happened if you hadn't found him soon after he fell."

Reid was right, Vincent hadn't talked to me about his fall that night. I assumed it was a sensitive subject. Even though he was supposed to rest in bed after he returned from the hospital, he had supervised most of the photo shoots yesterday and Thursday, sitting with his leg propped up on whatever elevated surfaces he could find.

Reid handed his fifty-dollar bill to Carmella and waved goodbye. "I'm heading home. I can handle only so much of this festival without feeling like a bee in a garden. Hadley, I hope to see you tomorrow night. Let me know if you'd like a ride."

I smiled and waved, then whipped my head toward Carmella as soon as he disappeared into the crowd. "What do think?" I whispered. "Hometown heartthrob or brother-hating psychopath?"

She stared in the direction where Reid had gone. "Criminals come in all shapes and sizes, but I've never seen one look as good as that man. Not even in the movies. I'd say give him a chance. Go on his boat tomorrow night for the party."

I shook my head, my mind clearer now without the presence of his Casanova cologne. "But the phone calls with Vincent…and Reid actually used the word 'unresponsible.' How many people do you know who use that word? Carmella, what if Reid is the one who pushed Vincent from the balcony?"

"Just because he's guilty of one grammatical error doesn't mean he tried to kill his brother," Carmella reasoned.

She had a point. Maybe I would go. Reid had invited Vincent's entire crew, which meant I would be safe with so many people around. "I'll think about it. But I'm definitely not taking him up on his offer for a private tour."

Carmella's mouth curved into a mischievous smile. "That's a shame. I'm afraid you'd be missing the best part of the evening."

We sold our last wreath at one o'clock, then helped Erin return the table and chairs to her storeroom. After an on-the-house lunch of chicken salad sandwiches at Whisks and Whiskers, Carmella and I ventured into the still-buzzing town square.

"Come on, let's go check our vases," Carmella said, pulling me by the hand.

I groaned. "No one's put any flowers in my vase. I have yet to go on any official dates."

"And who's fault is that?" she teased. "Maybe you shouldn't have canceled on Mr. Hottie last week."

Heading for the long line of tables, we wove through the crowd, which had grown livelier as the day progressed. Hands that had held coffee in the morning now held plastic cups filled with beer and wine. Children darted around us holding colorful mounds of cotton candy. I counted three young boys whose boutonnières now consisted of only a stem pinned to their shirt, the flower likely smushed somewhere in the street.

"How can there be so many single women in such a small town?" I asked, eyeing all of the vases. The line of tables started just past the water fountain in the center of the square and extended almost an entire block. Each table held twenty or more vases in varying shapes and sizes. About half of the vases held a single flower, a quarter of them were empty, and another quarter overflowed with flowers.

Carmella giggled. "This tradition used to be only for single women, but now married women join in on the fun. I suppose it's a good excuse for their husbands to buy them flowers." She paused, pointing to the table closest to us. "You know how you can tell which vases belong to single women?"

"Theirs have more flowers?" I guessed.

"No. Single ladies usually decorate their vase with more ribbons. The married women know they'll get flowers anyway, so they don't bother making it look fancy. She motioned to a tall vase in front of us holding a dozen carnations, a single strand of raffia ribbon tied around its center. "Case in point."

A young woman to my right squealed. Peering at a vase full of flowers, she tore into the little envelope wedged between two roses, read the card, then dashed off with a big smile on her face.

"Why didn't she take her flowers?" I whispered to Carmella.

"It's the tradition." She resumed walking toward the table holding our vases. "You aren't supposed to take your flowers until the end of the day."

We passed a man in his twenties holding an armful of pink and red tulips, leaning over the table while reading each vase's nametag. The trickles of sweat on the side of his face told me he had been searching for quite some time.

About midway down the row of tables, we slowed to look for our vases.

"Hadley!" Carmella cried. "*Look*."

It took me a moment to recognize my vase. It had never held so many flowers. There were pink and white tulips, hydrangeas, lilies, and roses.

I checked the nametag on the vase to make sure it really was mine. "I got flowers," I said, not believing what I was seeing. "Who would—"

"Open up the card," Carmella urged. She plucked a small white envelope from a pronged plastic stick and handed it to me.

I removed a bright pink card from the envelope. Inside, my name was written in all uppercase letters in blue ink. There was a small heart beneath my name.

I felt like squealing just as the other young woman had done, but I whirled around, searching for the man who had given me the flowers. Reid? Dennis?

"Well? Who's it from?" Carmella asked.

I continued searching the crowd. "There isn't a name on it."

She clasped her hands in front of her chest. "Ooh, a mystery man. I like it."

I returned the card to the pronged stick, then wiggled my phone free from the slender pocket of my small purse. I missed the single, large pocket of my tote bag. Taking a step back, I snapped a photo of my flowers. I'd send it to my mom and dad later so they could ooh and aah over them.

Two tween girls approached, waving to Carmella. "Hi, Ms. Jones," they said in unison, each holding something behind their back, looking as if they were fighting a smile.

"Hi, Addie. Hi, Samantha. You two look like you're having fun today."

They both turned giggly as they stammered out their polite replies, as if Carmella were an A-lister movie star. The girls spun around and slid a flower into Carmella's vase, then waved goodbye and ran off.

Carmella's vase, one of the largest on the table, was so full of flowers I didn't think it could fit any more. Tags from students at Darlington Hills Middle School hung from each flower, some signatures sloppy, some in better cursive than I ever managed.

It thrilled me to see so many flowers from her students. I doubted Carmella's long-distance boyfriend, Neil, bought her many flowers. From everything she'd told me about him, he didn't seem like the flower-giving type.

"Carmella, these kids absolutely adore you," I said, motioning to the vase. "You're a celebrity in this town."

She laughed. "I don't know about that, but I am blessed to have the best middle school students ever. They are a bunch of sweethearts." She paused, then held up a finger. "Except for the ones who aren't. They aren't all perfect."

I frowned. "Hang on a sec." I moved to the table next to us, toward another vase I recognized. It was the blue and white porcelain one that used to be my grandmother's. Two ribbons were tied around its middle: a thick white satin one and a thinner lacy ribbon. A small red plastic gemstone heart was glued in the center of the bow.

"It's Aunt Deb's," I said as Carmella joined me. I turned the scalloped note card hanging from the lacy ribbon toward Carmella. Aunt Deb had written her name with a calligraphy pen on the card. "Do all single women put out a vase or only those who are looking for a relationship?"

"I can't say for sure, but I don't see why someone would put a vase out if they didn't think there was a chance they'd get some flowers."

Staring at my grandmother's empty vase, my heart felt heavy. Did Aunt Deb want to date again? It had been five years since my Uncle Bill had passed, and even though she never talked about dating again, it was quite possible she wanted to.

I ran my fingers across the sparkling heart gemstone. Aunt Deb probably wouldn't have put so much time into decorating her vase, scalloping the edges of the notecard, and crafting perfect letters with a calligraphy pen if she hadn't hoped to find some flowers.

"Come on," I told Carmella, motioning her to follow. "Let's go find some flowers for Aunt Deb. If someone can randomly put some in my vase, then I can do the same for her. You know, pay it forward."

She hurried after me. "I love it."

Fifteen minutes later, I handed a twenty-dollar bill to a teenage boy at the Stems and Smiles stand-up booth. It had been more difficult than I thought it would be to find a bouquet of flowers at the Flower Festival. The first three flower booths we tried had sold out of everything but half-wilted single-stemmed flowers. Definitely not what I had in mind.

But I walked away from Stems and Smiles with a floral arrangement every bit as beautiful as the one I'd received.

On the first table we passed, a large green vase filled with dozens of long-stem pink roses sat perilously close to the edge. Nudging it closer to the center of the table, I peeked at the name tag: Shirley Decker.

I laughed. "Looks like Aunt Deb will be getting some of her friend's potted plants." I told Carmella about the bet they had made about whom Hal Stenner, the over-sixty heartthrob, would give pink roses to this year.

We arranged the flowers in Aunt Deb's vase and I drew a little heart in the accompanying card, just as my own secret flower-giver had done. Stepping back, I admired her flowers. I hoped they would make her feel special.

"Now the three of us will take home a bunch of flowers tonight," I said, gazing at the table holding my vase. "I still can't believe someone gave me—"

My eyes bulged. "Hey! Where did my flowers go?" I strode toward the neighboring table. In the place of my beautiful bouquet was a single white rose. A dead, drooping, nearly flattened white rose.

"What is *that*?" Carmella shrieked, staring at the pathetic flower. She pulled the pink card, which was now bent down the middle, from the pronged plastic stick in the vase. She read it. "Roses are red, but this one's..." Her eyes grew larger as she finished reading it to herself.

"What's it say?" I asked, reaching for it.

She held the card away from me. "You don't want to know. We need to head home, call it a day. You're going to call that police friend of yours and ask him to be your personal bodyguard."

"Please. I need to know."

Carmella's eyes darted around the street. "Fine, but then we're going home." Slowly turning the card upward, she read it again "Roses are red, but this one's dead. If you don't stop snooping, you will be too." The hand-drawn heart had been scratched out in thick, red ink.

The happy, sunshiny sparkles I'd felt since finding the flowers in my vase evaporated. But I wasn't scared. I was ticked off someone had stolen my flowers. Now I'd have to report this to Dennis, and I'd feel awful if he was the one who had bought me the flowers—or even worse if someone else had.

I snapped a photo of the dead flower so I could text it to Dennis. "What a lousy poem," I grunted. "The second part doesn't even rhyme."

Carmella led me away from the table. "Mmmhmm, you're telling me. The lunatic we're dealing with can't even follow a proper poetic rhyme scheme. Obviously, they never paid attention in English class."

# CHAPTER SEVENTEEN

"Based on these photos, you seem to favor a traditional interior design style mixed with some coastal and farmhouse elements," I said, clicking through the photos Gigi had saved on her computer. My hands trembled with nervous, excited energy. I needed this redesign project to revive my dormant consulting business.

We were sitting on her formal living room sofa, a nineties-era hunter green monstrosity with a dizzying pattern of gold and mauve flowers. Gigi's furniture and decor were elegant and expensive, but dated. Most of the walls in her house were covered with either striped or floral wallpaper, and thick, velvety, hunter green drapes hung from all of her windows. I understood why she wanted to make some changes.

I reached across the sofa and dragged my oversized handbag toward me. It was a many-zippered fortress that I had difficulty navigating through, but after the recent death of my tote bag, I had to resurrect it from the far corner of my closet. None of my trendy clutch purses would fit more than my phone and keys.

I set Gigi's laptop on the coffee table in front of us and pulled a slick, black binder from my bag. "I prepare a project portfolio for each of my clients. This one is from a former client in New Orleans, who gave me permission to keep hers to showcase my work."

Unlike the overstuffed four-inch design inspiration binder I started in college, the project portfolio was neat and organized with well-labeled tab dividers and glossy sheet protectors for every page.

Gigi slid her reading glasses down to her nose and scooted closer to me. "May I?" she asked, holding out her palms.

I opened the binder to the first section, then handed it to her. "My clients' portfolios include all of the specifics relating to their project, starting with a project overview"—I pointed to the first tab—"followed by a detailed budget, timeline, design elements like paint swatches and textile samples, as well as 3D renderings I create with interior design software to show what rooms will look like."

Gigi studied each section of the portfolio, carefully turning each page. "What was this client's interior design style?" She tapped a red, manicured nail against a photo of the redesigned family room. "I love what you did with this home."

"Thank you. This client's style is similar to yours—a mix of traditional and contemporary southern. And if you hire me for your redesign project, we will spend even more time honing in on your style preferences."

Gigi looked up from the binder. "Honey, I already know I'm hiring you. I'm sorry I didn't make that clear when I called you. I decided to hire you when I looked at all those client photos you put up on your website. And the hourly fee you posted on your site sounds reasonable enough. I also took the liberty to track down your previous employer in New Orleans—the one you listed on LinkedIn—and she raved about you." Gigi lowered her voice. "I didn't say this, but you don't have much competition in Darlington Hills...no one who I'd like to work with, anyway."

I got the job? My heart sprang into celebratory mode,

increasing its pace as though it were preparing my body to run around the room or jump up and down on the sofa. But I remained still, stifling a squeal of happiness.

"Wow, thank you! I can't tell you how excited I am to begin working on your home."

"When can we get started?" she asked.

"I'll get some photos and measurements today if you have time."

Gigi's eyes lit up. "Today would be wonderful. I have the rest of the afternoon open."

"We'll also talk about how you plan to use each space. Not only do I want your rooms to be aesthetically pleasing, I also want them to be functional. Color schemes are also something you'll select early on. And from looking at your inspiration photos, I can see you want to move away from the hunter green and mauve to something brighter, sunnier. You have some great windows in this room and I'd like to optimize the light in here."

She nodded vehemently. "That's what I had been trying to tell Willy."

"After I have a solid understanding of your goals and preferences, I will present my recommendations on paint colors, light fixtures, drapes, furniture, and so on."

"Don't forget kitchen countertops, appliances, and flooring," she said.

"Absolutely. We will refine the scope of your redesign project so I can give you a detailed timeline and estimate to ensure it fits within your budget. Do you know which areas you'd like me to focus on?"

"Downstairs."

"Okay, which rooms downstairs?"

"All of them."

My eyes widened. "*All* the rooms?"

"Only if you have the time. I would like new furniture, drapes, and decor throughout the first floor."

She wanted to know if I had enough time? This was a dream project. If I had to, I would petition Father Time himself to add more hours to the day. I would re-engineer my body to function on less sleep and I would put my entire heart into this project.

"I have the time, and I will make your project my priority," I assured her. "And although I work at Walnut Ridge, I am quite familiar with other home furnishing companies in the area." Since moving to Darlington Hills, I had spent most of my Sundays off driving to surrounding cities to visit furniture stores, textile companies, and suppliers of home accessories.

Gigi closed the binder and handed it to me. "After you've completed the first story, we'll move on to the second." She stood and returned her glasses to the top of her head, fluffing her shiny silver hair. "Come on, I'll show you around upstairs before you start taking measurements and photos downstairs."

All four of her bedrooms were on the second floor. To the left of the staircase was the owner's suite, which had endless opportunities for updating. Gigi closed the door behind us when we left her room. She led me down a long hallway lined with framed photos, pausing to open the doors to the three guest bedrooms so I could peek inside.

She motioned to the open room at the end of the hallway. "You'll recognize the furniture in my game room. I bought some Walnut Ridge pieces back in February when I returned home from a lengthy stay at my sister's place. As I've mentioned, I was ready for some changes to this old home, so I bought a few items to update our family room. Willy never came up here, so I didn't think he would care."

"Did he like it?" My guess was no, considering how much he had seemed to dislike Vincent.

Gigi resumed walked toward the game room. "He was furious. He never could handle change, bless his heart."

We stopped at the entrance of the game room. I recognized

the sofa immediately. "The Lazy Breezes sofa! This is one of my favorite—"

I gasped. It was the same sofa from the walnutridgejunk.com website. The left and middle seat cushions had large stains just like the photo on the website. Moving past Gigi, I made a beeline for the sofa. The stains were lighter than they were in the website photo, and the pilled upholstery told me someone—probably Gigi—had scrubbed them to death.

Slowly, I turned my head and scanned the room. It was all here, everything from the website: the mango wood bookcase with the lopsided shelves, the bent lamp, and the oddly shaped decorative pillows.

"It's a shame, isn't it?" Gigi asked, coming to stand next to me. "I hadn't owned this sofa for even one week when Willy accidentally spilled his coffee on it."

"Accidentally?"

She fluffed one of the decorative pillows, looking flustered. "Well, that's what he claimed, but I suspected it was intentional. Not only did he never come in this room, he also couldn't stand the taste of coffee."

I lifted the wonky pillow Gigi had just replaced on the sofa and studied it. The sides were not proportional and the fabric was bunched up in the middle. I unzipped the decorative pillow cover and glanced inside.

Ah ha! Someone—Willy, I guessed—had altered the shape of the pillow cover by pinching the interior seams and hand sewing a sloppy line of stitches.

I zipped the cover and returned the pillow to the sofa, then moved to the mango wood bookcase, which held books and knick-knacks despite the askew angle of its shelves. I removed several hardback books so I could see the holes for the shelf support pins. Someone had drilled extra holes between the evenly spaced predrilled holes.

Clearing the rest of the books and accessories from the

shelves, I pulled the support pins from all the extra holes someone drilled, replaced them in the appropriate holes, and lay the shelves on the pins. "There. Now your shelves are even."

"How did you manage to do that?" Gigi asked incredulously. "I was planning to get rid of them, but now I quite like them."

I replaced the books and accessories on her bookcase and stood. "Gigi, are you familiar with the website walnutridge-junk.com?"

"What an awful name for a website. No, I've never come across it."

"The site shows photos of defective Walnut Ridge furniture and complains about the company's noise levels and other neighborhood nuisances." Pulling my phone from my old hand bag, I navigated to the website and held up the photo of her stained sofa.

Gigi slid down her glasses again and peered at the photo. "Well looky there, this person bought the same sofa as me." She took my phone from my hands and narrowed her eyes, then looked back at her sofa.

She sighed. "Willy set up this website, didn't he?"

"That's what I'm thinking. Your bookcase, lamp, and throw pillows are also on the website. It seems as though he tinkered with the items you bought to make them look defective." I pointed to the pillows. "Turn those pillow covers inside out and you'll see what I'm talking about. And someone drilled extra holes on the inside of the bookcase so the adjustable shelves wouldn't lie straight."

Gigi puffed her cheeks out as she exhaled slowly. "I'm afraid to say that sounds like something Willy would have done. Setting up websites became something of a hobby for him recently. Once he figured out how to do it, he made one for our neighborhood HOA as well as our niece who runs a bakery in New York."

My phone dinged, signaling a new text message. Gigi glanced

at the notification, then handed it back to me. "You got a text," she informed me.

REID

U coming tonight? The Sutherland leaves at seven sharp. Hope to see you there.

I slipped my phone back into my bag. I would reply later, after I left Gigi's house.

"It's none of my business, but I happened to notice your message was from someone named Reid. Is it by chance Reid Weatherford?"

"Yes. You know him, I take it?" I raised my eyebrows, hoping she would take that as an invitation to gossip.

"Reid is an absolute doll. I don't have to tell you this if you've met him. From the few encounters I've had with his brother, I've gathered that the two of them are nothing alike."

She lowered her voice, shifting into ultra-secret gossip mode. "Reid and Vincent had a falling out not too long ago. It was over a woman, of course. Vincent's ex-fiancée, Claudia, left Vincent for Reid. But Reid wouldn't give her the time of day. Vincent didn't believe his brother's side of the story, and instead accused Reid of stealing Claudia. Things got heated between them after that. You do know that's why Reid's moving, right?"

I smiled, feeling a fresh spark of hope. I liked Gigi's version of the story much better than Gayle's. Gayle had made it seem like Reid swept Claudia off her feet on her way to the altar. Maybe Reid was a good guy after all.

"I heard a different version of that story. One where Reid ran off with Vincent's fiancée."

Gigi looked horrified. "Reid wouldn't do such a thing. You know, he hasn't dated much since his ex-girlfriend left him for another man." She narrowed her eyes. "Do you want to guess who that other man was?"

I shrugged. "I don't know many of the men in town."

"Oh, you know this one. It was Vincent, hon."

"Wait—what? Vincent's ex-fiancée was...*Reid's* ex-girlfriend?"

"That's right. I've never met her, but this Claudia woman is as fickle as they come. She dated Reid for just under a year before she left him for Vincent. Then, she went and changed her mind again, left Vincent and begged Reid to forgive her."

"And Reid turned her away?"

"Reid has a heart of gold, but he doesn't play those kinds of games. He was done with Claudia the moment she walked out his door the first time."

"Sounds like Vincent has caused Reid a lot of grief lately." First the woman, then Vincent's threat to report the *Sutherland* to the port authority. "Why would he host a dinner party to celebrate Vincent's recovery? I don't get it."

She smiled knowingly. "I told you, he has a good heart."

"You know him well?" I asked.

"Not really. I've only spoken with him a few times. Practically everything I know about Reid I learned from Willy."

"Oh, Willy and Reid were friends?"

She narrowed her eyes, glancing at the ceiling. "I don't know if friends is the right word. The two of them had a...how should I call it?...*reciprocal* business relationship. Reid allowed Willy to host a couple of at-cost business dinners on that lovely boat of his, only charging him for the food and beverages. In return, Willy agreed to sell his home without a commission. He was Reid's realtor."

# CHAPTER EIGHTEEN

I left Gigi's house at half-past five, my mind buzzing with all of the new revelations: the photos from the Walnut Ridge-bashing website were from Gigi's home; Reid had not run off with Vincent's fiancée; rather, Vincent had initially seduced her away from Reid. Last but not least, Willy was Reid's realtor and they had a 'reciprocal' business relationship, as Gigi had called it. Reid had mentioned his new realtor reshot photos of his home, but he hadn't told me he hired Willy initially. Was Reid intentionally withholding that information?

So much new information, yet none of it gave me a definitive answer to my ever-burning question: who was this honey-eyed heartthrob?

Was Reid the kind-hearted, benevolent man Gigi claimed he was, who helped Vincent while he was incapacitated and threw him a party despite the many ways Vincent had wronged him?

Or was Reid's newfound brotherly kindness all an act?

Walking briskly along Gigi's brick-paved sidewalk, I unlocked my car and jumped inside. I was done talking *about* Reid Weatherford. It was time to talk *to* him and find out for myself who he was. The *Sutherland* would pull away from the dock in an hour an half, leaving me just enough time to shower and get ready.

Yesterday when Dennis came out to see the dead tulip and threatening note, he wouldn't tell me who, if anyone, was a suspect, but he told me I needed to lay low until they make an arrest. I hoped 'laying low' didn't include going to the party. Besides, I would be safe with so many people on the boat.

I stopped at the intersection of Gigi's and Vincent's streets, craning my neck to see the colossal Walnut Ridge house at the end of the cul-de-sac. I felt drawn to it, as if something within that two-story home of contemporary southern charm held the answer to Willy's unfortunate death.

But the minute hand continued to race around my watch. If I wanted to board the Weatherford tonight, I couldn't waste time staring at Vincent's home.

The moment I flew through my apartment door, I took my second shower of the day, not taking the time to rinse all of the conditioner from my hair.

I checked the clock when I got out: 5:45 p.m. I relaxed a little. I would need to leave my place no later than 6:45, which left me a full hour to get dressed, put on makeup, and blow-dry my hair. Easy.

My phone dinged in the kitchen where I'd left it on the counter next to my car keys. I raced down the hall to read my text, a towel still tied around my body.

REID

Hey. I just picked up Vinn and we're heading to the dock. Want us to pick u up?

I thanked him, but told him I wasn't ready yet and would meet him there.

Slipping into a pale yellow spaghetti-strap dress, images of Vincent's home paraded through my mind. There was something there that held answers—I could feel it. His home was the epicenter of all the chaos in the past couple of weeks: Willy's murder, Vincent's fall, and even the knife sliced through Carmella's rain boots had been stolen from the Walnut Ridge home.

And whomever had broken into my design studio had taken the picture frame I removed from Vincent's attic. But how would anyone have known I took it? I'd been alone in the attic, and I carried it in my tote bag to my studio.

I froze, my zipper halfway up my back, as I recalled the hooded figure on the park bench during my walk from Vincent's house to my studio. Shortly before I noticed the figure, I removed the frame from my bag to look at it. Had the person on the bench seen me? Had they tracked me all the way from Vincent's?

And what would have been so special about the picture frame? Aunt Deb said Geraldine's grandkids used to visit until she had a falling out with her daughter. It was logical the photo was of Geraldine's daughter and grandchildren since it was taken in her home during Christmastime.

I had to see that photo again. Something about the eyes of the grandkids seemed familiar. And though I couldn't retrieve the picture stolen from my studio, it was possible there were other photos of the kids in Vincent's attic. There had been a bunch of keepsakes in the box where I found the frame.

I yanked my zipper up the rest of the way, ran to my closet, and tried on four pairs of heels to find the best match, then haphazardly threw makeup on my face as though it were a Jackson Pollock canvas, furiously swiping my lashes with mascara.

Six o'clock.

Stepping in front of my full-length mirror, my reflection told me I'd better get busy taming my wet crazy hair. But if I let my hair air-dry and just go with my natural curls, I would have time to stop off at Vincent's home and pop into his attic again. No one would be there, but the spare key was likely where I returned it, in the pot of marigolds.

I pulled my slender black clutch purse from the top shelf of my closet, then managed to squeeze my phone, pepper spray, lip gloss, and car keys into it.

Razzy followed me to the door, widening her blue eyes to guilt me into staying home with her.

"Sorry, sweetie. It's going to be another late night." I turned to open the door, then sighed. "Okay, okay, I'll give you an extra helping of food. Just this once."

My phone rang. I peeked in my purse to see who was calling.

Aunt Deb. I didn't have time to talk; I'd have to call her in the morning.

Razzy followed me to the pantry where I removed a small can of wet cat food—the stuff I saved for special occasions. My phone rang again.

Immediately, little sirens sounded in my mind. Was it Aunt Deb again? She only called twice in a row if something was wrong. I hustled toward my purse and, seeing her name on the screen, answered it.

"Is everything okay?" I asked.

"Hi, hon. I just wanted to ask if I can borrow that serving tray you keep in your studio. You know, the wooden one with the handles?"

I said a silent thank you that nothing was wrong. No reports of break-ins, vandalism, or assault. Praise be. "Absolutely. Please use whatever you'd like." After the break-in, I replaced the lock to my studio and given Aunt Deb a spare key, which she now kept in a locked safe in her home.

"Thank you. I'm having some ladies over for tea after tomorrow's hike, and I'd like to spruce things up a bit. Would you like to hear what I have in mind?"

Hugging the phone to my ear, I opened the can of cat food and spooned it onto one of my salad plates, then set it next to

Razzy's other food bowl. "I'd love to, but I have to run to a work event now. Maybe tomorrow?"

"That's fine. I don't want to take up any more of your time." There was an edge to her voice, one I wasn't used to hearing.

"Is…everything okay? You sound tired."

She paused a moment, then sighed. "I'm fine, I just had a terribly awkward conversation with Roy."

"Roy?" I asked, trying to recall if I knew anyone named Roy.

"Roy Sanders. You know, the detective who came out when someone broke into my office and your unit."

I checked the time again. It was ten past six—time to leave. I put my phone on speaker mode, locked the door to my apartment, hurried to my car, and headed toward Vincent's. I needed to get off the phone, but she sounded like she needed to talk. "Why was it awkward? You two seemed to hit it off just fine last week."

"Well, I thought so too, which is why when he called me to schedule time for a security audit, I thanked him for putting flowers in my vase at the festival yesterday."

"Uh…"

"Oh, Hadley, you should see them! They're absolutely breathtaking. But can you imagine how embarrassed I was when he kindly informed me the flowers weren't from him?"

I turned onto Picket Lane and headed toward the narrow bridge crossing Bonn Creek. "Listen, about the flowers, I'm the one who put them in your vase. I was trying to do something nice for you."

Aunt Deb gasped. "*You* gave them to me? Well, that's just perfect. The first flowers I've received at the festival in years, and they're from you. I should have figured as much."

"I'm sorry, Aunt Deb. I didn't think you'd assume they were from Detective Sanders."

"Of course I assumed they were from him. He's the first single man I've talked to in a long time, and he even offered to do a security audit for me. I must have misread his intentions."

I pulled into Vincent's driveway and turned off my car. "I need to go, but I'll call you first thing tomorrow. Again, I'm sorry I caused you any embarrassment. It definitely wasn't my intention."

We hung up. With a heavy sigh, I stepped out of my car and headed for the backyard. I hated getting off the phone mid-conversation, but I didn't want to be on the phone in the attic. It was 6:20, which would leave me less than twenty minutes in Vincent's attic.

The spare key was exactly where I buried it, along the back edge of the flowerpot, covered by a thin layer of dirt.

I opened the door leading to Vincent's kitchen, then hustled upstairs to the attic. I hoped none of his neighbors had seen me sneaking around his house and going inside. I'd have a hard time explaining myself to the police if they showed up, and even though Vincent had asked me snoop around for answers, I didn't want him to find out I was doing my snooping in his house, uninvited.

The familiar wave of musty, damp air greeted me the moment I opened the attic door. I pulled the string to the overhead light and the room lit up for all of five seconds before the bulb made a popping noise and went out.

Yikes. As creepy at the attic was, it was even more so in the dark. I considered backtracking into the game room and switching on the overhead light, but for the sake of time I opted instead to whip out my phone and use its built-in flashlight. I aimed it at the plywood flooring as I moved toward the box marked 'keep,' ducking under a horizontal support beam.

My phone's flashlight was bright enough to light up the entire attic. Sliding off my heels, I hiked up my form-fitting dress, careful not to tear the thin fabric, and crouched next to the "keep" box. I placed my phone on the top of an adjacent box.

I opened the box and started digging. There were no other picture frames, only piles of letters and dozens of other random keepsakes. I pulled a tall stack of hand-addressed letters and looked inside each one. Five minutes later, I set the first pile and lifted the other two stacks of letters from the box. I didn't take the time to read them, but peeked inside each one for any photos. My search yielded one photo, but it was of a man leaning against a blue, 1970s convertible Mustang.

I groaned. Nothing useful, and now I only had ten more minutes before I needed to leave. My legs were killing me from crouching so long, but I dealt with the burn because I didn't want to sit on the dusty floor and get my dress dirty.

Reaching into the box, I grabbed an armful of keepsakes and dumped them on the floor next to me so I could see the items in the bottom of the box. Under a cross-stitched floral tapestry, there was a leather journal with a stack of something white protruding beyond the worn edges. I flipped it open and removed half a dozen photos.

"Yes!" I cried, shuffling through them. They were similar to the ones in the picture frame. The same two children stood with goofy grins in the breakfast room in front of the bay window, but instead of the blonde woman between them, it was an older woman with brown hair. Most likely Geraldine, who according to Aunt Deb, was a brunette.

I turned over the photos and read the inscriptions in the bottom right. It was the same beautiful cursive that appeared on all of the boxes in the attic. Geraldine's, I presumed.

"Bubba and Noodles, Christmas 1991," I read.

*Noodles*. I had heard that name before. It was the username of the person who had made an ugly comment on the walnutridge-junk.com website. It was Noodles, followed by several numbers that I couldn't recall.

I recalled what Dennis had said about connecting the dots. Were these dots worth connecting? It did seem strange that a user with the same moniker as the child in the photo had made such an ugly, threatening comment on the website. I raised the photo at the top of stack towards the light from my phone. Again, the familiarity of the children struck me. I knew those eyes but I couldn't place where I'd seen them. The older child was a boy, but I couldn't decipher the gender of the scrawny toddler, who was likely the bearer of the nickname Noodles.

And something else about the photos bothered me. Something was off. The bay window behind them, its sectioned panes of glass fogged with frost, looked different.

No, that wasn't it. Frosted windows would have been expected in late December.

My phone chimed. It was my calendar alert telling me I had fifteen minutes before the *Sutherland* would depart.

I slid the photos into my tiny purse and swung my arm towards the box for my phone. My hand hit my phone, but my fingers failed to grasp it and it slid off the box, onto the floor, and then everything went dark.

I leaned toward the direction I'd heard my phone hit the ground, barely able to see the tall stacks of boxes in front of me with the dim light offered by the windows in the game room. Slowly, my eyes adjusted, and I saw a muted pink glow along the edge of the attic.

Squeezing myself between two stacks of boxes, I moved towards the glow. It was coming from below, just past the edge of the plywood flooring.

"Seriously?" I muttered, staring down into the deep abyss of pink insulation into which my phone had fallen. I dropped to my knees and reached towards the glow, but my phone wasn't within reach. If I had a broom, I could have swiped at it and maybe retrieved it, but I would waste too much time going down to his utility closet to get one.

I stood, then scanned the dark space below: fluffs of insulation, two-by-four support beams, a small network of insulated pipes, ladder rungs, cobwebs—

Ladder rungs? Why would there be built-in ladder rungs in the space between the garage and exterior wall? I closed my eyes, visualizing Vincent's garage. I'd only been in there a couple of times, but I recalled a door on the far wall, opposite the door from the mudroom. At the time, I assumed it led to his side yard, but maybe it was a door to a small closet or storeroom.

Keeping my eyes on the ladder, I turned my feet toward the door leading to the game room. *You don't have time to see what's down there,* I told myself. My fifteen-minute calendar alert had gone off several minutes ago, and it would take fifteen minutes to drive there.

Slowly, my feet turned back toward the ladder. I had to know what was down there. It would only take a minute.

I slid a stack of boxes out of the way, then turned around and lowered one foot into the dark innards of Vincent's home.

I hesitated. If curiosity had killed the cat, it certainly wouldn't do me any favors. But the ladder led to somewhere and I was determined to find out.

One rung, two rungs—so far, so good. I stretched my foot down another level, my bare toes touching the dusty wooden rung. The sudden sound of ripping fabric and a rush of cool air against my upper thigh made me yelp. Releasing the rung with one hand, I inspected the damage.

Whoa. The four-inch side slit above my knee was now at least eight inches, catapulting my dress from chic and flirty to cheap and naughty. It was possible Vincent had safety pins somewhere in his house, but I would surely miss the boat if I looked for them.

I hustled down the remaining rungs. The muted light from my phone struggled to reach the ground floor, making it impossible to see. I ran my hands along the wall next to the ladder.

Insulation ballooned out between evenly spaced two-by-four boards, and thin wires dangled from above.

I took another step away from the ladder into the darkness, feeling the wall as I inched to the left. It was a pattern: board, insulation, board, insulation. About five steps from the ladder, my left shoulder bumped into a wall. It rattled. I slid my hand along the wall until I found a pull handle about the size of one used on a kitchen cabinet. It wasn't a wall; it was a door.

I pulled the handle and the door shook. Pressing my shoulder against the smooth surface, I pushed. The door flew open.

There was a series of loud clangs, the sound of metal hitting concrete. I poked my head through the door. A sliver of dim light shone along the bottom of the adjacent wall, maybe ten feet away. Heading towards the light, I shuffled my feet against the cool concrete so I wouldn't step on whatever had just fallen.

I found the door. Wrapping my hand around the cool metal knob, I turned it and pulled. It opened to the garage, which was occupied by Vincent's car.

I blinked as my eyes adjusted to the soft light pouring in through the small windows in the garage door. There was a series of light switches on the wall and I pressed them until I found the one that lit up the storeroom.

Hustling back through the door, I scanned the small space. It held all the tools and equipment most people stored in their garage—tools, buckets, saws, bags of fertilizer. Opposite the door to the garage was another door. Turning the deadbolt lock, I opened the door and looked outside. Dense hedges at least as tall as the door lined the side of the house, explaining why I'd never noticed the door from the outside.

The footsteps. The night Vincent fell, I had heard someone running along the side of the house, away from me. Had someone left Vincent's house through this door? Had they climbed down the same ladder I just used?

I closed the door and turned the lock again. Now wasn't the

time to leave any exterior doors unlocked. I turned toward the hidden door that led to the ladder. The door and surrounding wall were covered with sheets of pegboard, which held rows and rows of well-organized tools. The separate sheets of pegboard were aligned so perfectly that it hid the door to the ladder.

Who knew about the secret door? Vincent? Reid? Considering the amount of dust on the ladder, I guessed it had been installed many years ago.

I bent over and picked up the screwdriver that had fallen from the pegboard when I opened the door. Not far from the screwdriver, a white cloth with brown stains lay wadded up, its edges protruding from behind a bucket of carwash supplies.

My throat constricting with sudden dread. "Please don't be blood," I whispered. Using the end of the screwdriver to lift the soiled cloth, I took a quick sniff. The stale, sickening scent of iron told me it was indeed blood.

A shrill clanging sounded, making me drop the screwdriver and cloth. I bent my knees, ready to run, then froze. I shook my head. It was just my phone ringing—possibly Reid calling to ask where I was. I wished I could leave Vincent's house through his garage door, but I needed to return to the attic to retrieve my shoes and purse, which held my car keys.

Leaving the light on and the secret door open, I hurried back to the ladder. It was easy to find with the light from the storeroom. I reached the top faster than I had reached the bottom, thanks in part to the greater range of motion afforded by the longer slit in my dress.

The attic was much darker, but I quickly located my shoes and purse. I slipped into my heels and ran toward the game room. My forehead collided with the overhead horizontal beam, making me fall back onto my bum.

The darkness of the attic seemed to swallow me, the door to the game room shrinking away. I took a deep breath, fighting to focus on anything other than the sharp pain in the center of my forehead. My phone rang again.

*The party. Focus on the party,* I told myself. I crawled towards the game room. I needed to call Dennis and tell him about the secret door and bloody cloth. But Vincent didn't have a landline, so I would need to use someone else's phone.

I slipped out of the attic door, into the game room, then hurried down to the kitchen, pausing to grab an icepack from Vincent's freezer. After locking his back door, I returned the spare key to the flower pot and ran around his house to my car.

I needed to make it to the *Sutherland* before she departed. Now more than ever, I was certain someone had tried to kill Vincent. They hadn't succeeded the first two times, and there was a chance they would try again.

I had to warn Vincent.

# CHAPTER NINETEEN

After traveling east for twelve miles, I pulled into the dock's parking lot. I hadn't needed my phone's map guidance since the dock was next to a ramshackle hardware store I'd been to a couple of times.

I threw the ice pack on the floor in front of the passenger seat and grabbed my purse. The *Sutherland*'s dock was behind the hardware store, so I couldn't see if the boat had already departed.

There were only a handful of cars, including Reid's, in the parking lot, which told me most people had arrived in cabs. The single, flickering light affixed to the side of the hardware store illuminated a sign pointing to the *Sutherland*. I crossed the lot and walked along a paved sidewalk behind the store.

A band played spirited folk music from somewhere ahead of me, and an indistinct glow grew brighter as I followed the long path that wound through a series of warehouses.

About a hundred yards ahead, a figure stepped onto the path from behind one of the buildings. I slowed, ready to run back in the other direction, but the person turned away from me and started off toward the dock. Maybe someone else was as late as I was.

I continued along the path, squinting to see who was ahead of me. The figure walked past the last warehouse on the path and was momentarily bathed in the light from a nearby floodlight.

Sonya. Her long, silver dreadlocks swung as she strutted away from me. She moved quickly, pumping her arms as though she were speed walking. I opened my mouth to holler at her, to ask her why she was out here, but she took an abrupt turn to the left where the pathway ended.

A fog horn bellowed, stretching its deep, sonorous tone for nearly ten seconds. Despite the increasing pain in my head, I jogged toward the sound. Reaching the last warehouse, a sign at the end of the pathway came into view: Welcome to the *Sutherland Paddlewheeler*.

Under the bold, black letters was an arrow pointing in the direction Sonya had just gone. I turned to the left.

The *Sutherland* was directly ahead, shining as brilliantly as a fiery festival of lights, its beauty matched only by its reflection in the still water around it.

I sucked in a deep breath and stepped onto the long wooden pier leading to the boat. Sonya had vanished. Either she had boarded the *Sutherland* or was taking a late-night swim, because there wasn't anywhere else she could have gone.

The *Sutherland* blared its horn again, and I hastened toward a young man in a white suit at the end of the pier.

"Come on, miss!" he hollered, waving his hands urgently. "Doors are fixin' to close."

I took his outstretched hand as he guided me from the pier to the entrance of the *Sutherland*. He gave me a strange look and pointed to my forehead.

"You okay, miss?"

"Never been better," I fibbed.

He motioned inside the *Sutherland*. "The party is on the first floor, the Jamestown deck. Restrooms are to your right, in the back of the boat. Men port side, women starboard side. If you need some fresh air this evening, take the staircase in either the front or back to the third level, the Williamsburg promenade deck."

I thanked him, headed down the short hallway, and hooked a left into the banquet room.

I stopped and stared. The *Sutherland*'s outward magnificence paled in comparison to her interior charm, which embodied the enchanting romanticism of Colonial Virginia. Acrylic paintings with chunky bronze frames lined the walls, depicting scenes from the Revolutionary War and life as an early settler. The room sparkled with mesmerizing arrays of light from crystal and brass chandeliers.

"Hadley!" Vincent called out from his table in the front of the ballroom. He motioned me over, a smile on his face.

I slipped around a group of Terence's crew who were standing in a circle with their dates, then headed for Vincent. There were about a dozen tables in the ballroom, each with a white tablecloth, six formal place settings and a centerpiece with fresh flowers. "Hi, Vincent. Sorry I'm late."

"Glad you could make it. I've been trying to call you. Reid said you were coming—" His smile faded. "What happened to your head?"

"I bumped it." *While I was in your attic.*

"Do you need some ice or something?"

I smiled, gently stroking the tender spot on my head with the pad of my index finger. "Nah, it's just a bump. It'll be fine." Lowering my hand, I caught a glimpse of my finger. Its tip was smeared with blood. "Oh! Guess I hit it harder than I thought."

Vincent's phone was half-hiding under the napkin in his lap, as if he were trying to conceal it. I needed to call Dennis to share everything I'd learned in the attic. "Would you mind if I borrowed your—"

I stopped, certain I'd seen someone with long silver hair from the corner of my eye. Had Sonya boarded the boat? I swept my eyes across each cluster of people standing around talking, but didn't see her.

"Is something wrong?" Vincent asked. His voice carried a surprising hint of concern. "You're jumpy tonight."

As much as I wanted to talk to him about my recent discoveries, now wasn't the time. There were too many people around and I didn't know who I could trust.

Leaning closer to him, I kept my voice low. "I saw Sonya on my way out to the pier. She was ahead of me, so I didn't see if she boarded." I did another three-sixty scan of the ballroom. "I think she's on the boat."

"She's here because I invited her."

I raised my brows, pain tearing through my forehead. "You didn't press charges against her for the roof stunt?"

He nodded. "Nope. In fact, Sonya Bean is the newest employee on my payroll, effective yesterday afternoon," he said, enthusiasm lighting his eyes. His wine-red dress shirt brought out the warm glow of his cheeks, which were typically void of color. Tonight he seemed happy, more relaxed. "She'll work part time as Walnut Ridge's sustainability consultant, making sure we source the paper for our catalogs from responsibly managed forests, and she'll develop a program to incentivize catalog recycling."

"Wow, that's great!" I said. As annoying as Sonya's bullhorn was, I cheered silently for her. She had fought hard for her cause and had, in a way, won. "It's a win-win for everyone."

Vincent turned his palms up. "There was merit to her complaints. I should have done this a long time ago and I'm hopeful she'll get us on the right track."

There was a low humming sound and the floor vibrated slightly. Out the window, the wooden pier slowly grew smaller. The band struck up another tune, this one louder than the previous one. The chatter also intensified as the circles of conversation drifted closer and closer to the bar in the middle of the ballroom.

Everyone looked stunning. Dress slacks, vests, ties, and shiny leather shoes replaced work boots, jeans, and threadbare T-shirts. Rachael, who was busy introducing her husband to Terence, wore a brilliant red chiffon cocktail dress, undoubtedly earning her the best-dressed award of the evening.

Although most of the crew and their plus-ones were standing, a handful of guests were already seated at their table, including Vincent. In front of his place setting was a flat-bottom wine cork with a slit along the top that held a name card bearing his name. The name card to Vincent's right had Reid's name, and the one next to Reid showed my name.

"He'll be down soon," Vincent said.

"Who?"

He nodded toward the front of the boat. "Your date. He's checking on the kitchen crew to make sure everything's on track for dinner."

"Oh, he's not...we're not..." I stumbled to find the right words. Did Vincent think Reid and I were on a date? *Was* this a date?

Vincent held up hands as if to say he didn't care, it wasn't any of his business. But his twitch of a smile told me he did indeed think his brother and I were on a date. It was the first time Vincent had spoken of Reid without getting grumbly.

Terence looked at Vincent and me, waved, then drifted with his circle of people toward our table. His snug white dress shirt was tucked into khaki chinos with no belt, achieving an effortless not-too-casual, not-too-businessey look.

Terence shook Vincent's hand. "Glad you're back, man. We were rooting for you." He swung his outstretched hand in my direction. "Hadley, you look lovely—" His eyebrows dipped. "What happened?"

"I got into a bit of a pickle on my way over. It's no big deal. Really."

Rachael, holding a wineglass that was one sip shy of empty, let out a high-pitched giggle. "Girl, you need a mirror, some tissues, and a hefty load of concealer to cover that cut of yours." She pointed to the back of my dress with the hand not holding her wine. "What'd you do, get into a fight with a bag of cotton balls?"

I inspected my backside. Fluffs of insulation clung to the yellow fabric. I had, in a way, gotten into a fight with Vincent's attic and had lost miserably. At least no one was pointing out my ripped dress.

When I looked up, Reid had joined the small group staring at Hadley the Mess. His smile was so big I could have counted all thirty-two of his teeth if I'd had the time.

My face felt hot. "Hi, Reid." I stepped toward a gap in the circle of stares. "The ladies' room is in the back? On the starboard side?" I pointed to the left and then the right. I had no idea which was starboard side, and the man on the pier hadn't elaborated.

"Come on, I'll take you there." Reid reached for my hand and led me away from the table. "If you're facing the front of a ship, the starboard side is the right side. Left side is the port side. Easiest way to remember the difference is both 'port' and 'left' have four letters. And you look lovely, by the way. I'm happy you were able to make it tonight."

"Thanks. I'm lucky I made it here in time. The *Sutherland* is amazing. It makes me want to re-read every American history book I've laid my hands on so I can feel like a more worthy passenger as we cruise along the Historic Triangle."

He smiled. "You're worthy of a ride, even if you can't name all the important historical figures from the Virginia Colony."

"Thomas Jefferson for sure...probably Washington and, I don't know—maybe Madison?"

"You'll have to join me on the *Sutherland* another evening. I typically share this factoid between the entrée and dessert course."

We stepped into a short, narrow hallway that, according to the sign on the wall, led to the stairs and restrooms. Reid stopped and turned to face me. "Can I get you something for your cut?" he asked.

"Thanks, but I'll just dab it with some water and tissues. I ran into a...wall as I was leaving, and didn't take the time to tend to it."

"I have a robust first-aid kit on board if you need anything," he offered.

"Robust?" I teased.

He dipped his chin and grinned. "Please ignore half the words coming from my mouth right now. I'm a little nervous, and I think it has something to do with that yellow dress of yours." His gaze boomeranged from my eyes to my dress and then back again. "Cotton balls and all."

I imagined his arm slung over my shoulder, pulling me in close. It was tempting to disregard my suspicions about him and enjoy the evening with Reid and his cologne, but I politely excused myself and headed for the ladies' restroom.

In front of the sink, I gawked at my reflection. The icepack I'd place on my head in the car had smeared the blood across my forehead, making my cut look far more serious than it was.

In high school when I first started dating, my mom gifted me advice passed down from her mother. "Do everything you can to look your best when you're getting ready," she had said, "but once you leave your home, don't give your appearance a second thought. Turn your attention to others."

Tonight I had taken that nugget of advice too far. If she were seeing what I was seeing in the mirror, she would retract every last word of her statement. Instead, she would tell me to never leave the house without a pocket mirror and to check it every five minutes.

I lathered my hands with soap and gently washed my cut, then patted it dry with a paper towel from the dispenser fastened to the wall. I would put antiseptic cream on it before bed, but the rose-scented bathroom soap would have to do for now.

If Reid hadn't been waiting for me on the other side of the door, I would have taken advantage of my solitude to study the photos in my purse. Something about them bothered me and I was itching to study them again.

But they would have to wait. I swatted my hands against the back of my dress to remove the remaining fluffs of insulation. I checked the mirror again and applied a fresh coat of lip gloss.

My reflection was less scary than when I had entered the ladies' room. The blood was gone, my hair was dry, and my curls hadn't crossed the threshold into frizz territory. I was fortunate most of my co-workers were taking advantage of the open bar because they would be less likely to remember what a mess I was tonight. I would have to make sure I steered clear of anyone's camera.

Reid was leaning against the wall opposite the ladies' room when I returned.

"Tour?" he asked. "How about it? I'd love to show you around if you don't mind missing out on a cocktail or two."

I hesitated. It wasn't the cocktails I minded missing. I had driven, so I wouldn't be drinking tonight. But considering my suspicions about Reid and the threats I had received, I didn't want to venture too far from the crowd.

"The bar will be open throughout the party." He seemed to sense my hesitation, but it was clear he wanted to show me around the *Sutherland*. It was reasonable to think he would want to show me his pride and joy. He was proud of it, justifiably so.

Or was there another reason he wanted me to be alone with him in some dark, deserted corner of his ship? As kind and genuine as he seemed, there were too many uncertainties surrounding him. And I had promised myself I wouldn't go off alone with him at the party.

Rachael bopped down the hallway. "There you are!" she cried when she saw me. "The party's in there, missy, not out here." Her eyes shifted slowly to Reid, embarrassment crossing her face at sloth speed. "Oh! I'm sorry if I interrupted anything."

"Not at all," Reid said. "I was trying to convince Hadley to let me give her a tour of the other floors. Would you like to join?" He swung his gaze to me. "That is, if I can convince Hadley."

Without waiting for me to reply, Rachael grabbed my hand and tugged. "Come on, I've been dying to see what's up there."

"Okay," I said. If Rachael was going, I would go. Considering her small frame and current state of mind, she was more like a tipsy Tinkerbell than a beefy bodyguard, but I felt safer in her company.

Reid pulled his sleeves a quarter the way up his arms, then motioned toward a door on the starboard side of the boat. "The stairs are outside on the wrap-around deck. We'll go to the second deck first."

Rachael and I followed close behind him. She nudged my arm with her elbow, pointed to Reid, then wagged her eyebrows up and down at me.

I answered her silent question with a shrug. She gave me a look that said I'd be crazy not to be into him.

Reid opened the door and I braced myself for a rush of wind. But the evening was still and the *Sutherland* wasn't moving fast enough to generate her own wind. Outside, the music from the band was joined with the rhythmic churning of the giant paddle-wheel in the back of the boat. Had I not been so eager to return to the party, I would have loved to watch the paddles whip through the water.

"The second floor, the Yorktown deck, has two banquet rooms," Reid explained when we reached the top of the stairs. He opened a door and flipped on the lights. "This one is the larger of the two up here. It's popular for corporate events and small dinner parties. Past the door at the far end of the room is a smaller banquet room used for more intimate events. I'm afraid it's not much to look at right now. It's being used as a storage area for my contractors' supplies." He cast a knowing look at me. It was the room he planned to take me to for dinner.

I walked further into the banquet room. Tables draped in floor-length white linens were clustered around a wooden dance floor, which sat in the middle of the room in front of an elevated stage large enough to fit a five-piece band. Opposite the stage was a bar lined with backless swivel stools similar to the one on the first floor.

Unlike the shimmering banquet room directly below us, this room was darker, moodier. It oozed the same historical charisma, but was more reminiscent of a prohibition-era speakeasy, where patrons could sip in secret.

"You've got a great dance floor in here," Rachael said. She pointed her toes toward it. "Bet it's a great place for wedding receptions."

"Actually, most of our larger events—weddings, quinceañeras, retirement parties—are held downstairs. The acoustics aren't great up here. I've had more than several bands complain about it. Apparently the hollow stage makes it too boomy, and having the subwoofers mounted underneath it doesn't help." Reid walked to the front of the dance floor and tapped his foot against the elevated platform, which yielded a series of hollow thwunks. "It's on my long list of improvements I need to make to this ol' boat."

"What about your historical dinner cruises?" I asked. "Are they on the first deck as well?"

He shook his head. "If the weather's nice, most folks prefer to stand on the open-air promenade deck for the tour portion of the evening. Then they eat dinner on the first level, and oftentimes go back to the top to enjoy the night view of the James

River. Would you ladies like to head up there now? We can take the stair—"

"Sure!" Rachael shimmied past us, heading for the door we'd just come through. "I've always loved the river at night. I might spend the entire evening up top—" The door closed behind Rachael. Through the windows, I saw her ascending the staircase to the third deck.

Laughing, Reid held up his palms. "What would you like to see next? The Promenade Deck? Or do you want to pop in and see the smaller banquet room?" He motioned to the door on the far wall. "It's my favorite room on the *Sutherland*."

"Um..." I looked longingly at the door through which Rachael had left. She hadn't turned out to be as good of a bodyguard as I hoped.

"It's your choice. Rachael seems perfectly content showing herself around. I don't think she'll mind if we don't follow her."

"Actually, I would love some fresh air." I moved toward the door, hoping to catch up with Rachael sooner rather than later.

Reid followed my lead, shutting off the lights in the room on our way out. He rolled his wrist over and checked his watch. "We might catch the tail end of the sunset if we're lucky."

At the bottom of the staircase, I gathered a handful of my dress' yellow fabric and lifted it slightly so I wouldn't step on the bottom hem. The last thing I needed was another tear.

Reid waited for me at the top of the stairs, holding his hand out as though he were going to pull me up the rest of the way. I hurried up the remaining steps, pretending not to notice his outstretched hand.

I stepped onto the polished wood of the promenade deck and was greeted by Rachael's shrill scream.

# CHAPTER TWENTY

Reid and I rushed toward Rachael's scream, which had come from somewhere on the other side of the covered bar in the middle of the promenade deck.

"Rachael?" we yelled in unison.

Again, her scream sounded, followed by the pounding of feet against the deck. We ran around the back wall of the bar and nearly slammed into Rachael.

"'*Sweet Caroline*!'" she said, squealing. "The band is playing my favorite song." She slid out of her heels and took off running again toward the stairs. "Thanks for the tour, Reid, but I gotta go dance!"

"Be careful on the stairs," he called out after her.

"Wow," I breathed, placing a hand over my chest. "I thought someone had...I thought she was hurt." I sank into the nearest chair, waiting for my heart to stop pounding.

Reid laughed it off. "Who knew she was such a Neil Diamond fan? I'd hate to stand next to her at a concert." He pulled another chair closer to mine and sat down.

For the second time in five minutes, Reid and I were alone, this time even further from the crowd partying below. I stood and turned toward the staircase. "We'd better head back down. Wouldn't want to miss Vincent's party."

"There's plenty of party left to enjoy," he said. "Why don't you let me show you around up here? The view from the bow is amazing this time of the evening." He stood and put his hand on my shoulder.

"Actually, I really like this song too. Neil Diamond's the best. I'd like to go dance." I slid away from his touch and moved toward the stairs.

He followed me. "So you and Rachael have the same taste in music. Interesting."

"Yes. It's quite the coincidence."

His eyes narrowed slightly as he studied me. "Listen, I understand if you aren't interested in dating or getting to know each other better. I totally get it. But it seems like something's bothering you. Have I done some to offend you?"

I appreciated men who said what was on their mind and didn't make me guess what they were thinking. It made communication much easier and I didn't feel like I was playing a game. Tonight, I was the one withholding all of my thoughts.

I raised my hand to wave off his concern, then lowered it when I realized how much it was shaking. "You haven't offended me. The past couple of weeks have been challenging and I'm not my usual self."

My usual self wouldn't have turned down a date with Mr. Heartthrob or shown up to a dinner party caked in dried blood and attic insulation.

His sharp eyes studied my face. "No, it's something else. I'd like to get to know you better, but I'm sensing there's something holding you back from feeling the same way."

I puffed out my cheeks, slowly releasing my breath. It wouldn't hurt to ask him a few questions, and I could sprint down the two flights of stairs to the party in less than ten seconds if necessary. "You know how this town is, with everyone in everyone's business. I've heard some...rumors around town about you, Vincent and his ex-fiancée. I believe her name is Claudia?"

Reid closed his eyes for a long beat, then nodded. "Yes, Claudia."

"One woman I spoke with said you might still be in a relationship with her."

"Gayle Nuñez told you that rumor, didn't she?"

"Bingo."

He nodded. "Not only is Gayle the town's biggest gossip, but most of what she says isn't true." He looked intently into my eyes. "I am not in any sort of a relationship with Claudia. She and I dated long distance for almost a year until she met Vinn at a New Year's Eve party, fell for him, and left me. They dated a while, got engaged, then she panicked and left Vinn a week after they moved to Darlington Hills. She drove to my house and tried to convince me to forgive her. Can you believe it? She actually wanted to get back together with me the day she left Vinn."

"I'm sorry. You didn't deserve any of that."

He shrugged. "She wasn't the first woman to break up with me. What stung the most was that she left me for Vinn."

This was my chance. He had left the door wide open for me to ask my questions about his relationship with Vincent. "I don't have any siblings, but I'm sure it would be hard to forgive something like that. I've heard it caused quite a rift between the two of you." I hadn't exactly asked him if he'd tried to kill his brother, but it was a start.

Reid flinched, as if I had struck a hot nerve. "Rift? Is that what people are saying? Because 'rift' doesn't begin to describe what happened. Vinn's and my relationship went from close-knit to nuclear, all because of Claudia. Then last year, the two of them moved to *my* town because now everyone wants to live here after the Ladyvale Manor became Instafamous, and Vinn can't stand to *not* have something I have. I was ready to forgive them and start anew, but then a week after they arrived Claudia ran out on Vinn. It was three months before they were supposed to get married. So of course, Vinn blamed it on me."

"It wasn't your fault Claudia changed her mind again," I said.

Despite the dim lighting on the promenade deck, I could see his face growing red. I opened my purse and stuck my hand inside, wrapping my fingers around the can of pepper spray. Just in case.

"One could argue it was my fault," he said. "The night Claudia drove to my house, we were having some of the worst weather I've ever seen. Tornado warnings and high winds. She refused to go back to Vinn's house, saying she was either staying with me or driving home to her folk's house in Delaware. I even booked her a room at Hotel Darlington, but she wouldn't leave."

He held up his hands and sighed. "So I let her stay that night. She slept on the couch of course and I barely said five words to her, but I let her stay. And then Vinn showed up the next morning, saw her car there and Claudia in her pajamas, and he assumed she and I had rekindled our relationship. He refused to believe the truth."

A gust of wind came, sending my untamed curls in every direction possible. "I have noticed some hostility between the two of you."

"Oh? Like what? Has Vinn said anything about what happened?"

"Not really, but I've noticed. Like when he called you while I was staging your house. You were livid. And when you called Vincent the morning Willy was killed, he was angry as well."

Confusion rippled through his eyes. "How did you know I was on the phone with Vinn those two times? He told you?"

I nodded reluctantly. I didn't want to lie, but now wasn't the time to confess to looking at Vincent's phone bill. "When you called the day Willy died, I believe Vincent told you to 'come take care of it,' whatever that meant."

"Yep. He insisted I come over to meet you so you could help me sell my house faster. He wanted me out of Darlington Hills as soon as possible."

"He was quite angry as I remember," I said.

"We've been arguing a lot. It's unfortunate because he's the only family I have left, aside from some distant cousins." He stared at the passing lights on the north bank of the James River for several moments. "So that's what's on your mind?"

I followed his gaze out to the shimmering lights of the Virginia Peninsula, pausing to consider how I could delicately ask my next question. "All families have disagreements, but I didn't know just how 'nuclear' things had gotten between you and Vincent."

"What do you mean?"

I placed my thumb over the pepper spray's trigger, ready to press it. "Earlier today I went to Gigi Ellsworth's home to discuss a redesign project, and I recognized the furniture in her game room from a website I came across—walnutridgejunk.com. Gigi told me Willy was your realtor and the two of you had a 'reciprocal relationship.' So it made me wonder if you set up the site because Vincent threatened to report your paddlewheeler to the port authority."

"I didn't set it up, Willy did. When he showed it to me, I told him to take it down, but he refused. I didn't press him too hard because it felt somewhat justifying after Vinn's threats."

Reid's red face told me I should wrap up the conversation, but I needed more answers. If I didn't ask him now, I didn't know if I ever would.

"Last Monday night, someone threatened me with a knife in a rain boot. I recognized the knife from a Walnut Ridge storage bin, so Dennis went over there to check it out. You were there and let him inside."

"Someone threatened you?" Reid's eyes were wide. "Officer Appley didn't mention that. Why didn't you tell me?"

"You texted me later that night, saying you'd just returned from work. You didn't mention stopping by Vincent's."

Reid looked down, his gaze sweeping across the wooden deck. "I did have a late night on Monday—a quinciañera that went on forever—and then I swung by Vinn's place for a few minutes. But I would have come over immediately if you'd told me about the threat."

"And where were you the night Vincent fell?" I blurted out. "After I called an ambulance I tried to reach you but you didn't answer. Later you told me you were driving around. You don't answer your phone when you're driving around?"

I cringed. If Reid was the culprit, he might try to harm me. If he wasn't, I was undoubtedly ruining any future chances of a date with him.

He held his palms up and gave a nervous laugh. "I don't always answer my phone right away. I probably had it on silent mode after the quinciañera. I don't understand why—"

Reid stumbled back, as if he'd been knocked off balance by an invisible quake. "Oh. Wow. I get what you're implying. You think I'm responsible for Vinn's fall from the balcony? That I pushed him out of rage because he said he would report the *Sutherland* to the port authority?"

The wind kicked up again, whipping my hair into my eyes. Letting go of the pepper spray, I pulled my hand from my purse to collect my wild hair. There was a tug on my wrist as I raised my arm. My pepper spray dangled from my wrist, the ring of its keychain caught on my bracelet. I shook my arm, which sent the pepper spray sailing across the deck.

Reid's eyes ignited. "You were going to spray me?"

I took a step closer to the stairs. I had seen how angry he could get and I wasn't going to stick around if he blew up. "No, of course not. Dennis told me to keep it close after the threats I've gotten."

"You've had your hand in your bag for the past five minutes," he snapped. "You were going to spray me!"

I stood there silent as my hair thrashed around my face. There was no point in lying about it. My finger *had* been on the trigger, ready to spray him if needed. "I believe whoever killed Willy meant to kill Vincent, and then later pushed him off the balcony." Bending my knees, I prepared to bolt.

"That doesn't mean *I* did it." He backed away from me, heading for the stairs. "You don't know me, Hadley. When Vinn fell—or was pushed—it was one of the worst days of my life, second only to the day my parents were killed in the car crash."

"I'm sorry, I was just—"

"Want to know why I didn't answer your call the night he fell? I was driving around Darlington Hills, second-guessing my decision to move. I didn't want to, but he threatened to report the *Sutherland* to the port authority if I didn't. That's why I went ballistic the day you came to my house. But despite Vinn's threats, despite my desire to move away from him, I drove around for over an hour that night, trying to think of how I could make amends with him."

Reid's eyes gleamed with a swell of tears. He paused to look out at the river, his lips slightly parted as though he had more words to say but couldn't find them.

"And then I got the call that Vinn had fallen and was unresponsive in the hospital," he said finally.

"I'm sorry I thought you were the one who..." I trailed off, too embarrassed to finish my sentence. "I know you must have been devastated when he fell. But I'm sure Vincent appreciates how much you helped out while he was in the hospital."

He nodded curtly. "He does. Since his fall, we've spoken more than we have in the past year and a half. And this party"—he held his arms out wide—"is more than a celebration of his recovery. He and I are on speaking terms again, and that's worth ten parties to me, if not more. Go downstairs, look at the welcome table with the champagne glasses. You'll see a framed photo of two boys climbing a walnut tree. *That's* what I was looking for in Vinn's room when your cop friend came by. I would never hurt Vinn or you. Even though you don't know me well yet, I'm shocked you thought I was capable of such a thing."

His tone was softer now, carrying heavy notes of sadness and regret. I felt drawn to him, felt the intense urge to wrap my hands around his.

But the gap between us could never be closed. I had killed my chances with a perfectly decent, eligible bachelor who had been interested in me up until the moment I accused him of trying to kill his brother.

Well done, Hadley. Well done.

Reid took the stairs to the first deck, claiming he had to check on the kitchen crew again. I sank into the nearest chair and buried my face in my hands.

Why had I confronted him during the party? If I'd been more patient, I could have shared my new discoveries with Dennis later in the evening or the next day. Not only had I destroyed my chances of dating Reid, but I had also hurt him.

Groaning, I kicked off my heels and propped my feet up on the chair next to me. The music continued to thump downstairs, but I wasn't ready to put on a happy face and join the party. I needed ample time to compose myself before I had to go sit next to Reid at the dinner table.

Reid had sufficient motives for attempting to hurt Vincent—the threats to his business and the ordeal with Claudia—and he had access to his home via the key in the flowerpot. But I believed him. Reid truly seemed to care about Vincent.

I closed my eyes filled my lungs with the cool evening air, which held traces of deep fried goodness coming from restaurants overlooking the James River. As much as I wanted to hide on the top deck for the remainder of the event, I needed to go downstairs. Tonight was about Vincent, and I wanted to show my support.

On my way to the stairs, I picked up my pepper spray, which had slid under a two-seater bistro table. As I slid it into my purse, my fingers brushed against the thin stack of photos.

The party could wait. Now was a good time to get a second look at the photos, away from all of the eyes in the banquet room.

I pulled them out of my purse and held the top one up to a light attached to a nearby rail. According to the inscription on the back, I was looking at the smiling faces of Bubba and Noodles. The older woman in the middle—likely Geraldine—had one arm around each young child. They stood in the breakfast room, the bay window behind them.

I narrowed my eyes as I studied the children. Both looked familiar, especially the younger, scrawnier one. I had seen that quirky grin before.

*Noodles*. The same nickname used by the person who left the threatening comment on the walnutridgejunk.com website. It couldn't have been purely coincidental. Noodles wasn't that common of a nickname.

My heart picked up its pace as I flipped through the other photos. They were similar, but taken at different angles. I stopped at the fourth photo. The photographer had moved, and now the bay window was no longer behind the trio, but to their left, and the dining room was in the background. The children made goofy faces at the camera while the woman kept her pleasant smile and looked directly at the camera. She didn't seem to care that the children weren't taking the photo session as seriously as she was.

The fifth and sixth pictures were overexposed. All three faces were washed out and blurry.

Hang on. I shuffled through the photos again, going back to

the fourth photo. Something was off. My eyes raced across the photo, sweeping over the smiling faces, the bay window, the blurred dining room table in the background.

The photo was backwards. Rather, the downstairs was backwards. The kitchen wasn't in the back of the house as it was now; the dining room was. Vincent had said he'd made significant changes to the home after he bought it, so he must have brought the dining room to the front of the house and sent the kitchen to the back. Architecturally, it made sense to switch the rooms so the more formal areas would be at the front of the home and private rooms in the back.

Vincent's contractors had done an amazing job of flipping the rooms. If I hadn't seen this picture, I never would have known.

My stomach lurched as a fresh memory rolled into my mind. The day Willy was killed, I had been standing in the breakfast room talking to Vincent, Terence, Josh and Willy. Terence had asked Josh to finish painting the dining room, and Josh had turned toward the kitchen.

Josh had worked in the house for nearly a month. How could he have gotten turned around? I studied the two children in the photo.

The younger child was Josh. AKA, Noodles.

I pinched my eyes shut, replaying the events of that tragic morning. At the time of the stabbing, I was in the upstairs bedroom, Vincent was outside trying to find Sonya, Terence was in the storage shed, and Josh was painting in the game room above the garage. If Josh had gone down to the kitchen via the stairs, I would have seen him pass by the bedroom.

My heart thumped faster as I considered another possibility: if Josh had spent time in the house as a young boy, he might have known about the hidden ladder. He could have accessed the attic from the game room, gone down the ladder, and through the garage to the kitchen. And then he could have gone back up to the game room the same way he'd come down.

My hand flew instinctively to my backside, ready to pull my phone from my pocket and call Dennis. Only my dress didn't have pockets and my phone was still buried in the innards of Vincent's home.

I stuffed the photos and pepper spray into my purse and ran down the stairs. I had to warn Vincent. Josh was at the party.

# CHAPTER TWENTY-ONE

"Hadley!" Rachael danced over to me the moment I burst into the banquet room. "Where've you been? We've been tearing up the dance floor and you are missing out. The band just played my favorite Aretha Franklin song, and I just requested a Lady Gaga song. They're going to play it next."

I looked between the jumping, swinging, and grinding bodies on the dance floor towards my table. It was empty.

"Have you seen Vincent?" I hollered, forcing my voice to soar above the music.

She giggled. "Don't tell me you'd rather hang out with him instead of dance with me. I wanna see your moves."

"But did you see where he went?" I pressed.

Rachael raised her arms and shook her body to rhythm of the music. "Nope, but why don't you stay and—"

I took off before she finished, heading for my table. Vincent's chair was pulled out and his crutches were missing. I stepped out of my shoes and stood for a brief moment on his chair to scan the room again. No Vincent, no Reid, and no Josh.

I hopped down and headed towards the restrooms, leaving my shoes by Vincent's chair. A table with champagne glasses sat along the wall adjacent to the entrance to the hallway. Giving it a quick scan, I noted an eight-by-ten frame with a photo of two young boys climbing a tree. This party really was celebrating the renewal of their friendship.

I ran to the men's restroom and pushed the door open. "Vincent? Reid?" After five seconds of silence, I took off towards the banquet room again weaving through huddles of people talking and dancing.

Sonya grabbed my arm. "Hey. Is everything okay? You're running around like the boat's about to sink."

"Have you seen Vincent?" I asked, searching the room as I spoke.

"He walked off a minute or two ago with another man, someone I've seen around the house who kinda looks like Vincent but has dark hair." She pointed to the doors leading to the kitchen on the opposite side of the room. "In there."

I sighed. Reid was likely telling Vincent about all of my accusations. "Thanks, Sonya. I hate to ask, but do you have a phone I could borrow for a minute? I lost mine and I need to make an urgent call."

Sonya gave me a once-over with narrowed eyes. "You sure everything's okay?"

"Don't worry, the ship hasn't sprung a leak," I said, trying to keep my tone light.

Sonya opened the clasp on her purse and removed her phone. "Here you go. Let me know if I can help with anything."

"Thanks, I'll bring it right back." I took off for the kitchen. "And congrats on your new job at Walnut Ridge," I hollered over my shoulder.

I hadn't memorized Dennis's number, but after a quick search on Sonya's internet browser, I found the main number for the local police.

One ring later, there was a click on the other end. "Darlington

Hills Police Department, Officer Stevens speaking. Is this an emergency?"

"I'd like to speak to Officer Appley or Detective Sanders." I glanced back at the party, then slipped through the doors to the kitchen. Men and women in white aprons scurried around three long stainless-steel counters, chopping, slicing, stirring, and drizzling.

"Sorry, miss, Sanders and Appley are both are out right now. Can I ask what this is in regards to?"

A young woman spooning dressing onto plates of salad looked up at me. "You can't be in here. The kitchen's off-limits to guests."

I covered the phone's mouthpiece. "Have you seen Reid or his brother?" I asked the woman.

She gestured impatiently to the other side of the kitchen. "They just went up the service elevator."

That made sense. Vincent was on crutches, so obviously he wouldn't take the stairs. I waved to signal my thanks, then hustled past the kitchen crew and pushed the elevator button.

"Miss?" Officer Stevens said. "You still there?"

I stepped into the elevator, debating which deck to try first. Reid might think I was still on the third deck, so if he didn't want to see me—I assumed he didn't—then he would have gone to the second deck.

I pressed the number two and the doors closed. "Yes, sorry. This is Hadley Sutton. We've got trouble out here and I think Vincent is in serious danger again. Can you please tell them I'm on the *Sutherland Paddlewheeler* boat somewhere on the James River? Could you send a patrol car? Or...um, boat?"

If I was wrong about Josh, I was wrong. The police wouldn't be too happy and I might ruin the party, but those consequences were better than those if I were right and Josh hurt Vincent again.

"Hello?" I asked, waiting for the man to acknowledge my

request. Maybe he was making a note or trying to reach Dennis or Detective Sanders. "Hello?"

I lowered my phone and turned the screen toward me. No signal. I had lost the connection at some point between the first and second decks. How much had Officer Stevens heard?

The elevator dinged and the doors opened. I stepped out and Sonya's phone's signal strength jumped immediately from zero bars to four bars. While navigating to the recent calls screen, I walked through the short hallway that led to the small banquet room where Reid and I were supposed to have dinner last Tuesday. But like he said, the room was a mess of aluminum ladders, paint buckets, and toolboxes.

Something slammed into the back of my head, and the room became a swirl of colors and lights as I hurtled face-first toward the ground. I caught myself clumsily with my hands, but my momentum sent me skidding across the hardwood floor.

Two hands wrapped around my ankles and pulled. Suddenly I was sliding backwards on my stomach across the room, away from the elevator.

"Let me go!" I screamed, kicking with everything in me to get away. Pain surged through my head, intensifying as I twisted and thrashed. The room started to fade, beginning in the periphery of my vision.

There was a grunt behind me, and my ankles were set free. A blurry form—a man?—bent over and grabbed something from a nearby bucket. Seconds later, two hands stuffed a thick wad of fabric into my mouth and tied it behind my head.

Fumes of paint and turpentine filled my nose. I tried screaming but ended up gagging and coughing as my body revolted against the stench. Once again, the hands wrapped around my ankles and dragged me on my stomach across the room and through the doorway into the larger banquet room.

"I warned you, Hadley." Though he whispered, the rough,

tremulous voice was unmistakable. It was Josh. "You're going for a swim, you nosey fool."

The floor seemed to sink while tables, chairs, and the ceiling spun into a dizzying blur.

And then everything went black.

Something was wrong with my arms. I couldn't feel or move my hands, fingers, or anything else below my shoulders. Everything was black. Something soft and wet filled my mouth, its sharp stench making me gag.

My head throbbed.

I opened my eyes. Darkness surrounded me.

Why can't I see anything? Why can't I feel my arms?

A rhythmic pounding drummed through my body and in my ears. My pulse? No. Too loud for my pulse.

I squeezed my eyes closed and shook my head, forcing myself to stay awake and focus. I raised my head to try to look around, but my forehead struck something hard above me, sending excruciating shock waves through my head. I lifted my legs, but couldn't raise either of them more than six inches. It was as if I was in a coffin.

The thumping continued, and was joined by a new sound: singing.

Music. The band. Vincent's party. Josh.

The fog in my brain lifted and I felt sharp tingles in my fingertips. My hands were bound behind my back, and I was lying on them.

*But I'm still alive.* The last thing I remembered before blacking out was Josh saying something about me going swimming. He must have planned to throw me overboard, but then changed his mind and put me here. But where is 'here'? The music was below me, so I was still likely on the second floor. I bent my knees as much as the low ceiling would allow and swept my bare feet across the floor. It was gritty and cold.

What part of Reid's boat was dark, dirty, and about a foot high?

I rocked from side to side until I regained most of the feeling in my arms. I seemed to have plenty of room to my left and right; just not above.

Josh couldn't have dragged me too far; he probably wouldn't have risked someone seeing him. I couldn't recall any small cabinets or compartments in the either of the banquet rooms. It was just walls, tables, chairs, the stage, and the dance floor.

*The stage.* Reid had said the stage was hollow. Something about subwoofers under there. I was trapped—bound and gagged—under the stage.

I wanted to scream and stomp my feet, but I feared Josh would hear me. Although I felt lucky to end up under the stage instead of in the river, it didn't make sense. Why go to the trouble stuffing me down here when it likely would be easier to throw me into the river? Was he planning to torture me?

One deep breath, another deep breath. Panicking wouldn't help anything. If Josh wasn't already in the room, he would likely return soon. I needed to get out. To do that, I needed to think clearly.

How had Josh gotten me down here? If I could find the access point, I might be able to get out. It probably wasn't too far from where I lay. I doubted Josh could fit in this small space, so he wouldn't have been able to maneuver me around much. He'd most likely shoved me in and closed the door.

Hopefully, a door without a lock.

Reid said the subwoofers were under the stage. Logically, they would have put them next to the access point in the flooring to make it easy to change or fix the subs. If I could find the subwoofers, I might be able to find the access point.

I swung my legs around wildly, feeling for the subwoofer. My dress ripped again, which allowed me to stretch my legs even wider. Shimmying from side to side, I turned around clockwise 180 degrees. My hands now ached from the weight of my body, and the pain from my head threatened to send me into another unconscious slumber.

My right foot kicked something and it screeched across the ground. Using both feet, I felt the object: four sides plus a top and bottom, mostly hard—except for a soft mesh covering on one side—and wires protruding from another. It had to be the subwoofer.

I raised my feet, running them along the rough underside of the stage floor to search for the access point. To the right of the subwoofer, the floor gave way and a sliver of light appeared above me. I pressed harder and the stage floor opened slightly and then closed. Something heavy was on top of the door. Scooting closer to the spot where I had seen the light, I pulled my feet towards my body and pressed up on the door with my knees. It opened again, wider this time, then closed with a thud.

I winced, not knowing how far Josh was from the stage. I waited, listening. If he was in the room, he would've heard the door shut. After thirty long seconds I tried again, channeling all my adrenaline into lifting the door.

The door gave and a loud thunk sounded, as though something large had fallen. I kicked the door open the rest of the way, scooted closer to the opening, then sat up and scrambled out of the stage. If Josh were anywhere nearby, he would come running.

My purse lay on the ground near the stage, its contents scattered around it—minus Sonya's phone. As I ran toward it, I strained to loosen the cloth tied around my hands. It stretched a little, allowing me enough room to slide my arms around my bum then step through my arms. I yanked the rag from my mouth, gagging as I caught a fresh whiff of the paint when I slid it over my nose and off my head. The smell of paint was forever off my list of happy-memory makers.

I snatched the pepper spray and stuffed it down the front of my dress, then dashed toward the smaller banquet room toward the elevator.

No. Not the small room. That's where Josh had been earlier when he struck me. I spun around and ran for the door to the stairs on the open deck. I pulled open the door, uttering a whispered thank you it wasn't locked, then aimed for the stairs. Terence and his guys would help. They could subdue Josh.

# CHAPTER TWENTY-TWO

Out on the deck, the sound of Vincent's voice drew my attention to the back of the boat. He stopped talking, then Reid's laughter drifted from the same location, somewhere around the corner.

I raced for the stairs, determined to make it to the party before Josh found me. I lunged for the stair railing, my feet flying down the first three steps.

*Vincent is in danger too.* This gut-punching realization sent me grinding to a stop midway down the stairs. Josh had tried to kill him twice before. He wasn't likely to stop trying now. I had to warn him.

Scanning the boat for Josh, I whipped my head around in every direction, then crept back up the stairs. He was around here somewhere, probably looking for Vincent.

I made a dash toward the sound of Vincent's voice, then peeked around the corner. Vincent and Reid stood against the back railing, Vincent on his crutches, Reid propping an elbow on the top rung of the white railing. Both were looking out at the open river. A dozen small tables and chairs similar to the ones on the promenade deck were arranged in front of a bar bearing a rustic wooden sign engraved with Paddlewheel Bistro. Any other day, it would be the perfect spot to watch the passing river and churning paddlewheel.

"She's probably not the only one," Vincent said, his voice booming. "I'd bet there's an entire club of women who think you look like a psycho killer." He was clearly teasing Reid about my misguided accusations.

I darted toward them, waving my arms and making shushing sounds. "Stop talking!" I whisper-yelled. "He'll hear you. Come on. Downstairs. Near more people. We need to go." My words slurred as they flew from my mouth faster than my lips and tongue could coordinate to enunciate properly.

They turned toward me, their smiles vanishing. Reid's eyebrows hovered low on his forehead while Vincent's stretched toward his hairline.

"Hadley, what happened?" Vincent eyed my dress incredulously, which had likely picked up more than a thin layer of dirt and grime from the underbelly of the stage.

"I said, we need to go back to the party. Near all the people." I punched out my words, keeping them just above a whisper. "Josh is around here and he's going to hurt you."

"You're blaming Josh now?" He was much louder than Vincent had been, loud enough for anyone in a sizable radius to hear.

"Josh is Noodles," I pressed. "Noodles is Josh. We have to go downstairs. *Now.*"

Neither budged.

Vincent looked concerned. "Exactly how hard did you hit your head this evening?"

"Josh is the grandson of the woman who sold you her house. I went through your attic before the party and found some old photos of him, then looked at them right after I accused Reid..." I trailed off, throwing Reid an apologetic look. "I think Josh killed Willy thinking it was you, Vincent, and then he pushed you off the balcony. And if you think this looks bad"—I motioned to the tiny cut above my eyes—"you should see the back of my head."

The pulsating stabs of pain told me it did indeed look worse than my forehead. "Josh hit me with a—"

"Who are you, Houdini?" Josh's voice weaseled through the thumping music and churning paddlewheel. He stood at the opposite corner from where I had come, aiming a small pistol at the three of us. "I would have thrown you over the side of the ship earlier, but people were outside taking a smoke break." Dark blue circles of sweat covered his pale blue dress shirt and he moved in a jerky, uncoordinated manner. I couldn't tell if he was drunk, hyped up on adrenaline, or nervous about holding a gun. Maybe all three.

The music seemed louder now. I prayed someone would take a break from the free-flowing drinks and dancing to wander upstairs and save us, though it was probably in their best interest to stay put downstairs.

I turned away from Josh, instinct telling me to run.

"If you move, I'll shoot," he barked.

I considered screaming, but that wouldn't put any more distance between the gun and me, and it would probably make him angrier. And no matter how much adrenaline was surging through my body, I couldn't outrun a bullet. The only weapon I possessed was my overly effeminate pepper spray, but it was no match for the death machine in Josh's hands.

Vincent raised a crutch at Josh as if it were a loaded weapon. With his leg still in a cast, he wouldn't be able to run either. Only Reid had a reasonable shot at hightailing it around the corner and down the stairs. But instead of running, he stepped between Josh and me.

My eyes met Josh's. "I already called the cops—right before you hit me and stuffed me under the stage. They're on their way." *Please let this be true*. Hopefully my call with Officer Stevens cut off *after* I told him there was trouble on the *Sutherland*.

Josh's mouth twisted into a snarl. "Well then, I'll have to make this quick."

Vincent grunted.

"I told the cops you're the one who killed Willy," I lied. "So you'd better think twice about adding any more bodies to your count. They know everything."

Josh didn't say anything, but continued pointing the gun at us. Was he reconsidering?

The paddlewheel whipped through the water below us, making the floor vibrate with its energy. I didn't like that we were standing so close to it. One hard push was all it would take to send us into the rotating wheel. Earlier, it had seemed enchanting. Now it reminded me of a giant blender set to purée mode.

Josh stepped to his left, leveling his gun at me. "I wasn't planning to hurt you tonight. But you didn't listen to my warnings, did you? You show up looking all fancy, except for the attic insulation hanging off your dress. You've been snooping around in Grandma's attic again, just like you were last week when you stole the picture frame and brought it to that ratty storage place of yours."

My eyes widened. "That *was* you on the park bench. You were waiting for me."

Josh shrugged. "I knew what you were up to; you were playing detective. And after I saw you in Vincent's room and up in the attic last week, I warned you not to stick your nose where it doesn't belong. But you didn't listen, did you?"

He swung his gun toward Vincent. "And *you*, you're like a disgusting cockroach. No matter how many times you step on 'em, spray 'em, those pests just will not die."

"What have I done to make you so angry?" Vincent asked. His voice was calm and steady. "I hired you, gave you a good job. I've been told I can be rather demanding, but I hope you never took it personally."

Josh snorted. "I can deal with a demanding boss. What I am *not* okay with is someone who doesn't care about the people he mows down to get what he wants. All you care about is your stupid catalog and the bottom line of your business."

Vincent pulled back his chin. "Mowed down? I don't know what you're talking about. I've never broken any laws or harmed anyone."

"You're so wrapped up in growing your little furniture empire that you failed to notice how many lives you're destroying along your way to greatness." Josh widened his stance and squared his shoulders. "The house you moved into, you stole it from me. Grandma was fixing to transfer the deed to me—her only heir—before she moved to some retirement community in Georgia. But then you came by and at the last minute convinced her to sell it to *you*."

"I'm sorry you didn't get the house, but I can't help that she wanted to sell it to me."

"Of course she wanted to sell it to you. You swindled her!" Josh snapped. "You promised her you'd name a new furniture set after her if she did. But that was a lie, wasn't it? I have yet to see any furniture pieces named Geraldine."

Vincent released the handles of his crutches and raised his palms. "These things take time. I can't snap my fingers and—voila!—have a brand new furniture set the next day. I have a new collection in the early design stages, and I will uphold my promise to name it after your grandmother."

Josh stepped closer to the three of us. "I don't care if you keep your promise. You won't be around to finish your new furniture. Your house should have been mine, but she sold it to you for far less than it's worth, and then she went and dumped the money from the sale into some charity, if you can believe it."

"Again, I can't help that she didn't give it to you. She mentioned she had a grandson, but said he hadn't called her in decades."

I gawked at Vincent. Now was not the time to try to win an argument.

"So what if I never called?" Josh said. "She's my grandma. She's supposed to love me whether I call or not. And I was counting on the deed to her house. I had planned to turn around and sell it because I needed that money. But you stole it from me."

I released a slow breath, staring at Josh intently. If we were going to make it off the *Sutherland* alive, this conversation needed an immediate change of course.

He was growing more agitated, and every precious minute that passed was one minute closer to when someone might come upstairs or the police, God willing, would show up. We needed to stall him. "Josh," I said calmly. "I've seen the photos of you with your grandma. It was clear she loves you very much. Do you think she would want her little Noodles threatening people with a gun?"

He reeled at the mention of his childhood nickname, momentarily lowering his gun. "How do you know about Noodles?"

"She wrote captions on the backs of her photos," I said. "Bubba and Noodles. I recognized it because you used the same nickname when you commented on that awful website about Walnut Ridge. She wouldn't want you to hurt anyone, and neither would Bubba."

He raised his gun again. "Bubba's gone but he would've congratulated me for what I'm about to do. And you're bluffing about the cops. You didn't tell them anything because you don't know anything. They're probably days away from arresting Vincent, because two days ago I gave the police a torn cease and desist letter Vincent hid in a storage bin the day he stabbed that man."

"You mean the day *you* killed 'that man,'" I clarified. "Willy Ellsworth was his name. And then you hid the letter to make Vincent look guilty."

Josh's lip twitched into a smile. "What can I say? I'm a smart guy."

"And I'm a smart woman. Which is how I figured out you took the secret ladder in the attic down to the storeroom, walked through the garage to the kitchen, killed Willy because from the back, he looked like Vincent, then took the same route back up to the game room."

"Secret ladder?" Vincent asked.

I nodded. "He took the same route out of your house the night he pushed you off your balcony—from the attic down to the storeroom, then out the door leading to your side yard."

For several long seconds, Josh was a statue before he shrugged. "So you found the ladder. That doesn't prove I killed anyone."

"Maybe not," I said, mimicking his indifferent shrug. "But the blood droplet in the garage that matches Willy's does. *And* the blood on the rag you tossed aside near the hidden door. *And* the blood droplets I'm sure the police will find when they scour the attic."

I paused to clear my throat. Panic was turning me into a soprano, which wasn't nearly as assertive as the lower end of my vocal range.

"You covered the blood on your hands and arms with paint. No one gets that messy when painting—not even accountants posing as handymen. I explained all of this to the police when I called them."

"Shut up!" Josh yelled, waving his gun erratically. "You can't stop talking, can you?"

I closed my mouth.

"I mean, who cares if you figured out I accidentally killed that man and pushed Vincent? You're bluffing about calling the cops and no one will know it was me. You know why? Because once you three go for a ride on that wheel behind you, you won't be talking to anyone. Not even to the fish at the bottom of this river."

I recalled Vincent's words the day he asked me to "go irritate a confession out of someone." His request had been ludicrous and insulting, but I was clearly irritating Josh and he had just confessed to Willy's murder. Check and check. I might have laughed at the absurdity of it all if Josh hadn't just told us we were about to swim eternally with the fishes.

An unnatural calmness settled over Josh's face. He leveled his gun at Vincent, his movements no longer jerky. "This is for stealing from me."

I thrust my hand down the front of my dress and grabbed my pepper spray. My fingers, shaking uncontrollably, failed to find the trigger. Panic exploded within me. *There's no time! He's going to shoot.* I whipped my arm back and hurled the canister toward his face.

Direct hit.

Josh shrieked, his hand flew to his left eye, and a gunshot sounded. Reid lunged toward Vincent, snatching one of his crutches. Vincent collapsed as Reid swung the crutch and pummeled the bottom end into Josh's nose.

I turned toward Vincent, who sat with his legs splayed apart. Just below his left knee, a hole the size of a small coin cut through his slacks. "You've been—" A glint of light by Josh's knee caught my eye. The shiny silver gun dangled from his fingertips. I bolted toward it and yanked it from his hand in one sweeping motion, then threw it as hard as I could into the black river.

Reid tackled Josh to the deck, straddling him across the chest to pin him down. Josh punched and kicked to get out from under Reid. Vincent scrambled toward them on his hands and right knee, then pounced on Josh's flailing legs. I grabbed a nearby chair, ready to swing it if necessary.

The music stopped and an uproar of voices sounded on the deck below.

"Up here!" I yelled. "Second floor. Help!"

Footsteps thundered up the stairs. Kyle, Terence, and two

other men ran around the corner, followed by a rapid flow of other party guests.

"Was that a gunshot?" Kyle demanded.

Unable to stand on my shaking legs, I leaned against the wall and sank to the deck. I nodded toward the tangled heap of men on the ground next to me. "Josh shot Vincent."

Vincent whipped his head toward me, his eyes bulging. "He did?"

I pointed to the bullet hole in his pants. Terence grasped Vincent's arms and dragged him away from Josh as Kyle and another man helped Reid restrain Josh.

Vincent hiked up his pant leg. His cheeks ballooned out as he released a long, slow breath. "It grazed my cast."

A new sound escalated above us, its staccato thumping louder the noisy churning of the paddlewheel. A helicopter with flashing blue lights cut through the clouds, sweeping a white spotlight across the *Sutherland*.

"See that, Josh?" I pointed to the police chopper. "Now tell me I was bluffing."

# CHAPTER TWENTY-THREE

I invited the cool afternoon breeze into my apartment through my front door, propping it open with a white porcelain garden stool. Razzy sat in the middle of the open doorway, too timid to venture outside but too curious to leave her post.

I sat at my kitchen table with Carmella, sipping lemongrass-mint iced tea while watching Razzy's little ears perk up every time someone walked by. It was Saturday, almost one week since Josh nearly killed me, and I had spent the majority of the week recovering on my couch, in my bed, or at my table. I'd sustained a minor concussion and the doctor had told me to take the week off to rest. I happily abided with his orders.

"Congratulations on your new client," Carmella said, raising her glass of tea. "When do you start?"

I clinked my glass against hers. "I've already done some of the preliminary work, but the real work begins next week. I plan to work on her project in the evenings when I leave Vincent's house."

After learning about my near-death experience on the *Sutherland*, Gigi had insisted I wait to start working on her house until my head healed completely. She had been so appreciative of my efforts in helping to identify her husband's killer that she brought three ready-to-bake casseroles in large disposable aluminum pans. I froze two of them and baked one on Tuesday, and enjoyed leftovers the rest of the week.

But tonight, I was cooking. I had felt good enough to run some errands: food for dinner and new rain boots for Carmella. It felt good to get back into my routine.

"Just don't work yourself too hard. You're still recovering," Carmella said.

I rolled my eyes. "Yes, Mother."

"Speaking of which, have you told your parents what happened?"

"Yes. Kind of."

Carmella lifted a brow.

"I may have left out a few details about how I got into the 'scuffle' as I called it. If I told them everything, they'd be on a flight back home right now, leaving Japan for good, and then—poof!—there goes their retirement plans."

Something dark skittered along the floor by the wall, and I sprang from my chair. Carmella spun around to inspect, then turned a curious eye on me. "You can swipe a loaded gun from the hands of a crazy man, but you're gonna let a little cricket scare you?"

Inching back toward my chair, I whistled to Razzy and pointed to the tiny critter. It was our unspoken agreement that I had litter box duty and she had bug duty. She looked at the cricket, blinked, then returned her attention to the chirping birds outside.

"That's right," I said. "I used up all of my bravado last week. If that bug gets any closer, I'm hiding behind my cat." I still couldn't believe I'd thrown my pepper spray at Josh and grabbed the gun from his hands. Strange things happen when I am moments away from death.

"And if I cross paths with any armed crazies, I'm hiding

behind *you.*" Smiling, Carmella reached for the open tin of homemade chocolate and walnut cookies Rachael brought over yesterday, plucking a plump one from the top. "But Josh is behind bars now, so we won't have to worry about that scenario."

I nodded as I eased back into my chair. In addition to the charges of attempted murder of Vincent, Reid, and me, the police also charged Josh with the murder of Willy Ellsworth.

After I told the police about the secret door and ladder, they found other evidence supporting the case against Josh. They confirmed the blood on the rag in the storeroom was Willy's, and it was mixed with traces of the paint Josh had been using at the time of the homicide.

"Happy Saturday!" Aunt Deb's voice sailed in through the open door. Moments later she strode into my apartment carrying a bouquet of white and pastel pink flowers twice the size of the one I had bought her at the Flower Festival. "These are for you, hon, since that misguided man stole your other ones at the festival."

Carmella laughed. "Misguided? That's the term I use for my wayward middle schoolers when they talk back to their teachers."

I stood to greet Aunt Deb. "Thank you, these are beautiful! I'll get a vase."

"No, no, you sit down and rest. I'll find a vase." Aunt Deb hugged me gently, kissed my cheek, then waltzed toward my countertop and set down the flowers.

"In the cabinet under the blender," I said, taking in her lavender dress. While most of her skirts and dresses brushed her ankles, this one fell just below her knees, showing off her five-miles-per-day hiking legs. "You sure look nice. New dress?"

Aunt Deb pulled a tall, square glass vase from the cabinet and set it next to the flowers. "Thanks, hon. I bought it yesterday." She turned her attention to the slow cooker on her right. "Whatcha got brewing this afternoon? Sure smells lovely."

"Enchiladas. It's a new recipe I found on Pinterest. It'll be ready in about twenty minutes if you'd like some."

"I'd love to, but I can't stay long." Aunt Deb lifted the lid and looked inside. "I suppose you mean enchilada soup?"

"No, just enchiladas." I hurried over to the counter and replaced the lid on the slow cooker. "And please don't remove the lid before it's done cooking. It said so like fifty times in the instruction manual. It's the cardinal sin of using a slow cooker. It'll let all the moisture out."

She pointed to my dinner. "Darlin', if those are enchiladas, then you don't have a problem of too little moisture. In fact, it might be best to leave the lid off while it finishes cooking."

There was a knock on my door frame, and Detective Sanders stepped inside.

I hurried toward the door. "Detective Sanders! Is something wrong?" A dozen scenarios flooded my mind, most involving Josh breaking out of jail.

It was the first time I'd seen Detective Sanders since last Sunday. Minutes after a helicopter from a neighboring jurisdiction arrived, a patrol boat carrying Detective Sanders, Dennis, and three other Darlington Hills officers reached the *Sutherland*. They boarded, arrested Josh, and hauled him to the police station after the *Sutherland*'s captain returned the boat to the dock.

My call with Officers Stevens that evening had cut off before I told him where I was, but not before he'd heard me say Vincent was in serious danger. That prompted Stevens to call Dennis, who had learned earlier that day Josh was the grandson of Geraldine Henkle. And while that wasn't proof of anything, it pointed to some irregularities in his initial police statement. Dennis knew Vincent's party was on the *Sutherland* that evening, so when he got the call from Stevens, he and Detective Sanders hightailed it out to the James River.

"Good afternoon, Hadley." Detective Sanders walked into my apartment, waving to Razzy as he passed her. He wasn't in uniform, but wore pressed khakis slacks and a dark blue dress shirt with gold-colored cuff links. "Nothing's wrong, I just had to take a call in your parking lot. I asked Debbie to go on in without me. I didn't want to keep her waiting."

*Debbie*? I swung my head to Aunt Deb, my eyes wide.

She beamed. "Roy and I have dinner reservations at six in Richmond, so we'll have to get going soon."

Detective Sanders joined us in the kitchen, standing next to Aunt Deb. I introduced him to Carmella, and when he turned to shake her hand, I gave Aunt Deb an open-mouthed 'why didn't you tell me about this?' expression. She lifted her chin and smiled coyly.

"We're trying a new Italian restaurant in the museum district," he said, his voice drawling. "Your aunt tells me chicken parmigiana is her favorite, so we're gonna see if this place tonight meets her expectations."

His phone rang and he glanced at the screen. "Excuse me, ladies. I have to take this call too." Then, turning to Aunt Deb: "I promise it won't be like this all night. I made it clear I'm off-duty tonight, but the Ladyvale Manor is up in flames and several of the responding officers need a little guidance."

"Oh, no!" I cried in unison with Carmella and Aunt Deb. The Ladyvale Manor was the ivy-wrapped house that had made Darlington Hills insta-famous.

"Is it arson?" I asked.

Detective Sanders took a step backwards toward the door. "Doesn't look like it, but your 'friend' Officer Appley"—he raised his thick gray eyebrows—"is at the scene right now." He spun around, leaving me to contemplate the teasing tone he'd used when he mentioned Dennis. And the eyebrow-raising thing? What was that about? What had Dennis told him about us? The thought both irritated and intrigued me.

"You're sure you don't need a rain-check on dinner tonight?" Aunt Deb called out.

Detective Sanders turned to face her, a smile on his face. "Half the town could burn down and I wouldn't miss tonight's dinner." He stepped around Razzy and through the doorway.

"You didn't tell me about your date," I whispered. "When did this happen?"

She fanned her face. "Shortly after I got off the phone with you last Sunday, when you informed me you had given me the flowers—"

"I'm sorry about that. I feel terrible I tricked you."

"Don't worry, hon. It was the sweetest thing in the world for you to buy those flowers for me. Anyway, no less than fifteen minutes after I got off the phone with you, Roy called and asked if I wanted to have dinner with him sometime. I don't know what prompted him to call back. Maybe he heard the disappointment in my voice when he told me the flowers weren't from him."

Another knock sounded on my door frame.

"Come on in, Roy, you don't have to knock," Aunt Deb said, her eyes still on me.

"Actually, it's Reid."

I whipped my head around. Reid stood in the doorway, marks of concern between his eyes.

"I just passed the detective on your sidewalk," he said. "Was he coming from your place?" His mind was likely running the same scenarios mine had when I saw Detective Sanders.

I smiled. "The only problem is my aunt has a date tonight with Detective Sanders and she didn't tell me about it until now." I put my arm around Aunt Deb, who was practically gawking at him. "Reid, this is Aunt Deb. Aunt Deb, meet Reid. He's Vincent's younger brother."

Aunt Deb laced her fingers together and gave a slight bow. "I've heard so much about you around town—all good things, of course—but I didn't know you and Hadley had become… acquainted. Please, do come in." She snapped her eyes to me, giving me a wide-eyed 'why didn't you tell me about this?' expression.

In slim-fitting blue jeans and a lightweight T-shirt, Reid took casual weekend wear to a whole new level of sophistication. The neckline of his dark gray tee hung low across his chest, showing off the smooth skin of his wide shoulders.

Giving Razzy a wide berth, he walked between my sofa and coffee table toward the kitchen. "I just left Vinn's house. I was helping him repack the boxes in his attic to send to the former owner—but I wanted to stop by and see how you're doing. How's your head today?"

"Better, thanks. Good enough to go back to work on Monday."

Reid had texted me a couple of times this week to check in, but he hadn't mentioned he would be stopping by today.

"Vinn owes you at least two weeks off work after what you did for him," he said, giving me a casual kiss on the cheek. "I'd milk your injury for all it's worth." He shook hands with Aunt Deb, then turned to Carmella. "Good seeing you again."

"Where do you live, Reid?" Aunt Deb asked.

He set down a brown paper bag slightly larger than a lunch sack on my table and faced Aunt Deb. "I'm in a house four blocks east of the town square…for now. I sold my home recently and I move out in a couple of weeks."

Aunt Deb's smile faltered. "Well, that's a shame. You're not moving too far, I hope?"

"Actually, I've decided to stay in Darlington Hills. I'll take my time looking for another home, but it'll probably be a teardown and rebuild. I love the idea of starting from scratch." He moved his eyes to me. "And I know the perfect person to help me decorate so it doesn't end up looking like a bachelor pad."

Reid was staying? My cheeks swelled with a smile.

Lifting his chin, he inhaled a deep breath. "Whatever you're cooking smells really good. It's making my stomach growl."

"It's enchiladas. Would you like some? I have plenty."

Aunt Deb recoiled, flipping her hand up as if to stop me. "Isn't it a little early for dinner? Reid, how about some lemongrass-mint tea instead? Hadley just made a fresh pitcher."

"Aw, come on, Aunt Deb," Carmella said. "Tea won't fill him up. I vote we give him tea *and* enchiladas."

Reid patted his stomach. "I second Carmella's vote. I'll eat or drink anything." He looked down at me with bright eyes. "Only if it's not too much trouble."

"Don't be silly," I chirped, opening my cabinet and retrieving two plates. "I'll have some with you." I doubted it would matter if I stopped the slow cooker twenty minutes before the timer went off. I grabbed a spatula and removed the lid.

Hmm. The enchiladas had drowned. I fished through the sea of soupy broth until I found one stuck to the bottom. Peeling away the soggy tortilla, I emptied its contents into the slow cooker. One down, eleven more to go.

Glancing over my shoulder, I sighed with relief when I saw Reid was busy talking to Carmella and Aunt Deb. He didn't need to know about my enchilada search and rescue mission. I exchanged the spatula for a ladle and the plates for a pair of bowls, filled them three-quarters of the way, topped them off with shredded cheese, and plunked a spoon in each bowl.

Aunt Deb poured tea into an empty glass in front of Reid. "Here you go, sweetie," she said. "Hadley has a gift for mixing drinks—teas, cocktails, coffee." She nudged the glass closer to him.

With the two bowls in-hand, I joined them at the table. Reid thanked us and dug into his soup. Aunt Deb watched him intently.

"This is really good, Hadley. It reminds me of a soup my mom used to make. Vinn's going to be jealous when I tell him about it."

I shot Aunt Deb a satisfied smirk.

After several bites, Reid set down his spoon and reached for the brown paper bag. "I wanted to bring this over today—" He paused and eyed Razzy, who had materialized below his chair. She looked up at him expectantly.

"She thinks it's for her," I explained. "Shows you how spoiled she is."

He dug into the bag, removing a plastic pouch of Fur-Rocious fish niblets. "She's a smart girl. Probably recognizes the Whisks and Whiskers bag." He dropped two treats on the floor next to Razzy. "Here, kitty. Sorry I can't pet you. I loaded up on allergy medicine before I came over but I don't want to press my luck."

My heart pitter-pattered as he talked to Razzy. He didn't hate cats, he just avoided them for the sake of his allergies.

"And this"—he stuck his hand into the brown bag again and looked at me—"is for you. I heard Josh destroyed, among other things, your favorite bag." He handed me a navy blue canvas tote bag imprinted with my Hadley Home Design logo. "No offense to Vinn, but I thought you needed something better than a Walnut Ridge bag."

I squealed. "Thank you! I love it." I held it up proudly for Carmella and Aunt Deb to see.

Carmella's eyes lit up. "Tell me where I can get one. I'm not usually a tote bag kinda gal, but this one's cute enough to carry around."

Aunt Deb looked bewildered. "Where on earth did you find this? How did you get her logo?"

"Easy enough, I just pulled the logo from her website, then had one of my buddies make the bag. He owns a company that sells promotional products." Reid dug another cat treat from the pouch and tossed it down to Razzy. "I buy all my *Sutherland* doodads from him. Pens, coasters, T-shirts, coffee mugs—you name it, he sells it."

Aunt Deb tilted her head. "Interesting. Stuff like that could help me spread the word about my storage facility. I might have to get your friend's number."

My heart leapt. If she was thinking about promoting her business, then maybe she wouldn't sell the facility and move to Chicago. I turned and leaned toward Reid. "This bag is perfect. I don't deserve it, and I'm honestly surprised you came over today after I accused you of…you know what. I didn't think you'd want to see me again." I dropped my head. "I'm sorry I was so far off base."

He waved off my apology. "You figured it out eventually. I don't know how you pieced it together—it's truly remarkable. And I don't blame you for having questions about me. Vincent and I were in a bad place in our relationship and you picked up on it."

"You are too good to me. First you give me those beautiful flowers, and now this bag."

His expression turned quizzical. "Flowers?"

"From the Flower Festival, last Saturday..." I froze. Uh-oh. Had Dennis given them to me? He hadn't fessed up to it when he came out to investigate the dead rose and threatening note.

Reid's laugh shook the table. "I'd say you have two admirers in this town—one who is considerably more thoughtful than me if he's buying you flowers."

Aunt Deb made a strange noise. "Alright, alright. I wasn't going to say anything, but now it seems I must." She turned a sheepish smile toward me. "Hadley, hon, I'm the one who put flowers in your vase last weekend."

"*You?*" I asked, reeling at the irony.

She tossed her hands up. "Your vase was empty, and I couldn't stand for you to not receive anything at your first Flower Festival."

I jumped from my chair and threw my arms around her. "How is it possible for us to be so alike when we aren't blood related?"

She patted my arm. "After twenty-five years of marriage, your dear uncle rubbed off on me somewhere along the way. Now I'm as Sutton as they come." She sighed, looking out my open door, where Detective Sanders' voice drifted through the afternoon breeze. "But now it's time for new friendships, new adventures. And that, my dear, is the magic of the Flower Festival."

I gave her one more hug, then made my way around the table, topping off everyone's glass of tea. With Aunt Deb, Carmella, and Reid at my kitchen table, and a town of opportunity awaiting me outside, I felt like I was home. Now more than ever before.

Want to join Hadley on her next whodunit misadventure? The next book in the series, *Berry Purple Betrayal,* is available now!

# BONUS SCENE

**First date fiasco: Reid resents murder accusation**

Curious about how Reid reacted after Hadley accused him of murder? Subscribe to my mailing list for an exclusive scene, "First date fiasco: Reid resents murder accusation," told from Vincent's point of view.

To access the scene, scan the QR code below with your phone's camera or tap this link.

If you're already a subscriber, check my latest newsletter for the link to all my exclusive content.

## BOOKS BY EMILY OBERTON

**Hadley Home Design Mystery Series**

Book 1 - *Lemon Yellow Lies*

Book 2 - *Pearl White Peril*

Book 3 - *Berry Purple Betrayal*

Book 4 - *Cider Orange Chaos*

Book 5 - *Wine Red Wrath* - Coming soon!

**Sweet Romance (Written as Emily Bradford)**

*Holly Jolly Christmas Derailed*

Want a FREE cozy mystery? Sign up for Emily's newsletter at emilyoberton.com

## A NOTE FROM EMILY

I started writing *Pearl White Peril* while living in Singapore during the so-called "Circuit Breaker," which was the country's name for the lockdown measures implemented to control the spread of COVID-19. Like many families during the pandemic, my kids were learning remotely and my husband and I were working from home.

I never realized how much our home echoed (and how loud my husband talks on the phone!) until the Circuit Breaker. My husband worked in our office, my daughter did her schoolwork at the kitchen table, and my son worked at a table near our bedrooms. I set up my laptop on a bookshelf in our hallway, where I could reach either of them in less than ten steps each time they had a question or needed IT support.

We worked this way for nearly two months during the Circuit Breaker, and I cranked out the first half of this novel at my bookshelf desk, typing on my laptop while fielding math questions and begging our overloaded, exhausted Wi-Fi signal to stay strong.

But I certainly can't complain about our situation during the

Circuit Breaker. As a family, we conquered math tests, conference calls, spotty WiFi, and the first half of this book.

I love hearing from readers! You can find me on Facebook and Instagram, where I share tidbits on all things related to my books, including links to my many sources of inspiration for this series, like recipes, interior design photos, and more.

You can keep up with my latest books at emilyoberton.com and join my newsletter for exclusive subscriber deals, bonus scenes, giveaways, and more.

# ACKNOWLEDGMENTS

Thank you to Miles, Noelle and Landon for your love and kindness. I appreciate you more than you'll ever know. Also, many thanks to my mom, dad and sister, Alli, for their constant encouragement and enthusiasm.

I'm also grateful to my extended family in Virginia who always welcome us with open arms when we visit. Dawn and Calvin, your amazing photography of the Virginian countryside provides spark after spark of inspiration for the fictional town of Darlington Hills.

Thank you to my tennis team friends, aka the "Slice Girls," for your friendship today and always, but especially during the Circuit Breaker, when our Wine and Zoom calls warmed my heart and kept me smiling. And finally, my deepest gratitude to the one who makes all things possible, Jesus.

I truly appreciate everyone who has read my books and I hope you have a blessed day!

For the latest updates on my upcoming releases, follow me on Amazon and BookBub. I can't wait for you to discover Hadley's next whodunit misadventure. Stay tuned for more twists, turns, and trouble!

# ABOUT THE AUTHOR

Emily Oberton is the author of the fun and twisty Hadley Home Design Cozy Mystery series. She's also worked in news radio, corporate public relations, and as an independent PR consultant.

When she isn't concocting clever clues or crafting capers, you'll find Emily playing tennis, decorating her own home (not just fictitious ones in Darlington Hills!) and spending time with family and friends. She lives just outside of Houston, Texas, with her husband, two children, and orange tabby cat.

Want a FREE book? Sign up for Emily's newsletter at emilyoberton.com

**Follow her latest book adventures here:**

Facebook: facebook.com/obertonwrites
Instagram: instagram.com/emilyobertonbooks/
BookBub: bookbub.com/profile/emily-oberton
Website: emilyoberton.com

Made in the USA
Columbia, SC
05 July 2024

38154512R10150